THE JEALOUS WIFE

*A psychological thriller with
a nerve-shredding ending*

James Caine

CHAPTER 1

Kelly

Tomorrow, everything will change.

I wake up to another perfect day in a small town.

I stretch, and immediately Lady, my miniature poodle, does the same on the bed beside me. She licks my face and I pet her white fur furiously.

Despite being alone now, I still sleep on the same side of the bed that I had when my husband slept beside me. A king-size bed for one woman was way too much, especially for me. Lady made it easier not to think about it.

I hate to admit it, but sometimes I miss him.

I look at the happy face of my doggie to help change my mood. "Walk, Lady?" I shout enthusiastically, and her tail wags faster.

She watches me as I get changed into my athletic gear. Walking into my office next door, I grab the gold pendant necklace from my desk and place it in my pocket. It's bulky, and I don't like bringing it with me on runs. It doesn't feel right wearing it around my neck either. Since I made the decision that would change everything in my life, I've been carrying the pendant more and more, and looking at the picture inside it, sometimes obsessively.

Lady watches me, turning her head.

I stretch out my arm further and do circles with my hands as I go down the spiralling staircase to my front foyer, while Lady scurries behind me, struggling with the steps.

Before I open the door, I stop at the small table near the entrance. On it are several pictures of Ryan and me, mostly while travelling. One from Italy, another from our month-long trip to Spain. The best vacation we had was the one where we travelled to Fiji. The ocean was crystal blue. The beaches were serene. *Beautiful* was a word lacking the power needed to explain how amazing it was.

I glance at our Fiji photo on the beach, and at the vase beside it, where his remains are kept. I read his name at the bottom. Ryan McDermott.

It's been nearly eight months since he passed. I let out a breath I didn't know I was holding.

It was a weird place to put my husband, on a table near the entrance of my house. It was almost as if he greeted anyone visiting. Most people would have placed him above a mantle in a family room or maybe a bedroom. I hated the idea. Why put a dead person in a living area? Why would I want to remember that my husband was dead every night I slept or morning I woke?

After what happened, I tend to stay away from the living room entirely.

I'm still in mourning, of course. Someday, maybe I won't even keep his remains in the house. Maybe my ex-mother-in-law will want him. There comes a time where I need to move on too.

What's an appropriate amount of time, though? Thinking of Ryan can bring up loving memories, and a lot of anger. Sometimes I think I keep him at my home to torment myself.

I've heard gossip from my single friends in town that some of the men are waiting for their shot at the now-widowed Kelly McDermott. I've already been approached a few times by male suitors looking to sweep me off my feet seeing that I'm vulnerable now. They probably hope that I'm some emotional mess after my husband died, but that's far from the truth.

I focus on myself even more than usual when I'm down or depressed. At thirty-one, my body is in the best shape of my life. Yoga twice a week. Strength training with light weights three times a week. A Zumba class. Pilates. Every morning, I have my run with Lady to start my day.

I look back at the large living room, with

a tall brick fireplace that reaches the ceiling, the marble floors, and the long dining table that Ryan and I used to entertain people at. This home is too large for one woman and her dog. Someday I'll be ready to move on in life, but not yet.

Not until I get my revenge.

Tomorrow, everything will change.

I smile, thinking of what will happen soon. The small town of Muskoka Lake is going to be getting a lot of attention soon. *I* will be getting a lot of attention soon.

Lady barks, getting more impatient. I bend down and pat her head. "Sorry, girl," I say. "Got distracted." I grab the leash from the closet and quickly put it on her. I make a kissing sound towards the vase as I open the front door. The sunshine blasts in my face as I do.

It's nearly ten in the morning, practically afternoon now. When you're single, unemployed, and wealthy, waking up early isn't exactly required. Ryan was the early bird. He was up, changed into his suit and out the door before I'd set foot out of bed.

I notice a white Escalade drive by, and the driver gawks at me. It's Dean Hemsbring. A neighbour a few blocks down. He's married with a young daughter, but that doesn't stop him from staring at me like I'm a piece of bacon waiting to be devoured. I wave and smile. He sheepishly waves back and quickly turns his head.

I'm used to this type of attention, which I receive more now that Ryan is no longer here. I wonder what Evelyn Hemsbring, his wife who I sometimes have brunch with, would think of her husband's gaze?

I'm aware that I'm pretty, beautiful even. Attention from men, and sometimes women, comes naturally to me without much effort. I've grown accustomed to it. Dean is harmless. A man with an imagination who'd need a reminder to not stare at the sun. He's probably more concerned I'll say something to Evelyn.

I won't, of course.

I close my front door. It's not locked. It never is. Crime is not a problem in Muskoka Lake. Everyone knows everybody. Some better than others. I feel I know every juicy piece of gossip this town has to offer, which isn't much.

Lady walks beside me as we head down the block. I stare at the empty home beside mine. There are only three homes on our block. Each home is larger than the next, with massive front yards landscaped beautifully.

A white picket fence stretches across the property of the former home of Mr. and Mrs. Miller. The senior couple moved out of Muskoka Lake to southern Ontario to be closer to their grandchildren. They were great neighbours who were always friendly to Ryan and me. I was sad to see them leave until I found out who was to move in.

I break into a jog, Lady keeping pace with me. I stare at the "For Sale" sign in front of the home, which now has a red sticker slapped across it. "Sold".

The idea of new neighbours can cause many to become anxious. Who will they be? Will they be nice? Young children who will scream their heads off all day? Uncontrolled dogs who bark into the night?

Not me. I can't wait for them to move in. I know exactly who they are.

That's one of the benefits of being in a small town. Everyone knows everything. The realtor, Shannon, is a friend of mine. When she sold the home, she was excited to tell me who my new neighbours would be, because one of them was someone I knew very well.

Nora Cameron. Now that she's apparently married, she goes by Nora Bowman.

My realtor friend had the assumption, like many, that Nora and I were the best of friends. That was never the case.

I stop running entirely as I get close to the driveway. Soon Nora and her husband will move in. It will be a happy day for them. Moving is always so busy, but exciting. It's the start of a new beginning.

I was happy when Ryan and I moved into our home. This is the best neighbourhood in town, and the wealthiest. Muskoka Lake's social elite live here. Nora, like Ryan and I, must have done well for herself since leaving town.

I breathe out. It was more like she ran away from here after what happened.

I grab the gold pendant necklace from my pocket and open it, staring at the picture inside. What was a memory of best friends became a nightmare, not only for me, but for this entire town.

It's time Nora got what she deserved.

Tomorrow, everything will change.

CHAPTER 2

Nora

I watch the two movers as they clumsily manoeuvre a large sofa through our new home's entrance. I make a face as the padded side of the furniture thuds against one of the double doors. Thankfully, it's the couch and not the wooden credenza that appears to be next when I peer into the back of the moving van.

My husband, Jameson, strolls behind me, wrapping his strong hand around my waist. He kisses the side of my face, his hand sliding to my belly. He's been more affectionate than usual now that I'm showing.

"I still can't believe this home is ours," I say.

Jameson kisses my cheek again. "When I saw the listing, I had to make an offer."

I smile, trying my best not to be upset at his comment. Buying a home is a huge decision, one that should be made together. Jameson, of course, took it upon himself to make it all on his own. When he showed me pictures, my mouth dropped open at how gorgeous it was. I asked to set a time to see it in person, but he had told me not to worry, it was already ours. He had bought it before even talking to me.

He was so happy with himself that he couldn't understand why I was upset at first. I wanted to be included, of course.

It's a seller's market, he told me in response. Had he not made an offer, the home would have sold to some other lucky couple the day it went on the market.

I couldn't get too upset. This is where I wanted to live the rest of my life with Jameson. Muskoka Lake is a beautiful small town that people often travel to during the summer. The lake's only two blocks away.

This is my hometown, and I always dreamed of returning. Because of Jameson, I'm back.

"Did I do right?" he asks, kissing me again.

I have to give it to him. He did. The house is beyond beautiful. As soon as the real estate agent gave us the keys this morning, we immediately ran inside. The pictures didn't do the property justice.

I nod at Jameson. "You did. Thank you."

"Anything you want," he says.

Lately he's been overly attentive attending to my needs. Jameson always wanted to be a father, and soon enough, that will be his reality.

No matter the time of night, he will satisfy my random food cravings. McDonald's fries dipped in vanilla ice cream. Pickles with a side of peanut butter and toast. He was now banned from eating chicken anywhere near me because the smell instantly made me vomit, along with many other scents.

He understands, though. He caters to me. It's endearing to see. He certainly wasn't like that when I wasn't pregnant, or even when we first started dating. Now that I'm to be the mother of his child, things have changed.

The movers come back to the van, taking their time before attempting to lift the credenza. As they lift it off the truck, Jameson pulls a face of his own.

"I feel like I should have requested three movers now instead of two," he says.

"Cheapo," I say under my breath. It was true, though, and he knew it. Jameson is good at saving a dollar, but can't see the big picture sometimes. I told him some of our furnishings would be too much for only two people, but he vetoed me.

I look back at my new home, and my annoyance quickly fades. When I was a kid growing up in Muskoka, I would come by this area just to gawk at the beautiful houses. There were only a few other people living on the block. A large white picket fence divided the spaced properties.

It's truly a dream.

As the movers near the entrance, one yells at the other to pivot. The other moves and is then yelled at to pivot the other way. As they enter the house, I hear another loud bang followed by one of the movers cursing.

"Okay," Jameson says. "I admit, three would have been better." I smile at him. "At least I had the wisdom to find insured movers."

My phone rings in my jeans pocket, and I quickly take it out. "It's Mom," I say, looking at Jameson.

"Go ahead," Jameson says. "Talk to her."

"I can call her back when we get more settled."

Jameson waves me off. "This is why we're here, Nora. We wanted to be closer to your mom when the baby comes. Talk to her. You know she wants to see you today now that you live less than ten minutes away."

I quickly hit the green button on my cell and put it to my ear. "Mom?"

"Eeeeee!" her high-pitched voice screeches into the phone. I swing my arm out to protect my ear drum. Jameson smirks at me. "My little girl!" my mother screams. "My little girl is back home."

"Not so loud, Mom," I laugh.

"Sorry!" she says, quickly lowering her voice. "Sorry. How's the big day going?"

"Good, Mom. Good."

"Is Jameson tired from moving all day?" she asks.

"No, Mom, we got movers. Jameson's not lifting a finger."

My husband makes a face. "Not true, Dorothy!" he shouts, leaning towards my phone. "I'm very good at pointing to where the movers should put things." Almost on cue, we hear a loud bang come from inside the house. Jameson curses to himself. "I should check on them."

"Yes, yes you should," I say in a deadpan voice.

My mom makes an overly loud sigh. "My girl is back home." The way she says it, you would think I'm moving back into my parents' home and not my own. "I can't wait to see you."

Finally getting to why she called. "I would love to see you today too, Mom. Give us a few hours and come by anytime. We can order pizza."

"Eeeeeeee!" she shrieks again.

I cover my ear once more and smile. Jameson was right about that too. This is why I'm back in Muskoka Lake. My mom was always the affectionate type, which is funny given how my father is.

I can already picture me and the baby going to Grandma's house. Having picnics in the park together. Enjoying the beaches for an afternoon.

When we lived in Toronto, everything felt

so distant. The buildings were darker. The people were all strangers. I hated it. I missed living in a small town. Now that Jameson works solely from home as a day trader, we no longer have to live in a huge urban center like Toronto.

"Eeeeeee!" my mom shouts again after I don't respond.

"I love being back in my hometown too, Mom," I say. I put a hand on my belly, thinking of those images of my mom and my baby playing together in the future. There are many perks to us living near my mom with a newborn. She could come over, allowing me breaks to sneak in a shower, or give me time to nap.

My friends in Toronto were sad when I told them I was leaving to go back to my hometown, but those of my friends with children immediately understood why. Raising a baby can be hard. I'm not naïve about what I have in store for me.

Jameson is the one completely romanticized by the idea of parenthood. I know I have a lot of sleepless nights and grumpy days ahead of me. Days that will require a lot of patience.

Being back in Muskoka Lake makes sense at this time in our lives.

"I'll see you soon, Mom," I say.

"Dad and I bought baby gifts too," she blurts out.

I hated it when she sent me gifts before the

end of my first trimester. I was worried it would curse my pregnancy, so I asked that she not send any more until I moved back home. Knowing my mom, she's already purchased enough toys and clothes to fill this moving van.

"Thanks, Mom," I say. "Maybe bring the gifts on a different day, though."

"Of course, of course. Just so you know, Dad and I are going to shower your little girl with everything she wants, like good grandparents do."

This is another thing mom does. She is adamant that I'm having a girl. She says my belly is carrying higher as I'm starting to show more, which means a baby girl.

I'm not sure if that's a myth or truth, but I feel strongly it's a girl too.

Jameson and I like to guess and talk about names, but we can't make up our minds yet. We can't agree on any name for either sex.

We have our next ultrasound in a few weeks, where we'll officially find out. Once I see my baby on the screen, and find out what they'll be, I hope I will have a better idea what to call it.

Jameson always tells me he doesn't care less what sex it is, even though I know he has his heart set on a little boy. Whenever he talks about our child, he calls it a "he", supposedly by accident. Jameson was the oldest of four siblings, all girls. Even his family dog was a female.

"I'll see you soon, Mom. Thanks for all the support. I can't wait to see you today."

"Love you, dear," she says in her high-pitched voice again. It's not exactly at her shrieking volume, but close to.

I end the call and place my phone back in my jeans pocket. I notice our neighbour's front door is open, and a young woman steps out onto the large wooden deck with a small white dog. Her blonde hair is tied in a ponytail that waves with every movement she makes. She's wearing a bright pink sports bra with shorts that are a little too short. She puts in her earbuds and touches the screen of her phone, before descending the stairs and beginning to jog towards me. Large, dark sunglasses covered her eyes.

At that moment, I realize I've been staring a little too long at her and look back at my home. It was hard not to notice her, though. For a moment, I hate myself for being envious of the woman's youth and beauty. I put my hand on my belly, which is getting larger each week, and try not to think what I'll look like when I'm nine months pregnant. I won't look like her anytime soon.

I certainly don't look like her now. After giving birth, it takes time for the body to recover from the trauma of childbirth. All the genetics play against you when you want to look thinner again. One of my friends in particular had a hard time with the changes in her body. She always comments on the loose skin around her stomach.

Of course, she doesn't regret having her child, but having a baby changes everything, especially your body. I've been trying to come to grips with this myself lately. My whole life I've been petite. Not because of hard work, like the young woman about to jog past me, but mostly genetics. I got lucky. I could eat pizza every day, soda pop, whatever, and for the most part it didn't show. I never really dieted before. Even when I was taking my medications, which tended to make people gain weight, I maintained mine.

In my peripheral vision I can see the young woman get closer, her blonde hair waving side to side faster as she picks up the pace, her dog attempting to keep up. Her face is stoic, and she appears to be concentrating.

I wonder how old she is. Perhaps college age. Anyone who lives in this part of town can't be struggling, so her parents must be well off.

It would be great when the time comes to have a babysitter live so close by. Although I'm sure my mom will be happy to take the brunt of watching over my baby, it'll be nice if we can someday find a reliable sitter who lives nearby. Of course, it'll take some time for me to trust anyone with my baby.

Jameson walks out of our house, shaking his head with a slight look of concern. I wonder how much damage our reliable movers have made in our new home. I share his expression.

Jameson walks towards me and notices the young woman running. Although he doesn't stare at her for long, he spends more time than needed on a random person. The woman is clearly gorgeous, something that strikes me immediately. It bothers me that my husband appears to have come to the same conclusion as well.

Maybe a babysitter gig isn't in our neighbour's future.

I turn to look at the woman again and realize she's not as young as I first thought. Maybe it's the bright colours she wears or her figure, but her face is noticeably older. Maybe late twenties. Perhaps older.

The woman smiles, and I notice a beauty mark above her lip.

Is that— No, it can't be.

I smile and shake my head for even thinking about it and glance at Jameson.

Can it be, though?

I look back at the woman. As if thinking the same, she slows down as she nears me, sliding the sunglasses off.

The smile vanishes from my face as the truth hits me.

She puts her head to the side and squints at me.

"Nora?" she asks. Her voice is still as

boisterous and confident as I remember.

I stare at her blankly, not responding. How am I supposed to react?

Kelly Van Patten is my new neighbour.

CHAPTER 3

Nora
Before

My best friend, Elizabeth Graham, who sits in front of me in class, reaches around and places a folded note on my desk. I continue to stare at my English teacher, Mr. Johnson, who is blabbing about the writing assignment for the week.

Without taking my gaze from the teacher, I quietly unfold it, glancing down at its contents.

"Beach tonight?" it reads. "Tap my back once for yes. Two no."

I smile and gently knock on her back once. Another note comes flying back a moment later, striking my chest. The girl whose desk is beside mine covers her face to conceal her laugh.

I try to hold back my own as I quietly open the new message.

"We should invite Ryan McDermott."

I smile, taking a moment to peer at the back of the classroom where Ryan sits with his other football buddies. As usual, they're chatting together, not paying attention to Mr. Johnson either. For a brief moment, Ryan catches my gaze and smiles back at me. He purses his lips together and blows a kiss and laughs with his friends.

His dark hair, effortlessly tousled, falls across his forehead in a way that makes my heart flutter. The way he leans back in his chair, exuding an air of confidence, draws me in like a magnet. There's an aura of mystery around him that I find irresistible.

Ryan's friend high-fives him, noticing the effect his air kiss had on me. The two of them laugh.

"Nora!" Mr. Johnson's deep voice booms. I quickly turn back and look at him, straightening my posture. "Why don't you explain to the class the writing assignment instructions I just gave, please." He raises an eyebrow, waiting for my reply.

Beth, who always has my back, answers for me. "You want us to write a short essay on the themes of jealousy and envy that impacts the characters in *Othello*."

"That's correct, Ms. Graham, but I asked Nora, didn't I?" Mr. Johnson walks down the aisle between desks towards mine.

Without regard for being caught, I quickly scrunch up the note about Ryan and place it between my legs, concealing it under my skirt. When Mr. Johnson looms over my desk, he only finds the first note that Beth wrote. He picks it up and examines it.

"Beach tonight?" he says with a laugh. "I don't suppose you and Mr. McDermott are planning on completing my writing assignment at the beach tonight, are you?"

The class erupts in laughter, Ryan's friends the loudest. I almost want to cover my ears in embarrassment until I notice the look on Ryan McDermott's face. Even though the date was with Beth, Ryan's face seems welcoming.

Maybe we *should* invite Ryan McDermott to our beach night.

Of course, if that happened, and he made a move on me, Beth would be destroyed. She's had a crush on him for years, even though he's never given her any attention to fuel it.

I look up at Mr. Johnson, pleading with my eyes for him to stop, and he catches on.

"No more love notes in my class, Nora," he says firmly. I don't bother arguing with him. I don't want to explain the note was from Beth. Instead, I give up and nod. He looks around the classroom with a smile. "This is the last month of high school for most of you," he says. "Try and keep what little attention spans you have left. We do have a final test coming that you will want to do well in."

A knock on the class door has everyone's attention. Mr. Johnson drops Beth's note back on my desk and opens it. "Can I help you?" he asks. I try to lean to the side as much as my desk allows when I hear a young woman reply. I can't see anything, though. Mr. Johnson's large body is covering the mystery girl. "That's great, come on in... Kelly, you said?"

Mr. Johnson turns back to the classroom, revealing a tall, thin girl with blonde hair. Most female students at St. Joseph's Catholic High School wear their skirts a little too high, and their dress shirts more revealing. She was something else, though. The skirt seems to barely reach her long legs. Her dress shirt had two or even three buttons undone, leaving little to the imagination.

It only takes a moment for one of the young men in the back of the class to holler something. I can't make it out what he says, but it's an obvious sign that he's happy with the new girl's appearance. Some of the boys in the back laugh again and Mr. Johnson quiets them down quickly.

"Enough!" he shouts. "This is Kelly..."

"Van Patten," the girl says with a thin smile.

"Right, Kelly Van Patten," Mr. Johnson announces. "She just moved to Muskoka from Toronto." He turns to her. "Why don't you grab any empty desk?"

Kelly nods, and looks around the room, spotting the one beside Beth. She quickly walks down the aisle and drops her backpack beside her.

"Hey," Kelly says to her. Beth waves back.

"This spot open?"

Beth nods. "I'm Beth," she says. "Did your family just move into the house on Meyers Street?

"That's right," Kelly says with a smile.

"I live down the block from you." Beth matches her smile.

Kelly lets out a laugh. "Well, you'll have to give me the lowdown on what's happening in this small town."

I hear chatter behind me. I turn and notice Ryan's friend whispering something in his ear. I see his gaze go across the room, but this time it's not on me. The new girl, Kelly, has his full attention.

I turn back and watch her continue to chat with my best friend. I watch them for a few moments before poking the new girl's back.

She turns to me with a wry smile.

"Hi," I say, reaching out my hand. "I'm Nora."

CHAPTER 4

Nora
Present

"Kelly?" I say, feigning a smile at the woman walking towards me. "Is that you?" I ask, even though I know it is. I'm trying not to react to knowing the terrible truth.

"Wow!" Kelly says. "I mean, it's been-"

"Yeah, forever," I answer, thinking that forever is too short a time.

"Wait, are you moving in?" she asks, surprised. "No way! Nora, I live right next door to you."

I know you do, I think. That's why I want to yell at my two movers to drag the furniture out of my new home and go back to Toronto. I don't care how much they damage the home doing so.

I can no longer live here.

"That's... crazy," I say.

"I almost didn't recognize you," she says, taking a moment to look me up and down.

I nod. "Yeah. Same for you." She smiles at

me, not saying anything. She used to do this to me when we were younger. She has a way of gawking at you, waiting for you to say something when you have no clue how to answer. It always made me feel small. "Well... I mean, you look great."

Kelly waves me off. "Oh, stop! I just can't believe we're neighbours."

Jameson walks up to us and puts out his hand to Kelly. "Hi," he says. Kelly looks at him a moment before grabbing his hand. She smiles before releasing it.

"Firm handshake," she laughs. She looks at me, and back at my husband.

"Sorry," I say, coming out of my daze. Or is it a nightmare? "This is my husband, Jameson. I'm Nora Bowman now." It takes another awkward moment before I realize I haven't introduced her. "And this is... well, our new neighbour, I guess, Kelly Van Patten."

"Nice to meet you, Kelly," Jameson says, nodding. "How do you two know each other?"

"Highschool besties," Kelly answers, although I'm shocked by her reply.

"Yeah, high school," I repeat. "Such a long time ago."

Her small dog barks. "Oh, and how could I forget? This is Lady." Kelly smiles at me. "Look at us now, though, all grown up. Who would have thought we would live in this part of town? You're going to love it here."

I don't answer. It may be the shock still in full effect.

"Thanks, Kelly," Jameson says with a laugh. "Kelly Van Patten, you said, right?"

Kelly gives a thin smile. "Well, Kelly McDermott now."

I almost scoff. If I had taken a drink, I would have sprayed it everywhere.

McDermott? Kelly actually married Ryan McDermott. How could anyone marry that scumbag? Of course it would be Kelly. Truthfully, they deserved each other.

What I don't deserve, though, is to be neighbours with Kelly and Ryan McDermott. A demon couple is living next door to me.

"Oh," I say, finally joining the conversation. "You married Ryan? That's great. How is he?"

Kelly lowers her head and takes in a deep breath. "Well, he's... he passed. Recently. It's been about eight months now." She touches the gold wedding ring on her finger. "I should probably change my name back to Van Patten now, I know. I just... don't really know what to do, to be honest. It was unexpected."

The lively expression disappears from Kelly's face. I'm suddenly overwhelmed with guilt for thinking so terribly of him. She's widowed at such a young age. I wonder if she has children. I touch my belly for a moment, trying to think of my life without Jameson in it.

The compassionate side of me comes back, and I put a hand on Kelly's shoulder. "I'm so sorry to hear. That's terrible." Jameson is quiet as he watches us.

"I'm still getting used to life without him," Kelly says. She turns her face from me and looks at Jameson. "I'm happy you found someone, too. Before I came out for my jog, I noticed this nice-looking couple standing outside. I hoped whoever moved next door were going to be good people. Now I know. It's even better than I could have asked for."

The movers come out of our home and walk back into the truck. They emerge, poorly balancing a large sofa.

Jameson follows them. "The main living room, right beside the kitchen."

"No problem," one of them answers, catching his breath.

"Well, I should let you guys get back to it," Kelly says. She looks at me a moment before reaching out with her hands and hugging me tightly. I'm not sure how to feel about it and thankfully she lets go almost immediately. "I'm so happy that we're going to be neighbours."

"It's great to see you, Kelly," I say, smiling back. "You'll have to catch me up on what's been happening in Muskoka."

She laughs. "As usual, a bunch of nothing. And it was nice to meet you, James."

"Jameson," my husband corrects her.

"Right, sorry." She waves at us both before turning and resuming her jog. Her little dog looks at me for a moment before Kelly gently pulls on the leash and she follows.

I watch Kelly for a moment before looking at my husband, who's still staring at our new neighbour as she continues down the block.

"Van Patten," he repeats, continuing to look at her. "You told me about her, didn't you?"

"Not really," I say. I've told many stories about her, none of which were good, but when I moved to Toronto, I thought it was better to leave Kelly and my past behind me as much as possible.

Kelly was one of the many reasons I left Muskoka many years ago. Now that reason is living right next door.

Jameson shakes his head. "Widowed." He turned to me and smiled. "I can't imagine what I would be like if you weren't in my life. That woman must be wrecked."

I nod in agreement. Here I am, digging up old resentments with Kelly, when I can't stop and appreciate what I have in my life.

Jameson puts his hand around my waist. "I love you, Nora." I smile up at him as he leans down and kisses me softly. He places his other hand on my belly and smiles. "And I have the perfect name for him: Oscar."

I laugh. "As in Oscar the Grouch? I hate it."

He makes a face. "More like Oscar De La Hoya, the boxer," he says. "But if you want me to focus on *Sesame Street* names, he should be called the Count."

I roll my eyes. "You need to start coming up with more girl names, I think."

"Oh, I have the perfect one. I've been keeping it to myself, waiting for the right moment to say it out loud."

"Okay, what is it?"

"Helga," he says confidently.

I sigh. "That's even worse. I pray for the baby to be named Oscar now."

CHAPTER 5

Kelly

That couldn't have gone any better.

The look on Nora's face was perfect.

It was worth my obsessive waiting by my front door for the moving truck to arrive. I'd been watching for Nora. She was easy to spot. A little larger than I remember, but of course, that's expected when you're pregnant. That was something else my realtor friend, Shannon, told me about Nora.

I have to say I wasn't expecting her husband to be so handsome. I saw the thick veins on his forearm that ran up his arm when he shook my hand. It was hard not to notice the bulging muscles hidden under his short-sleeved shirt.

If I didn't hate Nora as much as I do, I would have high-fived her for a job well done on finding a hot husband.

I continue my daily run, thinking about how our first interaction went.

If only Nora knew how much thought I

put into it, she would be much more worried. Maybe she would even hightail it out of town all together.

Let's hope not.

I may not know the next step in my grand plan, but I do know Nora can't leave until I get what I want. After that, she won't be going anywhere anytime soon.

I think of her husband, and it upsets me. He and Nora truly came off like the "happy couple".

That bothers me.

Even better for them, they have a little baby on the way. She has a beautiful home, a handsome husband, and soon a family. Isn't it just... perfect?

Karma isn't, though. I'm the dark cloud about to rain over Nora's beautiful day.

After our exchange, I look back. I half hope to catch her husband gawking at me. After all, it was part of the plan. I picked out my prettiest workout gear to get attention, not only from Nora, but the husband, too.

Perhaps that makes me wicked, but it's nothing compared to what Nora did. I slow my run, noticing Lady having a hard time keeping up, and lean against a fence overlooking the lake. It's one of my favourite places to take a break while jogging. The scenery is beautiful. It's something I can never get used to.

Despite its beauty, at times I think about what happened with Nora and me. I think about Beth. I try not to. I'd rather forget all about what happened, but I won't be able to, ever.

Images of Elizabeth Graham still haunt me. It haunted Ryan, too.

Instead of thinking of her, I continue my run. It helps you to avoid thinking about the past when you keep moving.

As I run into the downtown area, I spot Constable Tallie, a large cup of gourmet coffee in her hand, getting out of her vehicle in the Ontario Provincial Police parking lot. She closes her door, sees me and waves.

I smile and wave back. I watch as the larger woman enters the police building. Sandra Tallie was another graduate of St. Joe's High, along with Nora and me.

I never thought she would become a member of law enforcement, despite her always talking about it in high school. She was so shy. I didn't know her well back then. Nobody did; she was sort of a loner.

What she lacked in social skill she made up for in determination. She became a police officer stationed in her hometown. She always wore a short-sleeved button-up shirt with her black stab-proof vest over the top.

I take a moment and slow my pace, breathing more heavily than usual. Lady, struggling just as badly, looks up at me with pleading eyes.

Perhaps it's better to go back home. Now that I've reintroduced myself into Nora's life, it's time to think of what the next step should be.

Usually, my morning run makes me feel centred. I feel more at peace with myself. A calmness will overcome my emotions to the point where I'm numb to my past.

Today is different.

All I can think about is Nora.

I think about what I want to do and second guess myself. There's time to stop myself from letting this go further.

I thought about moving back to Toronto after Ryan was gone. After the Millers put up the "For Sale" sign on their yard and I saw how quickly it sold, I'd thought about putting mine up for sale.

I could travel a bit. Explore the world more. Find myself, or whatever.

Even my parents moved back to Toronto separately after their long and messy divorce.

There was nothing keeping me here in this town.

That was until I found out Nora would be my neighbour. That was until I saw an opportunity to get back at her. To ruin her. Or worse.

This doesn't have to go any further, a voice

inside me says, stronger this time. Just leave town. In this real estate market, I could put my house up for sale and it would sell before I could figure out my travel plans.

I've always wanted to go to Europe too. I could arrange for a nice, long vacation.

Then I think of the small bump in Nora's belly. The ball of happiness growing inside her. Her husband. This perfect life she will have.

It may be childish to think so, but it's not fair.

I feel like my mind is made up again. It's extreme, but Nora deserves it.

She deserves everything that she has coming. The only question is: how far am I willing to go to get what I want?

I think of the kiss Nora and her husband shared when I watched them from inside my home, and again I've made up my mind.

I will do whatever it takes.

As I run by Nora's home on my way back, I don't see her anywhere. I spot the two movers and her husband Jameson directing them.

The two movers slow as they spot me. Jameson waves at me, and I wave back.

I run past them, and after a few moments, turn my head to look back. As expected, the two movers are gawking at me.

What I find very interesting, though, is that Jameson Bowman is too.

CHAPTER 6

Nora

I hunch over the toilet bowl in my new bathroom, not holding back.

The nausea has gotten worse over the past week. Sometimes when I open the refrigerator, a waft of food will tickle my nostrils and I'll run to the bathroom to alleviate myself. A few days ago, I was walking around Costco and smelt rubber, causing me to immediately make my way to their facility, which I thankfully did just in time. It doesn't even have to be a smell. Thinking about raw chicken upsets my stomach to no end.

My mom told me that the healthier the baby is, the more nauseous you feel. I don't know if I believe that, but if it's true, I have a superhero growing inside me.

I flush the toilet when I'm done, taking a moment to watch the mess I made swirl away.

I just wish these symptoms would get better. I have a lot more pregnancy left and from what I understand, it's not peachy the rest of the way.

The things women endure to keep humanity alive.

I'm not even sure what caused me to get sick this time. Perhaps it was seeing Kelly again. Can seeing someone you don't like cause morning sickness?

I take my time standing up and notice Jameson at the door frame, his usual look of concern etched in his face and a glass of water ready in hand.

"Thanks," I say, sipping it.

"Was it the stinky mover?" he asked, making a face. "That one with the moustache had a stench that bothered even non-pregnant people."

I cover my mouth and wave at him to stop. "I don't know. I'm just a mess."

"A *hot* mess," he says playfully. He laughs at his joke and leaves me.

I wipe my mouth and wash my hands, rolling my eyes at him. Usually his playfulness lightens the mood, but it's hard to see anything as funny, having found out who I live next door to.

I experience a rush of nausea again, and in that moment I wish I could feel normal again.

Of course, I don't mean that. Having a baby is very important to me—to us. The feeling of being uncomfortable, sticky, and all around yucky can just be too much at times.

A month before our marriage, I stopped taking birth control pills with the hope I would be pregnant soon. I wasn't worried about it at first. My naïve assumption when I was younger was that you could get pregnant even thinking of a penis.

It was after eight months of trying that I got concerned. Was there a medical reason it wasn't happening? We bought ovulation tests to see when I was most fertile for months and months.

Nothing happened, though. Even science failed us.

We both met with doctors who assured us nothing was wrong medically. It just wasn't happening. That didn't make sense to me. We both switched our diets, took vitamins, and worked out more. We became a healthy couple, but frustratingly not pregnant.

Jameson really took to the new lifestyle.

After a while we stopped getting ovulation kits or even running to the late-night pharmacy when I felt I might be pregnant or that my body was different. I was so hyper-focused on any changes that I believed I was pregnant nearly every month and was let down each time when I discovered I wasn't.

It was only once I stopped caring that it happened. Our miracle. The stars aligned one night, and our baby was conceived.

It was an incredible feeling holding a positive pregnancy test.

It's completely disgusting, but we kept the urine test in a Ziploc bag. I felt like it was a trophy. It took nearly two years, but Jameson and I were going to be parents.

I tried not to get ahead of myself, knowing many women have issues during the first trimester. I would do my best not to even think about the baby until the first three months were over and it was still safe inside me.

Jameson comes back inside the bathroom with my pill bottle. "Thought you may be looking for these," he says, placing it on the counter. I thank him and he leaves again.

My pills are the last thing I want, but he didn't know that. I close the bathroom door and put the bottle in the medicine cabinet.

I take a deep breath, collecting myself, my stomach in knots. I place my hand on my belly.

"What's wrong, baby?" I whisper. "What's made you so upset today?" I sigh.

I hear a knock at the front door and breathe out heavily with a smile. Mom is finally here, although sooner than expected. There's something comforting even as an adult when you don't feel well, and your mother is nearby. I think of the times when I was sick, upset, and sad as a child and my mother comforted me until I felt better.

My mother can be too much at times with her support, but I always know it's there, and that's what matters most to me. I can put up with her suffocating love because she loves me. I hope someday to give my baby what my mother provides me, but maybe a little less.

I step out of the bathroom, the smile still plastered on my face as Jameson opens the door. Instead of bear-hugging my mother like he tends to, he stares outside a moment before nodding and saying, "Thank you so much."

I approach slowly, realizing it's not my mother, and almost panic when I hear Kelly's strong voice.

"It's no problem," she tells my husband. Jameson leans towards her, his head outside and out of view. I lean to the side to see what's happening, wanting to stay out of sight.

Jameson comes back inside with a large wicker basket filled to the brim with items. He looks at me and waves me over, nearly losing hold of the basket. "It's our new neighbour with a welcome package."

"It's nothing really," Kelly says.

I slowly walk up beside him and put my hand around his waist, which is difficult given the size of the basket in his hand.

"You didn't have to," I say with a smile, "but thank you."

"I wish I'd known it was you moving next

door," Kelly says. "I would have personalized it to what I remember. I bought this yesterday."

Jameson quickly looks inside the basket, trying to make out what he can through the film wrapping. "Oh, a bottle of wine; I guess I'll have to drink that on my own." He smiles at me.

"Oh!" Kelly says with an expression of surprise. "Are you pregnant?"

I nod and smile. "Yes, in the second trimester now."

Kelly laughs. "That's amazing! Congratulations. I thought you might have been, but I didn't want to assume anything. You never know, right?"

I feign a smile again, hating her for thinking I might just have gained weight. So what if I had?

"Thanks, Kelly," I say. "For everything. Such a wonderful welcome basket."

"I'll have to get another one for you when the baby comes," she says. There's something about the way she does so that bothers me. Back in high school, she had a playful way she spoke to people she bullied. I knew because I saw it firsthand. It was as if she turned into an infomercial salesperson, selling you some gadget that was complete garbage. She did it constantly to this schoolmate of ours named Sandy Tallie. For whatever reason, Sandy was the brunt of many jokes made in private and public at St. Joe's.

"That would be great," Jameson replies. "A baby basket like this would fill up our future nursery."

Kelly's bottom lip tightens. "That's lovely. Which room are you planning on having the nursery in? I've been to this home so many times before, when the Miller family lived here." She looks at me with a raised eyebrow. "Mrs. Miller was my wine buddy, which you will be too—once you can, that is." She laughs.

I smile. "There's this room beside the master bedroom. We wanted to make that the nursery. It's a little small, but once he grows out of it, he can upgrade to a bigger one."

"Right," Kelly says with an odd expression. It's as if her energy changes from fake info salesperson to whatever she's trying to be now. "You probably don't know much about the last owners, do you?"

Both of us shake our heads. "Why?" Jameson asks. "Should we have?"

"Well, I shouldn't say anything," Kelly says, putting a finger to her red lips. "It's nothing. I'm just superstitious, I guess."

"What happened?" I ask.

Kelly takes a deep breath. "I wouldn't have mentioned this, but since you said you wanted to make that room the nursery... The Millers lost a child. He was under a year, maybe only six months old. It was SIDS. It wasn't anyone's fault, but Mrs. Miller, Patricia, she really had a hard time after. I think she blamed herself. They put their baby boy down to sleep, and... It was a tragedy."

I can't hold back my expression, and it's plain as day to Kelly, who covers her mouth. "I didn't mean to upset you. Oh, my goodness."

"No," Jameson says in a sombre tone. "I'm glad you told us. Thanks. I should call that real estate agent to give her hell for not mentioning it."

Kelly nods. "I feel like I put a damper on your move-in day. I never wanted to do that to you guys." She suddenly smiles again. I always hated how she did that. One moment she would be sad and the next, flip a switch to the total opposite. Some people never change. "You said *he* does; does that mean you're having a boy?"

This time, I answer. "Jameson hopes so."

"Not true, not true." He shakes his head. "I will love anything. However," he says, smiling at Kelly, "if I notice a little noodle in the ultrasound coming up, I may open that bottle of wine you gave us."

Kelly laughs, putting out a hand and touching his chest. "So funny! Well, I should go. You guys have a great first night in your new home."

If I could have, I would have swatted her petite hand before it ever touched my husband, but instead I thank her again. Jameson tells her to have a good night as I shut the door.

"Such a nice woman," Jameson says when it's the two of us. He walks to the kitchen counter and takes the film off the basket. He starts taking out the items inside. I'm surprised by how many it could fit.

Out came several bottles of wine, specialty coffee, freshly sliced meat, crackers, and soft cheeses.

Basically, everything I can't have when I'm pregnant.

I shake my head as Jameson cuts open a large slab of salami.

I'm not sure I can handle this. How can I live next door to Kelly?

What the baby has been upset about hits me. It's been bothering me too since we pulled up to our new house. Seeing Kelly exacerbated everything.

I can vividly remember what Beth Graham looked like when we were teenagers. The thought of her makes me feel sick inside.

I knew it would be hard moving back to Muskoka Lake after what happened. I thought I could handle it. Kelly living next door changes everything.

All I can think about is Beth Graham and the terrible event that happened.

CHAPTER 7

Nora
Before

Beth and I sit on a rock on a short beach. We take off our sandals and enjoy dipping our feet in the cold water as we chat. The water isn't warm enough yet to fully enjoy, but will be in another week or so.

This is our special place. We discovered it when hiking on a trail nearby. The beach isn't sandy but filled with pebbles. The large trees and branches that hung over us make our spot nearly invisible to anyone on the water or the nearby trail. After our first few times coming here, we realized we had a gem of a place, all to ourselves.

It's as if we have our own clubhouse. A private beach just for us. Even though Beth joked about bringing Ryan McDermott here, I don't think she meant it. This is our place. Nobody else would enter it.

We share secrets here. Sometimes we write poetry together.

I've never really had a close friend like Beth before. Of course, I have friends, but when Beth's family moved into town from southern Ontario four years ago, we instantly clicked.

We had a passion for creative writing, which was evident in our English class. It's how we started getting to know each other. We decided to partner up for a project where we had to present information about the book *Lord of the Flies*.

We were also obsessed with this television show called *Gilmore Girls* and would watch it together each week.

She's easy to talk to. She won't interject with her own stories when I'm telling mine. She won't one-up me in conversation with something that happened to her. She genuinely listens to you.

It's something I admire about her.

"That was a close one with Mr. Johnson today," Beth says, and dips her toe in the water, collecting a bunch of seaweed with her foot. She makes a yuck face as she flings it across the water.

"Thank god he didn't find the other note," I say with my eyes wide. "You're going to get me in trouble."

Beth laughs. "Have you started applying for universities?"

It's something I hate talking about. Beth nonchalantly bringing it up is like being struck by a bolt of lightning.

"Not yet," I answer. I have no clue what I want to do next. I've only just turned eighteen. How the hell am I supposed to know what I want to do for the rest of my life? They expect us to invest a bunch of money in education when I can barely make up my mind on what to eat for lunch that day.

Worse though, is knowing Beth won't stay in town. She has grand plans to be a social worker. She's talked about getting her bachelor's in social work many times. She's already applied to the University of Toronto and to Windsor, although she's hoping for Toronto more. She applied early and hopes she'll get an answer soon.

Then off she'll go. Our private beach will be only for me then.

I've thought about applying to the University of Toronto too. I'm not sure what I would take, though. Speaking to our guidance counselor at St. Joe's, he told me when people struggle with a major, they can take a general degree at university for a year or two and it won't impact them too much. Once in college, and hopefully a little more mature, you can pick a major.

"You should apply to Toronto," Beth says. It's not the first time she's mentioned it. "We could be roomies. Find an apartment close by. That way, I don't have to stay on campus." She sighs when I don't reply right away. "Come on!" She shoves me, nearly causing me to fall off the rock.

"I'm weighing options," I say, cupping my hand in the water and splashing her. She laughs, making a bigger wave back.

"I saw that new girl walking home today," she says, changing the subject.

I've been trying to forget about her and the exchange we had in class today. "Kim, right?"

"Kelly," Beth corrects me. "Kelly Van Patten. She lives so close to me. We walked together for a bit on the way home."

I raise my eyebrow and dip my toe in the water. "She seems a little stuck-up to me."

"She was really easygoing, I thought. She's pretty, so I thought she would be a snob, too, but she's really nice. Really easy to talk to."

I think about how Ryan looked at Kelly when she entered class. How Beth so quickly opened up to greeting the new girl. Now they're walking home together.

I tilt my head. "I think Ryan McDermott has a crush on her already. I could hear him and his friends whispering at the back of the class."

Beth's expression changes and she looks down at the water. I knew that would get to her. How many times have we talked about Ryan McDermott at this beach? How many times did we fantasize about what kissing him would be like?

I've had a few boyfriends. Nothing long term. The three relationships I've had lasted a few months. Nothing really happened with those boys. A lot of making out, and some heavy petting, but that was as far as it went.

Beth had *much* less experience. One boyfriend that lasted only a week. She never even kissed him. She joked that she was keeping herself for Ryan McDermott. I didn't have to tell her that Ryan wasn't holding himself back for anyone. He has a reputation at school that goes much further than the three relationships I've had.

"I'm sure a lot of boys will be interested in her," Beth says with a thin smile. "She's an interesting person."

"And gorgeous," I say, shaking my head. "She'll have half the boys wrapped around her finger before graduation. Who moves their kid to a new school a month before high school ends? Talk about good parenting."

Beth scoffs. Her parents divorced when she was young. It was something that we've talked about many times, especially at the beach. It upsets her to speak about her father.

I shared stories about my dad, too. Even though my parents have stayed together, it's rocky at the best of times. There was a year where they separated and lived apart. I stayed with mom. My dad didn't visit me for six months until he eventually reached out to Mom and arranged to see me once a week.

I'm not sure how my parents got back together, but eventually they did. Maybe it was out of shared misery of being alone. Although I didn't see much difference in happiness once they were together again. They're just... different people. I wonder how the two of them could have even fallen for each other, being complete opposites.

Beth reaches down to grab her backpack that leans against the rock. "I have something for you," she says with a smile. "I was going to hold off till the end of the year to give it to you, but why wait?"

I smile back. "That's unexpected. I didn't know we were supposed to give each other friend gifts after graduating. Is this your 'I'll never see you again' parting gift to me?"

Beth rolls her eyes. "You have a way of ruining a moment, you know."

I nod. "I've been told."

Beth rummages around until she pulls out a gold necklace, a pendant gripped in her palm. She opens it up and inside is a picture of the two of us from last September.

I can't hold back my smile. "That's just amazing." She hands it to me, and I examine the photo. It was taken by her mom on a trip to

Wonderland. Right after the picture was taken we went on a rollercoaster that made Beth sick for the rest of the day.

"I have one for me, too," Beth says, grabbing another pendant inside her bag.

I immediately put it around my neck and look down at it. I wrap my arm around her. "Thanks. This means a lot."

"My dad took me out to this market last weekend," she says. Much like things were when my parents were separated, he sees her once a week, although now that she is getting older it's more like once a month. "When I saw the matching pendants, I had to get them. My dad bartered with the guy for ten minutes until he gave me a deal." She laughs. "It's not real gold, though."

"Could have fooled me," I say. "I love it, thank you."

The fact that it isn't gold doesn't matter. She could have given me a necklace made of Cheerios on a piece of string and I'd be happy with it because of the pendant and its meaning.

I lower my head. "I really don't know what I'm going to do in this town when you're gone."

Beth gives me a thin smile. "So don't stay. Come to Toronto."

"You don't even know if you got accepted yet."

Beth nods. "Well, just come wherever. You

don't know what you want to do yet, anyway. You don't even have to go to college. Just work for a bit."

I look down at my necklace. I hate talking about the future. It's Beth ruining this special moment now. I can feel a tear welling in my eye. "I never had a friend like you," I say.

Beth pats my back. "I know. I feel the same." We stare off into the blue water, dipping our toes in.

CHAPTER 8

Kelly
Present

I arrive back home and shut the door with a wide smile on my face. I can't hold back the laughter. I lean on the table in the foyer to catch myself from falling over.

The table shakes and so does the vase with Ryan's ashes. I stand and look at the picture of my husband.

He would have laughed, too, had he been there. That was something we always shared, a sick sense of humour. It made things fun during dark times to have some levity in our marriage.

An image of Nora's face when I told her the story of the Miller family's "tragedy" comes to mind, and I almost die laughing again.

Of course, it wouldn't have been funny had that story been real. The Millers had two children, both grown adults now. Mr. and Mrs. Miller are senior citizens. They moved to downsize to an apartment and live closer to their grandchildren.

It was bad enough giving her a basket of things she couldn't enjoy. I hope that immediately after I left her husband ate some of it in front of her. That would be the cherry on top. If only I could be a fly on the wall in their home. It would make this much more fun.

I'm already having a ball at Nora's expense.

I laugh again, and it's my echo that stops me. What would a fly on my wall think?

There's something pathetic about it. I'm letting the fun and games consume me. It's as if my body is a vehicle that I have no control over. Instead of gasoline, my engine is running on pure revenge.

When the laughter stops, the silence hits me. I look down at the table, at Ryan.

I think of Nora and her husband. That satisfied look on her face when she wrapped her arm around Jameson in front of me. She did that on purpose, I know.

I told them I was a widow. I mentioned he died, suddenly. They didn't even ask a follow-up question. Not an "oh, what happened?" or a "but you're so young to be a widow, how could this be?"

No more fun and games.

I've had my laughs, now it's time to figure out how to get even. I spend most of the night thinking of ideas, shooting them down because they are either too extreme or I know

I'll get caught. It will be important to maintain the image of the welcoming neighbour while executing my plan as well.

I sit at a desk in my office, fiddling with a notepad, writing down ideas. Every now and then, I look out the window, trying to spot Nora inside their home. Even though our large yards separate us, I still have a good view inside their house. I can see right into their master bedroom from here.

It was something that made me cringe when the old Millers lived next door. At night time, if a light was on, I could see clear as day what was happening inside, even from this distance. One night, Mr. Miller got a little fresh with old Mrs. Miller. I immediately shut my blinds, trying to get the image out of my brain. Apparently, I not only enjoy torturing Nora but also myself because I can still vividly see Mrs. Miller's fragile-looking hand unzipping his pants.

I shake at the thought. Although I must say well done on them for being their age and still wanting to get it on.

Near the end of my marriage, Ryan would barely touch me. No matter how good I knew I looked, he wouldn't put a finger on me. The times I forced him, he was quick. It was as if having sex with me was a chore. The last time, he couldn't get erect. I stopped trying after that.

A light turns on in the master bedroom

and Nora comes into view, followed by Jameson. They kiss each other and hold hands, walking around the room. Nora's pointing at the wall. I can imagine what they're talking about. What picture should go here or there?

Where should we hang our wedding photo? Where should we hang all the pictures that represent our happy life together to show it off?

I cringe again and close the blinds. I would rather watch the Millers get it on than another second of Nora and Jameson Bowman being happy together.

I take a heavy breath, shoving my notebook off my desk. It flies across the room, striking the wall. I put my hands across my forehead, slipping them down my face. I turn my head and Lady is lying in her favourite corner of the room. She'll be no help in figuring out what to do.

I suddenly think of an idea. It's funny how they pop into your head after a while, or when you're desperate.

What if I could be a fly on Nora's wall?

CHAPTER 9

Nora
Present

I've been back for one day and already had two encounters with Kelly. When my mom actually shows up, she at least makes things... better. More manageable.

I don't mention Kelly being my neighbour. My mom would likely remember her from when I was younger. I don't want to talk more about Kelly Van Patten today. I don't want to think about her husband, Ryan. I certainly don't want to think about Beth.

It's all too much.

My mom comes only for a short while. She makes us tea and chats in our new dining area. We give her the grand tour of the new home and at each space her mouth gapes wider and wider.

She loves the backyard. Who wouldn't? The pool's surrounded by foliage and overhung by trees. It almost reminds me of the beach that Beth and I would visit.

Mom can't wait to come back and says she wants to get out of our hair since it's getting dark. Moving in day has certainly wiped us out, even with the help of movers; Jameson's exhausted, spending most of my mom's visit laid out on the couch.

He had been moving furniture around from where the movers initially put it, at my direction, which he hated. Once the furniture was in its best placement, though, Jameson saw how much more beautiful our living spaces were. I have a knack for decorating and space management. Jameson says I just have a skill for bossing people around.

I'm sure the truth lies somewhere in the middle.

Of course, my father didn't come. Mom made up some excuse about him having errands to do, but you could tell she was just covering. His only daughter moves back to town to be closer to him and he can't be bothered to turn off the sports channel and visit. I'm sure it's finals time in one sport or another.

I never understood how someone as loving as my mother could be with someone so emotionally closed off as my father. How did Norman and Dorothy Cameron ever fall in love? How was I ever created from their love?

"We marry our parents" is a saying I've heard many times, and thankfully that's not the case for me. Jameson is nothing like my father.

My dad was a mechanic, used to working with his hands all day, melting in a humid garage. My husband works inside with air conditioning and has an ergonomic keyboard. My father was handy, and Jameson is anything but.

As I list these attributes, my father sounds more appealing, but I know he's not. He's a difficult person, unable to be open to anybody else's feelings besides his own selfishness.

Jameson is the opposite. Caring, empathetic, even vulnerable. During our first date, we watched a tear-jerker at the movie theatre. It was one of those mushy movies where one of the characters has cancer and you pray they survive, and of course they don't. I was nearly bawling my eyes out, as usual, and when I looked at my Jameson, his eyes were nearly decently wet.

My father would have joked about what a pansy he was had he seen him at that moment. My father wasn't one to care about insensitive words, either.

Where my father would have seen weakness, I saw husband material.

After my mom's visit to our new home, Jameson gives her a huge bear hug, as he usually would when he greeted her when she left. At first it had been a joke, but it's stuck. Even my father thought it was funny after a while, especially when Jameson would try to match my mom's natural enthusiasm, which she's infamous for.

They would shout 'Eeeeee!' together as they embraced. It was cute to watch.

Before leaving, mom and I make plans to do some baby shopping tomorrow. There's a lot to get ready, and we have nothing prepared.

Adding to the list of headaches is figuring out a new nursery. After Kelly told us what happened to the child of the previous owners, there's no way we can keep that room as the nursery. I'm not superstitious in the least, but it twists my stomach in knots thinking of the idea.

After Kelly left, Jameson gave me a look, and I knew exactly what he was thinking. He'd wanted the baby's room to be the larger one down the hall. I'd wanted the one closest to our bedroom. Of course, my choice was cursed.

I try not to think of what happened in that room, but it's hard to shake. I can't imagine having this wonderful child inside me growing for nine months and coming out into the world only to leave just as quickly.

How did the Miller family ever recover?

Did their marriage fall apart after the passing of their child? Is that why they left the neighbourhood?

The idea of Jameson and I moving into a home after a tragedy like that made my heart sink. I wish Kelly hadn't told us, but in the end, I suppose I'm glad she did. Had I known, I don't think I could have ever bought this home, despite how beautiful it is.

After Kelly left, while gobbling down some of the items in the basket she gave us, Jameson mentioned a few times how nice she is.

Maybe he's not wrong about that. Maybe I'm being too harsh on Kelly for what happened in the past.

People change, after all. I certainly have.

I thought I'd never be the same after what happened before I left Muskoka. All I wanted to do was escape, and Toronto seemed like the logical choice to flee to.

Staying there changed me. It took a long time, and a lot of therapy for me to let go of the past. I thought I had grown beyond my resentments, my rage. My sadness. I finally reached a place of peace with everything.

After two visits with Kelly today, I realize that may not be the case.

I walk upstairs to our bedroom and close the door behind me. I can hear Jameson snoring on the couch in the living room. It's only nine at night, but he's extremely tired.

I take out my cell phone and stare at the last text message I had from my therapist, Dr. Amy Albee.

"I wish you all the best, Nora, with moving back home to be with your family during this exciting time. If you ever need to talk, we can still arrange a phone session."

I thanked her in reply a week ago.

If I was being truthful with myself, I should call Amy. Tell her how I feel all my insecurities are simmering at the surface today after running into Kelly Van Patten. Dr. Albee had heard everything about her. She had heard all about Ryan. She knew what happened with Beth.

I thought I had changed after my long time working with Dr. Albee. I had worked so hard over the past several years in therapy. I thought I'd discovered the root cause of the trauma and why I felt so terrible all the time.

I finally knew after countless sessions why I felt the way I did, but even diagnosing it with the help of my therapist didn't change how it impacted me. I was still irritable. I was overly emotional. I was easily triggered, and a jealous human being.

I hated who I was.

Medications had a huge impact on me. Once I found the right prescription and dosage, it changed me at a molecular level. I still had feelings. I didn't turn into a robot because of a pill. The impact of my emotions definitely changed for the better. They were muted. I wouldn't get upset at the same thoughts that stayed inside me.

Dr. Albee taught me this mental health exercise that she called the Conveyor Belt. With my eyes closed, she would have me imagine I was standing beside a conveyor belt. On it were packages that would slowly pass by. Each of these packages would represent something. It could be the feeling of inadequacy I felt around my father. Another could be wanting to be an important person, even though I felt worthless. As these emotional packages came by me, I would imagine picking them up and feeling those emotions.

Rage, envy, or sadness would overcome me when I picked up these emotional packages. I would then put them back on the conveyor belt, and eventually they would go in a circle and come back to me. The idea of the exercise was that as these emotional packages returned to you it would impact you less and less.

Sometimes the exercise worked, and sometimes I struggled with it. After my prescription of Prozac kicked in after a few months, I felt almost cured. I would do the same exercise, imagine picking up the emotional package, try to feel those emotions attached to it, but it would have little impact. It wouldn't move the needle on my mood.

It felt great.

Then I found out I was pregnant. My therapist and doctor both assured me it was okay for me to continue to take my medication. I believed them, but my fear got the better of me. I Googled and saw blogs or forums where people talked about what they believed were negative effects of taking mental health medications while being pregnant.

Without telling anyone, I stopped taking them entirely. I didn't go cold turkey. I learned online that it could be very dangerous to do that. I found articles about how people safely weaned themselves off Prozac. It took over a month before I was completely off it.

I was worried a flood of negative emotions would come back, but thankfully, nothing changed.

Jameson won't understand if I tell him I stopped taking my medications. Dr. Albee definitely won't approve, either. It's not worth risking the health of my baby if there's even a slight chance of a negative outcome. I can always resume them after I'm done breastfeeding, or who knows, maybe stop altogether. I've felt much better. Being pregnant has made me happy. Sick, but overall happy.

Being neighbours with Kelly will test that.

Worse case, I can come clean to my husband and Dr. Albee about not taking my medications. If my mood changes drastically and I feel the same as I did before, I can do something about it.

Jameson opens the bedroom door, stretches and falls into the bed, headfirst.

"What a day," he says into the mattress.

"What a day," I repeat.

Jameson turns his head and looks up at me with a stare I've seen many times in the bedroom, especially at night. "So, Mrs. Bowman, how about we start off moving into our new home the right way? Christen the bedroom first, I'm thinking. Seems very logical to me. Maybe the kitchen after." He rolls over and climbs on top of me, leaning my body backwards onto the pillow.

I can feel how excited he is, and I wish I felt the same, but after the day I've had, I can't. I make a face of disapproval, which he misses, and begins kissing my upper neck, right below my ear. Typically, when he gives me the slightest attention there, it's on, but tonight I can't.

"Start taking off your clothes," he demands.

I let out a breath, hoping my lack of enthusiasm will catch on, but it doesn't. I put a hand on his chest, and he sits up.

"What's wrong?" he asks.

"I'm sorry, I just... feel sick today. Baby is really bothering me. All day. The non-stop nausea." He lets out a heavy breath and looks at me as if hoping that giving me more time to think about it will change my mind. "I'm really not in the mood," I say, putting the final nail in the coffin of the idea of sex tonight.

Jameson takes another long moment before nodding. "That's okay. Been a long day. I think I had too much of Kelly's wine. Such a nice gesture."

I turn away from him and stare at the wall of our new bedroom. The last thing I want to think about is Kelly and her basket of goodies. For a moment, I hate the idea that my husband has attempted to have sex with me and mentioned Kelly after I refused his advances.

It's as if Kelly has not only invaded my neighbourhood, but now my bedroom as well.

CHAPTER 10

Nora
Before

Beth's mom, Linda, drives us to the bowling lanes, with Beth's little sister Allison along for the ride. For nearly the whole ride Linda talks about the upcoming prom and what her and the committee are planning for us. Her mom is obsessed with prom, and Beth and I can't stand it. We don't exactly have dates yet, either.

It's Friday night in Muskoka, and if you're a teenager, this is likely where you will be. Most of us don't love bowling. It's almost like a social club where teenagers go because we can't drink or do anything else more fun.

On Friday and Saturday nights, though, it's Rock-N-Bowl. The bowling lane plays the top twenty songs with the lights off and a bunch of black party lights. I've noticed this young man who's at the shoe rental counter and whenever he works, he loves to play techno. At that point, the bowling lane almost becomes a miniature rave of non-intoxicated people.

Despite how I'm presenting it, it's fun. Besides, what else can we do?

Being eighteen in Canada, I can go to a bingo hall, but to be honest, that doesn't sound any more fun than bowling. Sitting beside old ladies all day, the silence broken only by the caller yelling out numbers and the occasional "BINGO!" screamer, followed by the disgruntled sounds of women, doesn't really do it for me.

Another year and we can start buying drinks. It's hard in a small town to try to get away with underage drinking. Everyone seems to know your age without you having to present a license to prove it. You need to know someone willing to buy you drinks, which Beth and I sadly don't.

There are house parties, but we don't exactly get invited to those often. While we're not exactly the lowest on the social ladder at school, we're not popular either.

Beth thanks her mom for driving us. Her little sister begs Linda to let her go to Rock-N-Bowl with us, but she refuses. Allison's only fourteen and Linda doesn't want her doing that yet. Who would have guessed that a bowling lane would be considered too much for a fourteen-year-old? Thankfully, Allison stays with Linda. Beth and Allison are like water and oil and can barely get along at the best of times. Allison has done a great job of being the stereotypical bratty little sister.

Beth and I are about to go inside when I notice Ryan McDermott and his friends standing outside the building, smoking cigarettes. They're hard to miss, all with their matching football varsity jackets on. A large J patched on the front, representing St. Joe's High.

Ryan is the type to be invited to house parties. It's usually him or one of his friends in his small circle that hosts most of them, from what I hear. Seeing him at Rock-N-Bowl was like spotting a celebrity walking through a Walmart.

"Well, this night got more interesting," Beth says, laughing. "I'm glad I brought my highlighter."

With the blacklights on, everything is illuminated. With all the hormones flying around the lanes, it's not atypical to see exchanges of phone numbers written on skin, the black lights brightening the digit trophies for others to see.

A few weeks ago, I gave mine out to a boy named Curt. He's from a neighbouring town. I hadn't seen him around before, which made him more mysterious and, therefore, attractive in a small-town kind of way.

It was upsetting when he never phoned me.

Ryan tosses his cigarette from his mouth to the cement, and rubs it out with his shoe. He gestures for his friends to do the same. They each do and, one by one, enter the bowling lane. Before

Ryan does, he turns his head and notices me.

"Oh my god," Beth says. "He's staring right at us."

Not us, I think. He's looking right at *me*. I look away shyly before glancing back at him.

He's still staring.

I can feel my heart flutter. He smiles and enters the building, leaving me in a puddle of admiration.

"Do you think I should ask for his number?" Beth says. "What's the chance of him saying yes? I mean, he stared right at me. That has to mean something, right?"

I don't have the heart to tell her Ryan McDermott wasn't looking at her. I'm not sure how she didn't see that for herself. I shouldn't be surprised though. She's had the hots for Ryan since moving to town, even though he's never showed any interest, just the kind she makes up.

I change the subject. "How do you think my new necklace will look under the blacklight?" I ask, holding the pendant out from my neckline.

Beth takes hers out from under her t-shirt and knocks it gently against mine. "Not sure, but I'm glad you're wearing it." We had made a pact to don them tonight. We called each other and chatted about what outfit we should wear. After a long conversation, Beth settled for a plain white t-shirt and jeans. Noticeably, though, she wore a black bra, which I questioned.

I was dressed down, too. Sometimes I enjoyed wearing a school uniform. It didn't need a lot of thought to figure out what to wear at school, as it was always the same. The only thing I needed to focus on was make-up and hair. I'm not the best at either, but Beth has been researching tutorials online and has been showing me tricks.

After consulting with Beth, I decided to wear a dark, slimming black shirt and blue jeans. It fit my body well, and I wanted to turn heads tonight.

If Curt was at Rock-N-Bowl tonight, I wanted him to notice me and kick himself for not calling me back when he could have. I didn't expect Ryan McDermott would be here though.

As we enter, I've already made up my mind that no matter how much attention Ryan may give me, I won't act on it. I fantasize about him writing his digits on my arm, and feeling like winning the lottery of cute boys at school. The girls would gush over the bright yellow digits on my arm and drip with envy.

It would upset Beth, though. Our friendship means more to me than some boy. As cute as Ryan is, as sexy as he looks, none of it matters if it ruins the best friendship I've had.

Right away, the techno music is blasting at higher volume than usual. I look at the bowling shoe rental counter and spot Techno Boy, as we now call him. As strange as he looks with his long curly hair, like he's straight out of the Eighties, I love the atmosphere he brings to this place. A group of people from school are already dancing near the arcade area, pumping their fists to the beat.

We go to the counter to get our shoes. Even though none of us bowled, renting shoes was mandatory if you wanted to stay. They must have made a killing from shoes alone each weekend. I scream at Techno Boy three times before he understood what shoe size I was. He asks if we want a lane, but I decline, of course.

We tend to mostly hang around the arcade area. I brought a bag of coins with me too, since we love playing arcade games when the night is dragging.

Tonight is different, though. You can feel the vibe in the air, and not just because Techno Boy created it. I already know it's going to be a great night. First off, Ryan McDermott and company are here. Secondly, I already spotted Curt in the back of the arcade with a group of boys.

"Want to play some games?" I ask Beth. She responds by nodding to the beat of the bass. Although she was already doing so before I asked, I assume this means she agrees.

As we get closer to the group of people dancing, we can't help but join in, especially with the rhythm of the music picking up. I turn my head and see Curt has spotted me. I look back at Beth and continue dancing, every so often glancing to ensure I have his attention. Suddenly I notice he couldn't care less. Surrounded by his friends is a girl with long legs, one of them leaning against the *Ms. Pac-Man* machine. It takes another moment for me to realize who it is.

Beth is the first to say it. "Hey! It's Kelly!" she shouts into my face. She starts to walk towards her, and I put my arm on her.

"What are you doing?" I ask. Why should it matter that Kelly is here? The only thing I'm slightly upset about is the group she's talking to.

"I told Kelly to come tonight!" Beth shouts.

"What?" Beth never mentioned this to me before. We spoke for nearly an hour on the phone before coming here. Her mom picked me up and the whole ride over she never mentioned inviting Kelly Van Patten.

I look over Beth's shoulder and see she's already speaking with Curt. I feel a touch of anger when he smiles at her in the blacklights, his teeth illuminated.

What's with everyone's obsession over her? Even Beth has fallen prey to her spell.

"I told Kelly to come tonight!" Beth repeats, assuming I didn't hear the first time. She continues to walk to the back of the arcade.

Once Kelly spots her, she enthusiastically raises her arms in the air and runs up to her, giving her a hug.

"Hey!" she shouts, squeezing Beth. When she lets go, Kelly sees me and smiles. "Hey Nora!" I give a short wave and smile back. Kelly pouts and bangs her head to the beat of the song that's increasing in intensity. "You never told me this place had kickass music!" she shouts.

"Techno Boy!" Beth shouts back.

"What?" Kelly asks, confused.

"Techno Boy!" I scream. "He's that weird kid at the shoe counter. He always plays this music when he works."

"Hell yeah, Techno Boy!" Kelly says.

"Who's that boy you're talking to?" Beth asks.

"Who cares?" Kelly says, starting to move to the music more intensely. Even the way she dances is perfect. She's wearing a bright white tank top and tight blue jeans. Her shirt shimmers under the blacklight.

The necklaces that Beth and I are wearing are dull and dark.

I look over at Curt, whose eyes are completely focused on Kelly now. I breathe out. Typically, Rock-N-Bowl lasts for a few hours. I stare at Beth and Kelly dancing together. Kelly is sliding her body around like a snack, while Beth laughs and tries to mimic her.

I wonder how I can leave without causing a scene. I'm not sure I'm in the mood for dancing. Not in the mood for Techno Boy's music, the arcade, or being third wheel tonight. I watch Curt as he gazes at Kelly like a child would a candy bar. I certainly can't watch the New Girl get all the attention all night, either.

Kelly reaches behind and grabs something from her rear jeans pocket. She shakes the small bottle of vodka at me.

"Who wants a taste?" she says, laughing.

"You got a mickey of vodka? How did you get it?" Beth asks.

"I have my ways," Kelly laughs, taking the red top off and taking a drink. She passes it to me, but I wave her off.

"I hate vodka," I say, making a face.

Beth grabs the bottle and takes a long sip. Kelly laughs. "Hey!" she screams. "Sharing is caring. Give it back before you drink it all."

It doesn't take long for the entire bottle to empty between them. I can tell Kelly is a little tipsy, but Beth seems over the moon drunk. I didn't think there was that much in the bottle.

I take a break from them and let them know I'm going to play the arcade games. Kelly doesn't respond but Beth nods at me, although again, I'm not sure if she actually heard me or is just bopping to the music.

"Come back to the dance floor when you're done," she shouts back at me. "We're just getting started here!" Beth puts her hand behind her head and raises one leg, swinging both to the beat.

Kelly laughs hysterically. "What the heck is that?"

"The sprinkler!" Beth screams. "They don't do the sprinkler in Toronto?"

"No! Please turn off the sprinkler!" Kelly says, and the two of them laugh as I turn and head to the back of the arcade. I walk past Curt, who doesn't even turn his head to notice me. He's standing by *Ms. Pac-Man*, so I decide to play a different game. If I hadn't, he and his friends would have probably asked me who my hot blonde friend was. I cringe at the idea.

My second favourite game Beth and I love to play is *Dance Dance Revolution*. In the back, Sandy Tallie is playing it with another girl from school. For a larger girl, Sandy knows how to play the game quickly.

The game ends and Sandy and her friend step off. She smiles when she spots me.

"Hey, Nora!" she calls.

"Sandy!" I say back. I feel like I can't hide my sour mood. It must be completely evident on my face.

"You and Beth just got here?" she asks. Her question annoys me. Why did she assume we came together? Were Beth and I tied at the hip or something?

"Yeah," I say. "You done on the machine?"

"Yeah, have at it. Just don't beat my top score," she laughs. Her friend pats Sandy on the back and whispers something to her. "Ugh, she is!" she shouts. She looks on the dance floor and I can't help but notice she's staring at Beth and Kelly.

"What's wrong?" I ask.

"Nothing," Sandy says. It only takes a moment for her to continue to say what she was thinking, though. "Are Beth and Kelly Van Patten friends?"

"No, just neighbours," I say confidently. She's only been at our school a week. How could Beth be friends with her that quickly?

"Good," Sandy says.

"You don't like her?" I ask. "New girl, I mean."

Sandy shakes her head. "It's nothing."

"Because I don't like her," I say. "There's something about her."

Sandy nods. "I don't want to get into it, though. You're friends with Beth. Please don't say anything to her or Kelly." Sandy waves to me and leaves the arcade area.

I step on *Dance Dance Revolution* and play a round. Usually, the game is meant for two players at once, but tonight, it's just me. I don't get the high score, or anywhere near Sandy's record. I decide to play a second game, but somehow do even worse.

When I finish, I try to spot Beth but can't find her on the dance floor. I look for the tall blonde girl but can't seem to find either of them.

For a change, I hear a lot of commotion off the dance floor near the bowling lanes. I spot Kelly waving her arms after throwing a ball down the lane and it going immediately into the gutter.

Ryan McDermott points at her, laughing hysterically. Beth grabs a ball from the ball track and tosses one after her, hitting the gutter on the opposite side. Kelly hugs Beth, consoling her, as Ryan and his friends laugh on.

My mouth gapes open. For one thing, people are actually bowling at Rock-N-Bowl. More surprising is that Beth is playing with Kelly, Ryan, and his friends. I walk over to them shyly and Kelly is first to shout at me.

"Nora!" she screams. "Where were you?"

I smile without answering. I told Beth and Kelly where I was going, and wondered why they didn't grab me to join them. They left me at the arcade area.

"Grab a ball!" Beth shouts.

Suddenly, Ryan McDermott walks past me, ball in hand. He drops it into mine. "Take mine. You're up." I look up at the screen. Apparently, it's "Butthead's" turn. Ryan laughs. "We're not keeping score, so who cares?"

I walk down the lane and take a step over a line, nearly slipping. Kelly laughs as I regain my stance. Ryan's bowling ball is, of course, much heavier than I would choose. I take the ball between my hands, bend and toss it with both arms. It slowly makes its way towards the centre of the lane until it collides with the pins, sending most down immediately. One single pin is left wobbling until it eventually joins its fallen colleagues.

Beth screams enthusiastically, followed by Kelly. Ryan claps while some of his friends holler at me.

"She's a pin assassin!" one of his friends shouts and laughs.

Ryan smiles at me. "Didn't know you're good at bowling," he laughs.

"She plays all the time!" Kelly answers for me, despite not knowing anything about me. The way Kelly laughs after, and the way Ryan and his friends do the same, it no longer feels like they are cheering me on but making fun of how good I am at such a lame sport. Beth doesn't join the laughter. I notice her staring at me with a thin smile.

"Hey," Ryan says, grabbing my arm. "We're heading to my place after. You and your friends want to come?" I shyly look away and he touches my side to get my attention. He certainly has it. "Come on. Just come." I look up at him and he has the same expression on his face that he had in class the other day and the same he had outside the bowling lane tonight. It's a look a woman knows all too well.

I don't even look at Beth. I hope Kelly is watching, though. "Yeah, I'd love to."

Ryan's smile widens. "Good. Tell your friends. We'll go soon."

We continue to bowl, if you can call it that. Almost everyone does poorly, except Ryan and I. Ryan hits a strike once and his boys jump and shout at him.

Ryan and his friends tell me they're heading outside for a smoke.

After they leave, Beth wraps her arms around me. "I think I should have eaten before I came here."

I laugh. "I think you should have eaten before you and Kelly downed that mickey."

"Can you grab me some fries?" she pleads.

"No problem," I say with a laugh. Beth plops herself on the seat in our lane, putting a hand on her head.

"Don't worry," Kelly says, sitting beside her. "I'll babysit this one. Grab a large fries. I'm starving, too!"

I smile back, thinking that I never offered to buy Kelly anything. "No problem." I go to the back of the building where the kitchen is. A long group of people are standing to order or gathered around, waiting to get their food. Ordering a large fries and a couple of drinks takes forever. Part of me worries about whether Ryan left without us. If it wasn't for Beth feeling sick, I would have stepped out of line a long time ago to check.

Once I finally have our food, I walk back towards our lane. Then I spot them and stop in my tracks.

Against the wall, Ryan McDermott is passionately kissing Kelly. His arm is around her waist as he leans against her slender body. The way they're kissing, you would think they were the only two in the room.

In the blacklight it's easy to spot the seven digits written in highlighter on Kelly's arm.

CHAPTER 11

Nora
Before

I walk past them as they continue their hardcore make-out session. Neither of them notices me. When I get back to the bowling lane, Beth is by herself, slumped over in her chair.

So much for babysitting her. Kelly said she would stay.

While Beth was reeling from her lack of food and excess drink, Kelly had alternative plans. How could she hook up with Ryan so quickly? I only left them for twenty minutes or so. Within that timeframe, somehow Kelly Van Patten hooked her claws into him. I gaze across the room and can still see them locking lips. Only now it's Kelly with her hand on the side of his head, caressing him.

I sit beside Beth and put the fries between us. I grab one and munch on it, staring off into the empty bowling lanes.

"Oh, thank god... food," Beth says,

grabbing a bunch of fries. "You're an angel, Nora."

If I'm the angel, what does that make Kelly?

Beth has been nothing but good to the new girl since she sauntered into town and how does Kelly reciprocate? She steals the boy Beth has a crush on.

I look at Beth, who continues to eat her fries one at a time. Despite how terrible she looks, she continues to bob her head to Techno Boy's music.

I think for a moment about not telling her. She's already looking miserable. Why make her night any worse? Telling her that her new *friend* stole the boy she likes would destroy her.

Kelly is no friend to Beth, obviously, but I am. I have an obligation to tell my friend when something is very wrong, even if it hurts her feelings.

"I need to tell you something," I say to her. Beth looks up at me with a misshaped smile.

"Don't worry. I'll be okay. I still want to go to Ryan's party—like, really bad," she laughs and concentrates on putting another fry in her mouth, missing at first.

I look across the room. Even sitting down, I can spot Ryan and Kelly in the dark corner, the tips of their heads visibly interlocking over the top of the chairs in front of me.

"I don't know if you do," I say, taking a deep

breath.

"What do you mean?" she asks.

"There's no easy way to say this to you, so I'm going to just say it." Beth looks at me confused. "Kelly and Ryan are hooking up right now."

Beth immediately looks confused. "What?"

I nod. "They're making out in the back of the room right now. I had to tell you. They're right there." I point at them, and Beth tries to follow my finger. Of course, once I do, Ryan and Kelly kiss a few more times and finally realize they're actually in public and stop making out to breathe again. Upset that Beth likely didn't see it in time, I look at her. Her head is slumped over even more than before.

Ugh. She missed it.

I look back and Ryan and Kelly are slowly coming back towards us. They take their time, laughing to each other about whatever's being said, until they reach us.

Kelly stands over Beth and I. "Hey, let's get out of here," she says. "Ready to go to Ryan's house?" She looks down at Beth and makes a sad face. "Oh, sweetie. Are you okay?"

I remove her hand from Beth's back. "She's sick. Drank too much." I look at Kelly for a moment and back at Beth.

"Do you guys still want to come?" Ryan

asks.

Beth doesn't answer, so I do. "I think I'll just help Beth get back home. You have fun," I say, looking at Kelly. She smiles back at me, but the expression is not returned.

She made my friend sick. She stole the boy she's obsessed about. How could she make the night any worse?

"Okay," Kelly says. "I'll see you guys at school on Monday."

Beth doesn't say anything, and I fake a smile, satisfied to watch Kelly leave. Enraged that it's with Ryan McDermott.

I look at Beth, who doesn't change her position. She continues to hang her head, slumped over.

I put my hand on her back. "Beth? Are you okay? I got you a pop too if you need to sober up."

She doesn't respond with words, but I can hear the faint sound of her crying over Techno Boy's music.

❊ ❊ ❊

When Monday arrives, nearly everyone at St. Joe's hears the news. Ryan McDermott and the new girl, Kelly, are together. Some rumours I hear are that they're actually dating. Sandy Tallie tells me during homeroom that they already had sex at Ryan's house. Rumours are flying in the hallways and it's hard to know who to believe.

All that anybody knows is that Ryan and Kelly are a *thing.*

I tried to call Beth on Saturday and on Sunday, but she didn't pick up or return my phone calls. In Mr. Johnson's class, Beth seems fine. Kelly sits at her desk beside her. I even catch Beth smiling at Kelly, as if nothing happened.

Beth doesn't turn to look at me. She isn't sending me notes. She barely gives me attention. I realize that it's because Ryan is sitting in the back of the room with his friends. The last thing Beth would want is to look back and see him right now.

She must be hiding her frustration well. She must be having a hard day. She likely had a terrible weekend after Rock-N-Bowl.

Kelly leans over and whispers something to Beth. Beth smiles back, nods, but doesn't respond.

For a moment, I worry that Beth is upset with me. She's barely said anything to me. Now, she sits beside Kelly and acknowledges her. Is this what they mean when they say don't shoot the messenger? Is Beth somehow madder at me for telling her about Kelly and Ryan?

I realize I'm overthinking this. She's wearing the pendant necklace. I'm wearing mine as well. If she was truly upset with me, she wouldn't be wearing it at all. I reassure myself that it was okay. She's likely going through a lot of emotions at the moment.

At lunch I wait by the table we typically sit at. Beth is usually the more punctual one, first to be there waiting for me. Today she's nowhere in sight. I sit at our spot and keep waiting. As time passes, I unpack my lunch and start eating the sandwich my mom made.

Sandy Tallie walks by with a tray of food she bought from the food court. "Can I sit with you?" she asks, and I nod.

We have lunch together and make small talk while I wait for Beth to come. She doesn't.

After lunch, Sandy and I walk by the tennis court at the rear of the school. On a typical lunch break, Beth and I like to walk around the area to work off our meal.

To my surprise, Beth's there, only she's not alone. Kelly is standing beside her, taking a deep drag from a cigarette. She puffs out a thick veil of smoke and nods at me, waving.

I give a thin smile back. Sandy and I walk up to them as Kelly lets out another puff.

"Hey, I was looking for you," I say to Beth.

Beth smiles back. "Yeah, I went by our table but didn't see you."

Kelly laughs. "You guys have a lunch spot?" She rolls her eyes but doesn't explain why she reacts that way. Is it weird to have a spot you go to meet up with a friend for lunch or something? I shrug off her comment and try not to get annoyed, but her smoke irritates me.

"I didn't know you smoked cigs," I say, waving the smoke near my face.

Kelly raises an eyebrow. "Well, it's great for weight control. I rarely eat lunch. I don't crave food until dinner." She looks at Sandy, awkwardly leaning against the wall beside me. "You should try one, Sandra." She smiles.

Sandy lowers her head with a sigh. "Hey, Nora. Maybe I'll catch up with you later, after school. See you." Without looking back, Sandy Tallie scuttles down the court area, quickly getting away from us, and I know exactly why.

"You don't have to be mean to her, you know," I say to Kelly in a harsh tone.

Kelly takes another drag and shares her second-hand smoke with us before answering. She points the cigarette towards Sandy. "You mean her? I wasn't being mean. I was offering her a smoke. That's a nice thing to do."

"For weight control, right?" I scoff.

Kelly glances at Beth a moment before looking back at me. "You know, you can be a little intense. Do you want a smoke? It's not pot, but maybe it will chill you out."

Beth sighs. "Well, I could use some weight control." She grabs the cigarette from Kelly's mouth and takes in a breath, coughing terribly.

Kelly laughs. "Not like that."

Why is Beth hanging out with Kelly after what she did to her? How can she not see how Kelly is ruining her life? Now she's coerced Beth not only to drink but to smoke.

"How was Ryan's house?" I ask Kelly, trying to make the subtle point to Beth.

"Fun," she answers curtly.

"I heard you two are dating," I say blankly. I'm not going to sugar-coat anything. Beth needs to hear it for herself so she can come to the real understanding of how rotten Kelly really is.

Kelly laughs. "Well, dating may be too much. I really don't know what we are."

"Heard you went all the way with him, too," I say, taking a quick moment to look at Beth.

Kelly breathes in her cigarette and blows out smoke from her nostrils. "You guys need to find more to talk about in this small town." She doesn't answer the question, though.

"So, did you? Go all the way?"

Kelly looks at Beth and at me. "Is that a problem for you if I did?"

I scoff. Before the conversation can continue, the warning bell rings.

"I got to go to the gym," Kelly says.

"Beth and I have math class," I say.

Kelly tosses her cigarette and rubs it out with her white shoe. "Well, I'll see you after school?" she asks Beth.

"Yeah, we'll walk home," Beth answers.

"Maybe on the way home you can show me that beach area you were talking about," Kelly says. I can feel my pulse quicken. If I was a teapot, I would be visibly steaming.

Beth nods and I watch as Kelly heads the other way towards her class. I can barely conceal how angry I am. I would love to erupt and spew out everything I'm thinking to Beth.

I walk with Beth towards math class without saying a word to her.

Did Beth actually invite Kelly to our beach area in the woods? What is she thinking?

What has Kelly done to my friend? She steals the boy she loves. She tricks Beth into thinking they're friends. How vindictive can Kelly Van Patten be?

CHAPTER 12

Kelly
Present

I have an obsession. I know it's sick. It's like watching a train wreck, only it's seeing myself and how… weird I've become. This is not what my normal day would typically be like.

I put the binoculars down for a moment, taking a break from staring into Nora's house.

I must be crazy, I think. I've been literally watching her home for the past hour, doing nothing else. I'm not usually someone who can do something like this. I would typically be on my phone or watching television.

Staring into my neighbour's home isn't a normal Tuesday night for me.

There's nothing I can do about it at this point. It's as if curiosity has taken over my body and I'm just along for the ride.

I watched as an older woman entered Nora's home. I watched Nora show her around. Given her resemblance to Nora, I assumed it was her mother. I don't remember her from when we were younger, though. I maybe only met her once or twice in passing.

I don't remember Nora talking much about her parents at all, really.

After the woman left, I continued to watch Nora and Jameson unpack. Jameson passed out on the couch as far as I could tell, although the blinds were halfway down, making it hard to see clearly.

Why did I care what they were doing? Part of me wanted to get ideas for what to do next.

I wanted to understand who Nora is as an adult. Who her husband is. It could make the next step in my plan easier if I know this.

I think of what a private investigator would do. They have a target and need to understand them better. To do so, they track their target's actions and develop an understanding of their routines.

A PI wouldn't have a hard time figuring out my routines. I tend to work out at the same times every day. I go to the same social events each week. There's nothing too mysterious about me.

It's been years since I've seen Nora, though. I have no clue what kind of things she's into, or how she spends her time. It will be important to know this for what I have planned next for her.

What exactly do I have planned? Well, I'm struggling with that.

The notepad where I wrote ideas for my

master plan is full of stupid ideas heavily crossed out.

I hoped that once I started watching her, I'd become more inspired as to what to do. I've watched her movements and written my observations, which were not very many.

I only made a few written notes. "J kisses N." I'm sure it's easy to decode that one. I wrote that a few times. Next I wrote, "They seem happy" and then crossed it out.

If Jameson is completely happy with his wife, why did I catch him checking me out?

There had to be a way for me to manipulate this, I know.

I watch Nora as she goes into the bedroom and closes the door. Soon after, Jameson gets up from the couch and comes into the bedroom.

This is where I leave off and lower my binoculars. Curiosity, I'll continue to call it, makes me raise the binoculars again to watch inside the room, but by that time, the action is done. Nora's turned on her side of the bed, Jameson's flopped on the other.

Even the Millers had more action happening than Nora and Jameson Bowman.

I curse myself for even wanting to see anything at all.

When I'm certain they're asleep, I stand up from my desk. Lady, who's been in her favourite corner all night, does the same, and follows me to the bedroom.

I lie in bed, thinking of the day and my actions. I look over at Lady and she's already passed out again. Sometimes I'm envious of animals. They can easily sleep without guilt about the things they do, the wrongs or harm against others they commit.

It must be peaceful.

At one point in my life, I was into meditating. As weird as it sounds, I felt more centred when I practiced it, but it's been some time since I've tried it. The last time I attempted to find my inner self was before Ryan... left.

After that, my life was more chaotic. Interviews with the police. Interviews with insurance companies. Dealing with lawyers. My life was one terrible nightmare until I found some stability.

Now in comes Nora, a nightmare from my past, coming back into my life, living next door, no less. At first, I thought I was cursed until I realized the potential.

I question how strongly I came on today. The lies I told. I think about what I have planned for tomorrow as well. I wonder if Nora has any idea what's in store for her.

Likely not. I've done a good job concealing my actions.

Tomorrow, that will be much harder to do.

Sam's Spy Store on Main Street opens at

nine in the morning.

CHAPTER 13

Nora

I'm excited when I see Mom's van come up my driveway. I open the front door immediately and smile at her.

"Hey, Mom," I call out.

She rolls down the window with shrieks of joy. "I can't believe I'm taking my baby to go baby shopping. *This* is exciting. I'm going to buy so many things today!"

I knew she would want to as well, but Jameson made sure I took our shared credit card with me today, demanding that I pay for the bulk of things, especially the big items.

I raise a finger to my mom, gesturing for her to give me a moment while I run back inside. I call out to Jameson, who's sitting at the dining table with his laptop open. I have no clue what he's doing exactly. How can a day trader trade with no net? The cable guys are coming next week. Jameson said he needed to do a few things, whatever that meant.

The world of day trading doesn't make much sense to me, and what I do understand scares me. One day you can make a few thousand, and the next your entire account can be wiped out by a few mistakes. Jameson's been doing it for several years now and was a banker before. His whole world is money and risk, so I trust him. Because of his work, I don't have to work if I don't want to. His income is more than enough for any family to live off of.

Even though our home is huge, and I can only imagine how much hair I would pull out each day if I was in control of the finances, Jameson assures me we're doing well. We're both better off if I don't have anything to do with the money aspect of our life.

I run up to him and wrap my arms around his waist as he types away at the kitchen table. I kiss his cheek.

"Someone's in a good mood," he says with a smile.

"It's nice to be back home," I say. Today I feel better about everything. Mom and I have a whole day of shopping planned. A whole day of planning for my baby. "I was looking forward to today. I mean, this is why we're back, so my mom can help."

"That's right. Well, try not to fill your Mom's van with baby stuff. I can't unpack anymore," he whines. "I'm still exhausted from yesterday."

I kiss his cheek again. "Love you. I'll probably be back after dinner. Going to visit Dad after we're done shopping."

Jameson makes a face. "Tell him to come anytime." He doesn't have to tell me what he's thinking. We've already talked about my father many times in the past. "Tell him I say hi."

"Will do, thanks."

I quickly gather my purse and shoes and jet out the door. I smile, thinking of the fun day I'm going to have with Mom. The expression vanishes when I see her.

Kelly is standing beside the van talking to my mom. She's wearing skimpy black Lululemon leggings that fit her long legs well, with a loose shirt. I'm surprised she's not wearing her pink sports bra again—or working out topless since she loves the attention.

Her small white dog barks at me when I get too close.

I try to hide my face as I get to the van. Kelly smiles when she sees me. "Good morning, beautiful, or afternoon now, I guess," she says in her cocky voice. "Well, it was good catching up with you, Mrs. Cameron. We'll have to get some tea sometime. The three of us could catch up." Kelly waves at me and my mom before walking down the block and breaking out into a jog, her dog trying her best to keep pace.

I get inside the van, my face void of any glimpse of happiness.

"That was Kelly, right? Kelly Van Patten," my mom says blankly. She looks at me.

"Yeah, she's my neighbour."

Mom nods. I put my seatbelt on and wait for her to put the van in reverse, but instead we sit in the driveway. I look at her and Mom has a worried parent face I've seen before on numerous occasions. It was the same face she had made many times when she and Dad separated. Mom would come into my bedroom and continuously ask how I was doing with the same face of concern.

"Are you okay?" she asks, getting to the point.

"Yeah. What happened—that was all in the past."

Mom nods again, but I know she can sense the dread inside me. It must be a motherly instinct. Hopefully, I'll have that someday with my own child.

"I'm okay," I repeat, although I'm not sure who I'm trying to convince, my mother or myself.

"Have you visited *her* since you've been back?"

Mom doesn't have to tell me who she's referring to. "No. It was the first day coming back to town," I say with a nervous laugh. "I didn't want it to be a heavy day. I wanted it to be happy."

"When you want to go see Elizabeth, I can go with you, if you want."

I lower my head. "I'll go... at some point. Can't we just... have some fun today, though? I'd rather not talk about any of this."

"I was worried about you," Mom says. "What are the chances that you're *her* neighbour? I should have known."

Muskoka Lake is pretty small, but not tiny enough to know who lives in every house. It's not Jameson's fault that he bought the house beside someone I can't stand. It's not my mom's fault for not knowing. It's not even Kelly's fault.

It was a series of happy events that brought Kelly back into my life. First, meeting Jameson. Becoming pregnant. Wanting to move back to my hometown. All things that made my life better, and that now feel overshadowed by someone terrible from my past.

Perhaps I'm being dramatic, though.

I reach out and grab my mom's hand. "I'll be okay, Mom, really."

"I just don't like it when you get... stressed. I don't want you to go through anything negative right now. You're pregnant. Are you still talking to that psychiatrist?"

"She's a psychologist, and sort of," I lied. "We're going to have some phone appointments. You don't have to worry about me, Mom. I'm fine."

Mom nods. "Okay, I just don't want things

to be how they... used to be. Promise me you'll reach out to me and your psychiatrist if you need help."

"Psychologist, Mom. Dr. Albee is a psychologist, and of course I will."

It's nobody's fault, I remind myself. What happened with Beth was a terrible accident. It's not my fault. It's not Kelly's. People make bad decisions.

CHAPTER 14
Kelly

My run today was later than usual and completed within a much shorter distance. Lady seemed to have trouble keeping up this morning, nearly pleading with me to return home. She would stop suddenly in the middle of the sidewalk, causing me to nearly trip over her a few times.

As soon as I felt confident that Nora and her mother had left, I quickly turned around towards my home.

I had no clue how long they would be away for, and I needed to use every moment I could. I tried to get some information from Mrs. Cameron. They were shopping for baby today. That could mean they would be away for an hour, or a few. Before I could get more intel, Nora interrupted us.

As soon as I was home, I quickly showered and got changed. Ryan always hated how long it took me to get ready, but I thought I was good on time. In less than an hour, I could be ready for a special date night at a fancy restaurant or a hang around the home date with Netflix.

Given how casually Jameson dressed, I felt a dress-down look would be ideal. In the two days I had seen Nora's husband, he wore a flannel shirt with his sleeves rolled up. I would do the same. I donned a nice green and black flannel shirt and rolled my sleeves up high. I buttoned my shirt, leaving a few undone to show my white tank underneath. It was an outfit Ryan had liked, and I knew it would get attention.

I walk to Nora's home and knock on the door. When Jameson opens it, he tries his best not to look at my chest and does a fair job.

"Hey, neighbour," I say.

"Kelly, how's it going?" he asks, pushing his hair back with his hand. "If you're looking for Nora, she just left with her mom. I think she'll be gone until after supper."

That's great to know. I have plenty of time.

"Well, this seems cliché of me to ask, but I need a cup of sugar. I'm baking and completely ran out."

Jameson raises an eyebrow. "Uh, wow, sugar? I think I unpacked that yesterday. Umm… come on in. I'll see if I can find it."

I thank him and walk inside. I follow him to the kitchen, and comment on how nicely placed the furniture is, even though I feel it's a bit dated.

"That's all Nora, of course. I just work here." He smiles and pushes back his hair again. I sit at the island counter on a stool as he rummages through some cabinets. "Sugar... sugar. Where is— ah." He takes out a large bag. "And a cup," he says thoughtfully. He opens a cabinet by the sink and grabs a mug. He pours sugar, filling it to near the top. He turns to me and slides it across the counter. "There you have it. A cup of sugar. Maybe not an official cup size, but my version." He smiles and I laugh at his joke, a little more enthusiastically than I would normally.

"How did you meet Nora, anyway?" I ask. I'm genuinely interested. Jameson appears wealthy, handsome, and has a fun sense of humour. The Nora that I knew barely had two cents and was boring as could be. *Plain* would be a generous adjective to describe her.

"I was her bank rep," he says with a smile. I smile back but fight the urge to roll my eyes. Even how they met was boring. "When she went to university, she needed a loan, and she would meet with me at the bank each semester. After she graduated, I asked her out."

I notice his laptop at the kitchen counter facing the backyard and the lovely pool that looks pristine. The real estate agent had told me she had it professionally cleaned for a quick sale.

"Do you normally work from home now?" I ask. "Are you still with the bank?"

Jameson nods. "Yeah, I work from home every day. I'm actually a day trader now."

"Ohhh," I say in awe. "That sounds dangerous."

"It can be," he says with a smile. "You have to know how to handle risk. Assess the potential outcomes of a trade. It's a lot of research, and a little luck... or maybe the other way around. I'm not sure, exactly, but I've been doing it for some time and I'm still here."

"Assessing risk?" I repeat. "Jameson, I thought you were more of an exciting guy, and that sounds... boring. You don't take risks?"

Jameson laughs. "Not at work, no. I try not to."

I look out at the pool in the backyard. "That was something I was always jealous of, your pool. Your backyard is beautiful. I always admired it from afar."

"Thanks," Jameson says. "I noticed yours is large, too. And you have a pool as well."

"It can be a lot to care of, though," I say. "I really miss my pool. I need to replace the liner and the heater broke. I'm waiting for some quotes to get the work done to jump back in. Being summer now, most of the companies are lined up until late August or early September. It's too bad. Swimming is one of the best exercises you can have."

Jameson nods. "Well, you know, since we're neighbours, come on over anytime to use ours."

I smile, seeing the opportunity I was hoping for. "Really? That wouldn't be intrusive?"

"No, not at all. After all, you're not only a friend of Nora's but our neighbour, too."

Friend? I laugh. Did Nora not tell him much about me? "Thanks," I say. "This is probably too much to ask, but... well, is it okay to go for a swim now?"

CHAPTER 15

Nora
Before
One week before prom

I can nearly count the days left of my high school life on my hands. It's nerve-wracking. Everyone has an idea what's next in life, and I have barely thought about it. More like I try to do anything else but think about it.

Beth got a letter last week. She's been accepted to the University of Toronto social work program. If she were a rocket, she'd blast off with the amount of excitement she has built up.

I think of Kelly. Like me, she hasn't shared much about what she wants to do next in life. She just moved to Muskoka Lake too.

She and Ryan McDermott are now *official*. Boyfriend and girlfriend. With prom only a few days away, and them being the IT couple, it's easy to see them taking the crown as Prom King and Queen.

Not that it matters.

I thought about not going. I even voiced it to Beth. Until recently, I had no one to go with. Beth's mom overheard me talking about not going and she demanded I attend. I'm a pretty girl and she told me I needed to go to prom. I'm not sure how beauty has much to do with going to an overhyped high school party. Beth's mom went on and on about how she never went to hers when she was our age and deeply regretted it.

A week later, at Rock-N-Bowl, I ran into Curt again. We started talking, and this time he actually called me when he said he would.

He's okay, I guess.

I agreed to go to his school prom, too. So I went from going to no proms to two. Beth's mom will be overjoyed when I tell her the news.

The prom committee that she's a part of spent the budget on fixing up the gymnasium. They wanted to go all out with a jungle theme for some reason. I'm not sure how symbolic that is.

Are the teenagers now free to roam the jungle? Many have another three to four years of post-secondary education left. Not exactly freedom.

Beth's mom has been extra busy now getting the school ready for the big weekend. Beth and I were recruited to help out. Sometimes it's not voluntary.

At times I come up with excuses not to help. Decorating for parties doesn't exactly excite me. I feel bad for Beth, though, who is almost forced to help at this point. The stress in her mother's face on getting the big day, as she keeps referring to it, as perfect is palpable.

With all the work being put into preparing for prom, I wonder if Beth has told her mother the truth. She has no date.

It almost seems history is doomed to repeat itself with Beth not going to her prom either.

She and I talked endlessly about who she could ask to go with her, although there were slim pickings left. She didn't seem to understand that, though. She wanted to have some level of attraction to the guy, which I understood. She had high standards, though. She wanted the boy to ask her to prom. That's how it's supposed to go, she told me countless times.

Curt had friends. I even talked to him about it, and he said he would likely know one who would take out Beth as friends. That way, the four of us could have a blast. After prom, we could find a party, or just have fun on our own. Even though Beth wouldn't know Curt's friend, we would be together, and Curt and his friend would be together. It could be fun.

Not to party pooper Elizabeth, of course.

Not only did she want the guy to be attractive, ask *her* to prom, but she also wanted to at least know him on some level.

That would be impossible to arrange with

Curt with the weekend coming up.

Where did that leave Beth for prom? A miracle... or going stag, which she already told me she wouldn't do.

I walk down the school hallway amid the usual rowdiness around me. It's busy in between classes, as many students run to their lockers to get their texts for the next class.

I spot Beth and Kelly walking towards me.

For a long time, Beth and I felt like a dynamic duo. Kelly came into the picture and suddenly changed things. More and more she would be included in our plans. We had gone to the beach together one time a few weeks ago, before Kelly officially started dating Ryan.

That had to have been the worst night at the beach I ever had. All Kelly talked about was how infatuated she was with Ryan. I hated listening. I hated even more the impact I saw on Beth when she talked about it. I wondered if Beth had told Kelly about her history with Ryan.

Thankfully, their friendship slowed down. After being officially together, Kelly spent more time with Ryan and his friends. It was surprising to see Beth and Kelly walking down the hall together. I was getting used to being the duo again.

I wondered how long Ryan and Kelly would last. Most relationships in high school have a short shelf life. A few weeks. Long ones, maybe a few months. Hopefully, Kelly and Ryan will be together forever. Beth and I can move on from her friendship and Ryan. Neither of them was good for Beth and me. Someday I hope Beth will see this for herself.

"Hey," Kelly calls out to me. She looks back at Beth and laughs. "See you after school." Kelly continues down the hall. A gust from her stride flaps a prom poster tacked on a bulletin board as she passes.

"What's after school?" I ask Beth. We already had plans, her and I.

"I invited Kelly to come with us to the beach tonight."

Of course she did.

"She's not with Ryan?" I say. Beth shrugs in response. I don't understand how she doesn't care. She must be hiding it well.

I open my locker as she stands beside me, waiting. We have geology next together. I close my locker a little more loudly than I intended, out of frustration. "Doesn't it bother you?" I ask.

"What?" she says.

"Ryan and Kelly? Together!"

"Can you keep it down a bit?" she says in a low voice. "Kelly didn't know I had a thing for him until after."

"So you did tell her?"

Beth nods. "Yeah, I mentioned it. It's... no big deal. Ryan and her... they go well together.

Can you stop talking about this now? We can talk about it later. Not here."

"Okay, sorry," I whisper back. "Can I come to your place after school?"

Beth nods. "So long as you're okay with my mom badgering you about prom... it's driving me crazy."

"She means well," I say. The bell rings and we hurry to our last class of the day.

The last period of school is always the worst. It drags on forever, and with a topic like geology, I feel more like banging my head against the wall than listening to the teacher.

Thankfully, the class passes faster than usual. I wave to Beth, letting her know I'll meet her at her locker at the end of class. I want to put away a few things before leaving school. Once I do, I quickly make my way down to Beth's locker. I spot her through the crowd of teenagers, but something seems off. In between students walking past me, I get a better picture of what's happening.

Beth's head is against her locker. She lightly bangs it against the metal door. Taped to her locker door is a smaller poster for prom. No doubt it was her mother's idea to have her put it there, promoting it to others using her daughter's prime real estate locker space. Beth lightly bangs her head against the locker again, harder this time, striking the poster.

"Beth?" I ask as I get closer. She ignores me and covers her face with her arms. Despite her attempts to conceal herself, it's easy to see the tears coming down her face.

I look around and, thankfully, no one else notices. It's the end of the day. People are more interested in leaving school as quickly as possible than noticing a girl weeping at her locker.

"Are you okay?" I ask, trying to understand. On the other side of the hall, I see Kelly wrapped in Ryan's arms. They're kissing and embracing each other against a locker. Watching them is like seeing a high school romance movie in action.

The two do look perfect together, though it's obvious to me now why Beth is so distraught.

"I'm sorry if I upset you before," I say. "What I said about Kelly and Ryan."

Beth lowers her hands. "You have no clue. You know how much stress my mom is putting on me right now? Every day she reminds me of what a failure I am. She doesn't do it directly." Her voice is raised and drawing the attention of others now. I look around and give a thin smile. "Has a boy asked you yet to prom, dear? She asks me nearly every morning and night. You're so pretty, dear, why not? Ugh!"

"Let's talk later," I say. "At the beach. Let's just leave."

"I don't want to go now," she says, turning away. She bangs her hand against the locker, catching a few more students' attention. One of them is Sandra Tallie. Kelly and Ryan are still in a different romantic dimension, one where all that exists is the two of them making out.

"We can go, just us, to the beach," I say. "It's better when it's just us, anyway." I put my hand on her shoulder, but Beth quickly brushes it off.

"I don't need anything from you right now. Just leave me alone." Beth quickly makes her way down the hall, slowing to look at Ryan and Kelly embrace.

They don't notice her.

Sandy stands beside me. "Is Beth okay?"

I breathe out deeply. "I'm not sure."

Had I known better, I would have run up to Beth and stopped her from leaving the way she had. I would have tried harder to reason with her. I would have confronted Kelly and her scumbag boyfriend, Ryan.

There was no way for me to know at the time that it would be the last day I saw my best friend Elizbeth Graham alive.

CHAPTER 16

Nora
Present

Jameson's nightmare was coming true.

My mom not only purchases almost everything on our shopping trip, but the van is packed with items. Everything's needed, though, for the baby. With Mom retired and Dad leaving the workforce soon, my mom told me she had extra income and wanted to spend it on things that mattered most. It touches me when she tells me Dad approved of splurging on my child.

Not knowing the sex of the baby is making things more difficult.

I know from other mothers that the first few months are mostly sleeping, eating, and changing diapers. They don't necessarily need cute baby clothes at that time. Gender neutral clothes will be fine until baby gets older.

I find the perfect crib at a store downtown on Main Street, affectionately called Boots and Mittens. The store has kid hand and footprints on all the windows made by the babies of happy customers. At the cashier I see a sign that lets parents know they can add to the decorations. It's a cute way to build loyalty to their store around town instead of customers travelling to Walmart.

They don't need special tactics like that, though. You can't find the quality of baby items at a big box store.

I fall head over heels for this rustic wood framed crib. I pretend to be unsure of it when Mom catches wind of my interest and reaches for her credit card. I tell her I need to check with Jameson, though. I take a picture of it and a few other cribs. I tell my mom I want Jameson to be a part of the decision on the crib, even though I'm sure he doesn't really care about these things.

Decorating a nursery isn't something that excites him as much as me. After our marriage and us trying to conceive, I nearly gave up the idea that I would ever have the opportunity to do this. After I found out I was pregnant, I would Google nursery pictures online trying to figure out which would be right for my unborn child.

The crib's perfect and matches a picture I kept of an image I loved. After we find out the sex of the baby, we can dress it up to match the nursery.

When Mom parks in our long driveway, she helps me bring all the items to the door before leaving. I was supposed to go for dinner at my parents', but the shopping day has wiped me out. I want to rest.

Mom was upset, but understood. I'm sure when she tells my dad that I'm not coming over, he'll be upset too. Yeah right, that'd be the day.

He can come and visit me, though. It's not like I live hours away anymore. A few minutes and he can see his only daughter.

I open the front door and call out for Jameson. I know his face will drop when he sees the number of things we bought.

He comes into the foyer and smiles, shaking his head at the bags in my hand.

"A successful shopping trip, I see," he says with a laugh.

"Even more bags outside." I smile. "I couldn't help myself. Everything is so cute, and tiny... and cute." I put a hand on my belly. Although I can't be sure, I feel like it's gotten larger since moving into our new home, even though it's only been a night.

Jameson grabs the bags from my hands and brings them to the kitchen counter.

"Can you take the bags to the nursery room?" I ask.

He nods and turns to me. "And which room is that?"

I give him a stare. It's obviously not the one Kelly told us about. He takes the hint and takes the bags to the other room we talked about.

Thinking of Kelly gives my stomach an uneasy feeling. After the awkward conversation with Mom in the van before leaving, we didn't talk about her, or Beth even.

It was nice not thinking about either. I almost forgot for a moment that Kelly lived next door until I came home.

Mom was even more excited during our shopping adventure. My baby's going to be spoiled in life. Not only by my mom, but Jameson and me. While my mom and dad do okay financially, they've never really been wealthy. We were always a paycheck or two from having to change our lifestyle completely.

Jameson is wealthy, though. He has money in the bank outside of the finances he gambles in day trading each day. I shouldn't call it gambling. He obviously knows what he's doing, and I trust him.

I trust him enough to know he wouldn't do anything that would put our soon-to-be family at risk.

I sit at the kitchen counter, slipping off my sandals. I'm not sure why I ever thought walking in sandals all day was a great idea.

I notice a splash of water from outside. I look at the branches of the trees, wondering if one fell into the pool. I love the lagoon look our pool has. Had I come to this house in person before purchasing it, I would have fallen in love with it, anyway.

More water springs into the air, and I see a long arm swing into the water, followed by another. Soon the body of a woman jolts across the pool. Her movements are serene as she breaststrokes across.

My mouth gapes open when I come to terms with the fact that Kelly is in my pool.

My pool.

Why the hell is she in my pool?

Kelly turns over as she nears the edge and pulls herself out. Her slim body glistens in the sunshine pouring through the branches. Her two-piece bikini doesn't leave much to the imagination.

Why is Kelly on my property? In my pool?

I look at the kitchen table where my husband was supposedly working all day. On it is his laptop, a notepad with a bunch of numbers written down on it, and a coffee mug. Nothing that would look out of the ordinary to most, unless you realize like I do that the chair he was sitting in is facing the backyard window, looking directly at the pool.

Was my husband enjoying the show? Did watching Kelly swim give him what he wanted?

"Hey," Jameson says, coming back, "I forgot to mention, our neighbour asked if she could use the pool. I figured that was fine."

"She has a pool," I say blankly. I noticed it

the day we moved in. I noticed many things about Kelly's home when I realized it was her living next door to me. One of them was that thankfully her home was spaced so far away from mine that I could feel more comfortable living here.

That doesn't appear to matter anymore now that Kelly feels my backyard is her resort to use.

"She said it's under repair, and asked to use ours," he says.

"And you just let her?" I say confused.

Jameson shrugs. "Yeah, why not?"

"Did you—" The backyard patio door opens, and Kelly comes in, the towel wrapped around her midsection. She does nothing to conceal her bikini top. I stop talking and try to hide my anger. "There's more bags outside," I remind Jameson.

He looks at me, surprised, and nods.

"How did baby shopping go?" Kelly asks, walking up the other side of the kitchen counter.

"Great," I say curtly. "I hear something is wrong with your pool."

"Yeah," she says, raising a hand. "Needs a new liner. Heat pump isn't working. I missed swimming. Thanks for letting me use yours. I love the saltwater pump. I'll have to look into getting that installed in my pool."

I give a thin smile. "No problem."

Kelly sees her welcome basket open in the pantry. "Looks like you guys enjoyed the basket."

"Yes," I say. Kelly always had a way

of demanding thank you's and attention from others. It's as if her kind actions always come with the price of remembering what she did for you. "Again, very thoughtful of you. Thanks."

Kelly waved me off. "No problem, love." She brushes her hair back, and as she does, it's hard not to notice her thin body move and jiggle in the right places.

It disgusts me.

My body continues to go through so many changes and hers still looks like a teenager.

It sounds childish, but it's not fair. I'm bringing a life into this world at the expense of myself, and Kelly gets to go on looking like a model, only thinking of herself.

I glance at the kitchen counter and at Jameson's laptop placement. I look back at Kelly, trying not to reveal how upset I am, but I could strangle Jameson at this moment.

"Well," I say standing up, my feet killing me but trying to stop the pain showing, "a lot to unpack from the day's trip."

Kelly walks around the kitchen counter and puts a hand on top of mine. "I just wanted to say again how happy I am that you're living next door." Jameson comes back into the kitchen and drops a few bags on the counter. Kelly doesn't look at him and continues to stare at me with her blue eyes. "I was hoping we could catch up better. Would it be okay if I come by tomorrow? Instead of having a wine night together, we could have teatime or something."

Jameson looks at me, an eyebrow raised. I can nearly read his mind. Say yes, establish your friendship with her.

He doesn't know everything. He doesn't know our history.

"I would love to," I answer, coerced, and she smiles for a moment until I continue, "but we still have so much to do here. So much to unpack and I was hoping to get most of it done before Jameson starts work again."

Jameson butts into the conversation. "I'm fine, babe, really. I got a lot done today. You two can catch up. No big deal."

I breathe heavily. I look back at Kelly, who's waiting for me to say something. Her boobs are barely covered by her swimsuit.

"Maybe another time," I say.

Kelly nods. "Of course. No rush. Not like I'm moving anywhere." She smiles. "Let me know when you're up for a visit. We can do it at my place or yours."

I fake a smile and thank her. She thanks us for the pool access. Jameson thanks her for the basket again. It's a huge thank-a-thon until she leaves.

I turn to my husband, and he immediately knows I'm upset.

CHAPTER 17

Kelly

"So now Kelly is going to be in *my* backyard every day?" Nora says to Jameson.

"I still don't understand what the problem is?" he says innocently.

Nora audibly scoffs. "I bet. You get to enjoy watching her in her bikini every day now, don't you?"

It's hard to make out what Jameson says with no visuals, but I can imagine he's playing stupid. "I wasn't watching her."

I smile as I listen with my headphones on to the exchange between Nora and her husband inside their home. I was worried that the listening devices wouldn't work well. Thankfully, I can hear everything as if I was in the room with them. I only wish I had a camera to see Nora's expression.

Maybe another trip to Sam's Spy Store is in my future. I smile.

"Your workstation in the kitchen is facing

the backyard," Nora yells. "You had a front-row seat, literally."

"I was sitting that way when she arrived. What are you accusing me of?"

"Nothing!"

"No, say it," Jameson says in a harsh tone. "I love you, Nora. I don't care if I have Playboy bunnies, swimming with no tops on in my backyard. You're who I'm married to. You're the mother of my child."

There's a long period of silence. After a while I worry I didn't install the equipment right. The clerk at the store told me it was extremely user friendly. He even joked about how you could toss the listening devices around a house, and with them being so small, you would barely notice them, which is exactly why I purchased several.

I planted one bug in a nook I spotted underneath the kitchen table where Jameson worked. Where else would I get more juicy information than the kitchen table? Many of the fights I had with Ryan were at ours. I assumed a lot of action and arguments came from dinner talks.

I managed to sneak into the master bedroom quickly and put one behind the headboard. I worried what the sound quality would be on that device. Hopefully tonight I will find out. I begin to fret that I didn't switch the bug on properly. It only has forty-eight hours of battery life, which is astounding for such a tiny thing. I need to come up with a plan for how to get the bugs back once they die.

Coming up with an excuse to visit their house tomorrow was a nice touch, I think. Teatime there seems like it could offer many opportunities to try and get the three listening devices back unnoticed.

The first bug I planted is the one I question most. Maybe the anxiety and rush went to my head. A bathroom doesn't seem like such a great idea now. It wasn't even the ensuite in their bedroom. I was too nervous about being caught in there by Jameson.

I cover my forehead in shame. A bathroom. What exactly did I expect to hear there?

I try not to think about my blunder as a secret spy. This isn't something I do for a day job. It's my first time attempting something like this, and I have to say I'm not bad at it.

On my first attempt, I infiltrated my target's home and planted three listening devices. One of them for sure is working. Hopefully, the other two are just as good quality-wise.

"You know I love you, right?" Jameson says. "You know all I want is you." They go silent again. I can hear movement.

After a few moments, I can hear the sounds of lips smacking together.

"You know I want you," Jameson whispers.

"No," Nora responds harshly. "Just stop," she says louder.

"What?" I can almost hear the surrender in his voice.

"You watch Kelly in the pool all day and now you want me?" she says coldly. "Now you want to have sex. I wonder why?"

Jameson scoffs. "What the hell are you saying?"

"You know exactly what I'm saying. You see this gorgeous girl in a bikini and after she leaves, you want to have sex with your fat wife?"

"Stop!" Jameson shouts. "I won't hear that. I wanted to have sex with you last night, and you said no. I just want *you*, my wife. Is that so wrong?"

I smile again. I wish I could put this on pause and grab a bag of popcorn. After I left their home, I ran back to my place to start listening. I sidestepped Lady, who was looking for affection as always, when I entered and nearly jumped for joy when I realized I was successful in not only planting the devices but them actually working.

I'm already nailing the spy game. The next James Bond will be a female at this rate.

"I wasn't feeling good last night," Nora says. "I want to, I do."

"Well," Jameson says. "Let's just—"

"Just leave me alone," Nora snaps. I can

hear movement again on the microphone and a faint sigh from Jameson.

Suddenly, a green light on my other device lights up on my desk, letting me know it's active. It's the bathroom bug.

I quickly pick up the separate headphones I have plugged into that one to listen.

I can hear the faint sounds of crying. "I hate her," Nora whispers. "It's her fault." For a moment, I wonder what she means by that comment. There's silence for a few moments. I'm about to give up on my bathroom device, worried I'll start hearing an array of farts and other bodily noises from Nora using the facility.

"She's just... nasty," Nora says.

She's talking about me, I know, and for a moment I feel terrible.

"She's a terrible person." I wonder where Nora is in the bathroom as she talks about me. I picture her standing in front of her mirror, talking to herself. "She's always been that way, you knew that. It's in her DNA."

When she makes the comment, I raise an eyebrow. I hear the sound of her lifting what sounds like the toilet seat, and I immediately take the headphones off.

I smile, thinking about the last comment she made.

Of course. I've been trying to figure out how to put my plan together, and Nora has given me the answer.

I open my laptop and start a search.

CHAPTER 18

Nora

It takes me some time to collect myself. I don't go back to the kitchen where Jameson is. I can't face him right now.

Part of me knows I overreacted. I hate myself when I do that. I used to be worse. I used to be a *lot* worse.

I can almost hear Dr. Albee talking to me about my insecurities. I did homework after our sessions together to reflect on the triggers that would escalate my mood. I came up with strategies on how to bring myself back down. Taking a break was one. Talking to my support network was another.

I just came back from seeing my mom. I don't want to call her now. Jameson is a huge part of my support network, and with him being the source of my issues, I can't talk to him. I think about calling some of my old friends from Toronto.

None of them know the type of person I

was when I lived in Muskoka. I never talked about Kelly Van Patten. I especially never talked about Beth.

I went to Toronto to leave everything from this town behind. And now that I'm back, the same problems are welcoming me with a slap in the face.

You can't run from your problems.

I had heard the line before but did not fully appreciate it until I came back here.

If Dr. Albee asked me to fill out what my triggers were today, I would write in bold: Kelly.

I try to not think about the woman. Ever since I moved back, it's all I've managed to do. She's in my head, rent free, and I can't get her out.

I think about the pill bottle still half full of Prozac.

I could start taking them again. I weaned myself off them successfully, and I'm sure I could restart them in a similar way. I wouldn't feel their effect, though, for some time.

That's all this is, I tell myself. I have a chemical imbalance in my head and my medications helped me with it. I should never have stopped taking them. I see now how stupid I was. After all, would a diabetic stop taking his insulin for no reason?

I take out my cell phone from my jeans pocket. I walk quietly down the hallway, opening the new nursery door, and closing it behind me. I look at the empty white room. The only things in it, besides me, are the bags and bags of baby stuff I bought today with Mom.

I click on Dr. Albee's name in my contact list and hit the green button. It starts to ring, and I immediately feel like a failure as I wait to hear her calming voice.

I wonder how Jameson and I will decorate this room. Soon it will be filled with so much love. Our baby will be sleeping here. I lower my phone, realizing she won't pick up and I'm thankful for it. I disconnect the call and put it back in my pocket.

I can do this, I tell myself. I don't need to take medicine. I stopped taking it for a reason. I was worried about the baby's health. That hasn't changed. I know Kelly is my trigger. I need to do my homework, knowing this. Dr. Albee gave me the tools to deal with it. I need to start using them. I can't go on my whole life running back to my therapist with every issue life puts in front of me.

My phone buzzes in my pocket. I take it out and realize it's Amy Albee. I take in a deep breath and pick up.

"Dr. Albee? Hey," I say, surprised. "Are you just checking in?"

"Hey Nora," she says with her usual tranquil voice. "I saw that you just called. Did you want to chat?"

I raise my hands as if lying about it like she

was in the room with me. "No, that's weird. I must have butt-dialed you."

"How's the moving process going?" she asks.

I take a moment. "Great. It's been amazing being back. I just got back from baby shopping with my mom."

"That's amazing, Nora. I'm so happy for you."

It's a half truth, I think. The time with my mom has been great. I can't wait for more of it. I just need to learn to deal with the Kelly factor better.

"Were you able to find a doctor to refill your Prozac prescription?" she asks.

"Just a walk-in for now," I say, this time completely lying.

"Perfect, Nora. I know we talked about how worried you were moving back, but it sounds like you've handled everything so well."

"It's been busy here," I say, giving a fake smile, even though she's not in the room. "With all the unpacking, I haven't had much time to do anything else."

"When you have a chance, I would love it if you could text me your new address. I would love to send something for your baby when the special day comes."

"Of course," I say.

"I would love to send a baby basket to you,"

she says, and I cringe thinking of the unwrapped one Kelly gave us that sits in my pantry. "Are you finding out the sex soon?"

"In a few weeks. I'll message you when I know."

"I'm so excited for you and Jameson. So," Dr. Albee continues, "you're not having any bad symptoms, being back in town? You were worried about the nightmares starting again."

"Nope," I say, completely lying again. I woke up in a sweat last night, out of breath. I wasn't sure if it was thoughts of Beth or seeing Kelly that caused them. I calmed myself and managed to sleep the rest of the night. "I've been managing well."

"Great. You can still call me if you need some extra support. I can always make room to speak with you, Nora. Please know that."

"Thanks, Amy." It's nice to hear. That's why I loved working with Dr. Albee. I know it's her job to empathize, but she does it so well you forget she's a therapist sometimes.

"We can always figure out how to bill you later," she says curtly. That comment brings me back to reality. Dr. Albee is not my friend. She is not a pal to talk about my woes with. This is her job.

I'm her job. I suddenly feel much better not telling her everything that's been happening.

I don't need to be someone's job anymore. I

could use a real friend, though.

We end our call after I reassure her I will call if I need anything.

I lower my head, looking at all the baby clothes and items in the bags around the room.

I think of Beth again, trying to get the last image of her out of my head. It's been something that has plagued me when sleeping and awake since I left town.

I wonder where the box with all the pictures of us is. I did keep a few and would look at them from time to time, usually when I was having a down day.

I consider trying to look for the box, and wonder if that would help improve my mood or make it worse. I open a search on my phone instead. I type in her name in the browser. I breathe out heavily as I read the first article that appears.

Local Girl Found Dead in Muskoka Lake. Foul Play Suspected.

CHAPTER 19

Nora

I push past some low-lying branches, making my way to our special beach. I look beside me, but Beth isn't there. How many times have we taken the trail? I hike past the weird-shaped rock whose base is thin and top is making it look like a mushroom, and leave the path, heading north. I remember how we would laugh and gossip the rest of the way to the beach when we knew no one else was around to hear us.

Now I'm alone. It's nighttime. I think about turning back but need to keep going.

"Don't go."

I hear a whisper and turn my head, but nobody is there. Certainly not Beth.

"Don't," the voice calls out.

Even though the voice is low, I recognize it immediately. Kelly Van Patten's voice becomes stronger. "It's your fault." Her voice is stern and commanding. I almost believe it when she says the words, even though I know the truth.

I arrive at the beach, ducking under another branch. I look around, but still don't see Beth anywhere.

I look around the dimly lit shore.

Then I see the white mass floating at the top of the water. I get closer, stepping into the cold lake. I continue walking slowly towards it, the water hitting my stomach. I know it's frigid, but I don't feel a thing.

When I get closer to the floating white clump, I dip my fingers in the water and feel something slither between them. I attempt to lift my hand, but it's stuck in the seaweed that grows close to shore. I yank hard and look at the water plants in my hand. Mixed with green are strands of brown.

I realize quickly that the long, thin, brown strings are not plants, but hair.

I look down and notice hands stretching out from both sides of the floating white material. I can feel the brown hair slithering at my thighs.

As the waves crash against my body, the white mass moves and bobs in the water, getting closer to me. It's a dress. A white dress. The neckline of the person in the water reveals a gold-coloured chain. I dunk my hands under the water, cringing as I touch the lacey material. I slowly turn the body over.

I cover my mouth, wanting to scream, but no words escape.

Waking in bed, I let in a quick breath. I'm sweating and feel my heart pounding. I sit up, trying to calm my pulse.

Jameson isn't beside me.

I panic until I realize he didn't sleep with me last night. I come out of the bedroom, walking quietly into the living room area. I let out a breath when I see Jameson passed out on the couch, breathing heavily.

For some reason I worried he wasn't in the house. Where else would he be? I feel silly for being as worked up as I am.

I can remember when my mother and father would have major blowouts when I was a kid. Usually, my dad would storm out and spend a night or two somewhere else.

Not Jameson, though.

I hate it when we argue before bed. Usually, we iron things out before turning in, so we always sleep together. Last night was different. I'm not sure if I was being too stubborn or him.

Instead of kissing and making up, I had to go to sleep with all the thoughts of our fight fresh in my head, not letting me close my eyes peacefully.

We haven't argued like this in a while. Not since...

I go back to the bedroom and lay out my clothes. After taking a long shower, I get ready for the day. I half expect Jameson to knock on the door so we can talk about last night, but he doesn't. When I'm changed and have gone through my morning routine, he's still on the couch.

I look at the stove in the kitchen and squint to see the time. It's nearly nine in the morning, and my husband isn't awake. That's not like him. Usually, he's up at the crack of dawn looking at bar graphs of stocks and analyzing the pre-market activity. Not today.

I wonder how long he was up last night. I hate myself for how stubborn I can be when I'm upset. Many times, I'll wait for him to come to me to talk.

I struggled with sleeping so much last night I should have come out of the bedroom to broker peace first for a change.

The baby store on Main Street is now open. I want to go back and look at the crib from the day before. If Jameson was up, I would talk to him about the purchase. It could be a good lead into talking again after our little fight.

Ugh. What was the fight even about? Why was I upset, exactly? He didn't cheat on me. He wasn't flirting with Kelly in front of me. Kelly imposed herself to get a swim in our backyard, and my husband, being the yuppy nice guy he can be, allowed it.

His laptop was facing the backyard window, though. That part bothers me. I tried so many times last night to recall where he was sitting before I left the house with Mom, but couldn't for the life of me remember.

Jameson has never given me a reason not to trust him. So why did I immediately freak out?

He's not a cheater, I know. I don't trust Kelly. How can I? The woman is *so* overbearing and aggressive. Who comes over to their neighbour's house for a swim?

She told Jameson that her pool needed repair. Is she not wealthy? Fix your damn pool. Stay out of mine!

I look at Jameson, sound asleep, and peaceful. A glob of saliva stains my decorative couch pillow. I try not to get upset about that, knowing it's because of me he's sleeping out here to begin with.

I grab my keys from the kitchen and head outside, closing the front door quietly behind me.

I don't want to bother Jameson. I'll buy the crib. He likely won't care too much which one we choose, anyway. When I come back, we can chat about last night.

I *will* apologize.

Kelly is what bothers me, not him. I need to remember that she is my trigger, not my husband.

I should also tell him about the nightmares. I need to involve my support network when they bother me. Jameson's heard about my dreams before. He's always there to listen.

I just want him to think of me as strong for a

change. I want him not to worry about me all the time. It was after everything that I went through that he gave me a choice either to stop working or maybe go down to part time. Work was getting to me, and he knew it. He wanted me to take time off and focus on myself. Of course, the first thing I did was get pregnant instead.

I start my car and look in the rear-view mirror.

What has Kelly really done to me since I've been back in town that I can truly hold a grudge against her for? She bought me a welcome basket. That was nice. Had I not known anything about Kelly, I would have thought she was a great neighbour from the gesture.

The problem was, I *did* know Kelly.

We were teenagers, though. I fix the rear-view mirror and look at myself.

What happened to Beth wasn't because of Kelly.

There was a time when I felt certain she played a role. After years of therapy, I let that go.

How much longer will I blame her for everything?

CHAPTER 20

Nora

I park my car on Main Street. I'm surprised at how busy it is. I noticed the day before with Mom how much more active downtown Muskoka was than I remembered. There are a number of new restaurants, many franchised ones, that you wouldn't expect in a small town.

A few years ago, Mom called me, excited to announce that they were building a Costco nearby. A number of new home developments were under construction as well. It seemed like my quaint little town had changed since I left. It had become posher, caught up with the times.

Despite the number of new buildings, Main Street still looked as rustic as ever, which is why I loved coming here the other day. Boots and Mittens store, for instance. Mom told me she had bought a crib for me at the same store when I was a baby. It feels nice to be able to do the same for my child.

I get out of my car and cross the street at

the pedestrian crosswalk. Cars on both sides of the street stop immediately to let me pass, which is something I can't get over.

If I had attempted to cross a busy street in an urban mega center like Toronto, I would have been run over multiple times after a few steps, without any of the drivers stopping to check on me.

In this town, they not only stop but the drivers smile and wave as I crossed. I wave back shyly. I guess I'm not used to small-town charms and politeness anymore.

Rows of trees line the street. All the parades happened here as well. I can't wait to come here someday with Jameson and our baby. It took a lot for Jameson to hang up his big-city mindset and move to a small town. With all the cute and fun family events here, I'm sure he'll be happy with the move.

A few buildings down from the children's store is the Ontario Provincial Police office. A few police cruisers are parked in the lot outside and on the street. I walk past and head towards the children's store, and then the door is flung open, nearly hitting me.

I'm about to turn around to give the person exiting a look of *appreciation* when I hear her voice.

"Thanks so much, officer." I immediately know it's Kelly. For some reason, she says the word *officer* in a funny way, almost demeaning. I don't look back and quicken my pace to the children's store.

When I hear the door close behind me, I pray that Kelly won't be walking the same way as me. I don't want to talk to her, not after last night. The reason Jameson and I fought was because of her. Despite me having mixed emotions about who's really at fault, I would still rather go about my day for once not thinking about or seeing Kelly.

I hear her loud steps walk the opposite way and let out a breath I didn't know I was holding. I almost feel like at any moment I might hear her arrogant voice call out my name, and I'll be forced to greet her.

I get to the children's store door and open it. Before I enter, I look back and see Kelly opening the door of her hot pink Porsche; if you were to give me a line of car pictures and ask me which would likely belong to Kelly, this would be it for sure. It's bright, expensive and beautiful.

I've never been so annoyed looking at a car before. Kelly tosses a large basket that's film-wrapped in the back seat. Inside is what looks like chocolate, cut fruit, and other items.

Did she exit the police station with a gift basket? How many gift baskets does Kelly give out?

Why was she there?

I sigh, wondering if the police are under Kelly's spell, as everyone was when she first moved into town so long ago. She must have everyone in town wrapped around her finger by now.

I realize I'm staring, and that Kelly can easily spot me gawking at her if I don't move when she turns around to get into her car. I quickly enter the store.

I let out a breath again as I look around. The air is filled with the delicate smell of cotton, and vibrant-coloured tiny clothes, soft blankets and stuffed toys instantly catch my attention.

Being in the store immediately calms my nerves.

I put a hand on my belly and smile. When I was here the other day with Mom, I had the same feeling of contentment. I knew I would be spending a lot more time in this store buying everything I could for the baby.

A saleswoman greets me and asks if I could use any help. I immediately let her know about the crib I was looking at. I describe the one I want, and she knows it exactly.

"Isn't it beautiful?" she asks. I nod in agreement. "I love how it looked when we got it in the store. I'm Theresa, by the way."

I shake her hand. "Nora."

"You know," she continues, "we also have a dresser with a built-in change table that matches the crib."

She's a great salesperson, because I'm immediately interested. She shows me where the dresser is, and I fall in love with it as quickly as I had the crib. I'm surprised I didn't notice it the day before, but Theresa mentions it was just assembled late last night and put onto the show floor today.

Not only that, but there's a twenty percent sale on buying a dresser if you purchase a crib. It's my lucky day, Theresa says, and I feel it. Jameson, I'm sure, won't mind me spending the bucks. We need this furniture, and if anything, he'll be happy that I got something at a discounted rate for a change.

She brings me to the checkout area, and I arrange for delivery next week. I thank Theresa again and go back to the show area, taking pictures of what I bought to show Jameson.

"Nora?" I hear a voice say behind me. I slowly turn. Allison Graham smiles back at me. "I can't believe it. I haven't seen you in—"

"Forever," I say, smiling back. She opens her arms, and we exchange a quick hug, but her large belly gets in the way.

"Look at you," I say. "How far along are you?"

"Seven months," Allison says, a hand on her belly. "Are you here for…"

"Myself," I say. "I'm nearly four months'

pregnant. Not showing nearly as much as you." I laugh. "I can't wait, though."

She rolls her eyes. "I just want this thing out of me." She laughs, but I'm surprised. "Sorry, I'm just ready for her to come."

"Her," I repeat. "That's so nice to hear."

She smiles. I'm so happy for Allison. I remember as kids, Beth and I talked about what we would name our future children, mostly joking and coming up with ridiculous ideas. One time, Allison nosed into the conversation and said how she never wanted kids. Mind you, she was only fourteen at the time. They ruin your body, she said, which was weird for a young girl to talk about.

Now Allison was an adult, staring back at me with a huge belly with a baby girl inside.

Much how Allison was before she didn't ask me questions about my pregnancy. She was always prone to focusing on herself, even as kids, which is why Beth, being such a people pleaser, never got along with her little "bratty" sister. Allison was the self-absorbed child, while Beth would take off her jacket to give it to you if you were slightly cold, even if she herself was freezing.

"I'm having an ultrasound soon to find out the sex of ours, too," I say. "My husband, Jameson, thinks it's a boy, but I have a feeling I'm having a girl."

Allison smiles again. "Well, congratulations. I can't believe I ran into you here. Are you visiting your mom?"

"I'm actually living in town again. We moved to the Winchester area."

"Wow," Allison says. "Beth and I loved that area. We would always bike there to try and peek inside the homes."

I laugh. "We did that too."

There's a moment of silence, as if we're each remembering our time with her. Thankfully, Allison breaks the silence.

"So, I guess this means we will both be off on maternity leave at the same time. We should —"

"Yes," I say. "I would love to see you again." We exchange numbers and catch up a little more. I tell her about my husband, and she tells me about hers. He's in financing as well, and I mention how Jameson was a banker himself until he got into stock trading.

We both agree they would get along and talk about setting up a man date. Even though Jameson never talked much about it, I worried about what leaving Toronto would be like for him. He's had the same social group since he was a teenager. While he agreed to pack up and leave Toronto for me, I wondered how he would deal with the lack of friends now.

He's a sociable person. Likeable. He's very

agreeable most of the time. He also works from home. There won't be a lot of opportunities for him to meet other guys at work. It was a strange concept, having to make friends as an adult.

Soon we'll have a baby, and the opportunities to meet new people while caring for a newborn will be even scarcer. It would be nice if somehow Allison's husband and Jameson hit it off.

It's also nice to see Allison again. It makes me think of Beth, of course. It's not like how it was with Kelly, though. Kelly made me think about all the terrible things that happened. Seeing Allison made me think of the happy times I had with Beth.

"You know who else lives in your area?" Allison says. "Do you remember Kelly Van Patten?"

I let out a sigh. "She's actually my neighbour."

Her eyes widen. "Get out!" She puts a hand on my arm. "I remember how much Beth talked about her, like she was some sort of goddess. I always hated her."

Suddenly, I know Allison and I will get along very easily.

"Ugh," I say with a sigh. "I can't stand her."

"She was just so much! Oh, listen to me, talking poorly about her even though it's been years. I'm sure she's a better person than I remember. It's hard not to feel for her after what happened."

"Her husband, Ryan, you mean?"

Allison nods and tightens her bottom lip. "That guy was such a goofus, too. Beth was... obsessed with him. I couldn't see why. I was happy when Kelly got to him first, but that—" She stopped herself from finishing the sentence. "Anyway, it's still really sad what happened."

"What do you mean?"

"She didn't say anything? I guess, why would she?"

"What happened to him?" I ask. It's something I had thought about. Ryan would have only been in his thirties. A young man who passed away so suddenly. The way Kelly talked about him, I assumed it was cancer or some terrible illness.

"Suicide." Allison shakes her head. "I heard Kelly found him, too. He shot himself."

"He killed himself," I say, surprised.

She nods. "Terrible. Right in the living room. I can't imagine coming home to find something like that."

"Why?" I ask. "Did he leave a note, or has Kelly ever said anything?"

"It only happened a few months ago. Word spreads in this town so fast, too, but I'm not sure why he did it. He owned several fast-food stores in town. A few have closed since it happened. He was wealthy, too. I always thought they had this perfect life. Kelly especially," she sighs. "I feel like such a fat ass anytime I look at her." She raises her hand. "I know, I know, I'm pregnant, but... that woman has a way of letting me know every insecurity I have."

I laugh. "I get it."

We talk some more about planning a meetup for us and our husbands. Before she leaves, Allison smiles at me. I'm not sure why she does, and it seems odd until I see a tear welling in her eye.

"Look at us," she says. "Both pregnant. Talking about arranging a meetup for our husbands. Beth would be happy to know we're talking to each other." She turns away and wipes her eyes. "It's been so long since her accident, and I still get emotional."

I notice she calls it an accident. Sometimes I refer to what happened to her that way as well. Many times, though, I've questioned what really caused her death.

"I miss her too," I say.

CHAPTER 21

Nora

I stand beside the gravestone, not wanting to look at it, even though I came for this purpose. It's been decades since I've visited her. It takes me a few moments before I can stomach gazing at the cold stone with her name on it.

Elizabeth Graham, it says in bold letters. A cherubic angel is etched in the top right corner.

The cemetery has a large, beautiful garden in the front. The yard is well maintained. The smell of freshly cut grass comforts me as I look at the resting place of my best friend.

I have had many friends since Beth, but none came close to being like her. She was special. When we hung out, I felt like we were the only two people in the world. We laughed until our bellies ached. She accepted me for the flawed person I am, and I did the same for her, at least I hoped.

All the fond memories we had, and now she's in the ground, and I'm standing above her.

It's a morbid thought that, six feet below, what remains of Beth continues to decompose.

An image of her body on the beach strikes me, and I force my brain to think of a happier time.

I was the one who found her all those years ago. It was only a few days before prom. Her mom, Linda, called me on the house phone that night asking if I had seen her. I told her I hadn't seen Beth since school earlier that day and we had gotten into an argument. I thought Beth was upset over something, but she wouldn't tell me everything. She seemed mad at me, even though I thought she was more upset over Kelly and Ryan dating.

Linda didn't know what to think or do. She called me again after midnight, asking me if I had seen her or heard from her, but I hadn't.

We were both worried. The police were called. They said to call them back by the morning if she didn't return home. It wasn't uncommon for young girls to run away from home when they're upset.

They didn't know Beth, though. She wasn't an unruly teenager. She was, for lack of a better word, a good girl.

The next morning, I knocked on Kelly's door. She had already spoken to Beth's mom as well and hadn't seen Beth either. I was half hoping that she was lying, and Beth was hiding in the house somewhere, ready to pop out with her usual smile, making us worry over nothing.

Somehow, I knew that wouldn't be the case. I'd had a sick feeling in my stomach that whole day after the exchange by her locker.

Kelly agreed to come with me to the bowling lane to look for her. It wasn't Friday, and it wasn't Rock-N-Bowl that night, but we still hoped she would be there. Kelly spotted Techno Boy and questioned him for a long time, explaining what Beth looked like and asking if he had seen a girl like that there that day. He hadn't.

We went to the local mall, if you could call it that. It was a handful of stores inside a large building with a tiny food court.

We searched every store but didn't find her.

We tried to think of places where she could be.

The beach. Our beach. Beth never went on the trail at night on her own, though. She hated how dark it would get out there.

Would she have slept overnight at our spot by herself? Was someone else with her? If so, it wasn't Kelly.

Beth's mom said she didn't notice any clothes missing or anything like that when I asked her. Nothing was gone from her room, except Beth.

Beth wasn't the type to run away, but

maybe she'd got so upset that she'd actually decided to sleep outside at the beach on her own, as hard as that was to believe.

I told Kelly, and she couldn't see Beth being there. I asked her to come with me to find out, but she refused. She said she would go to school and talk to some of the girls there. She would speak with every student she could to see if anyone remembered seeing Beth the day before.

I felt uneasy going to the beach on my own. I again tried to get Kelly to come with me. It was as if I already knew what I would find in the water.

Kelly again refused, and I went on my own, determined to find my friend, or rule it out as a place she could be.

I hiked the trail until I saw the funny-shaped rock. I walked into the treeline, passing the low-lying branches until I arrived at the beach.

Then I found her. Her body bobbing in the water. I can still remember screaming and running into the lake, checking the pulse of my dead friend. Her skin felt cold. I wasn't sure if it was because she was deceased or because of the water. Her blue eyes, wide open, stared back at me blankly.

I think of these terrible memories as I stare at Beth's tombstone. I feel tears streaming down my cheeks now. I wipe one away and put a hand on the cold stone.

The police investigated her death. Initially, they thought someone had done something terrible to her. The water was only a few feet high. How could someone drown there by accident? Beth knew how to swim.

I had read years later that the police found skin cells that didn't belong to her under her nails. That didn't seem like a coincidence. She must have fought someone off who was trying to hurt her. That person could very well be the one who killed her.

The police said they found no marks or bruises on her body that would suggest a struggle. A small bottle of vodka was found at the beach.

The police concluded that she either drowned by accident or intended to kill herself. Her family and I disagreed. That didn't make any sense.

In the end, her death was ruled an accidental drowning.

I knew exactly where she got the bottle of vodka from. I made sure to tell the police that as well. They said they had already questioned Kelly Van Patten, who had an alibi that night. I'm sure Ryan McDermott gave the police a story that made it impossible to link Kelly to anything.

Beth's family took her death hard, of course. She was only eighteen. She had her whole life ahead of her. Her mom went into a long depression. Allison didn't come to school for the rest of the school year.

With Beth's mom being so heavily involved in the prom planning and preparation, after what happened, she was in no way able to finish. Given the death of a student, the school decided not to finish where she'd left off.

Beth's mom had wanted her daughter to attend prom so much, but the terrible irony was that nobody would have one that year.

I'd had a date lined up, too. After prom was cancelled, and after what happened with Beth, I stopped talking to the boy.

I had my first near-breakdown around that time. I hadn't realized how much my mental health had deteriorated. I'm sure finding a corpse would impact anyone. Finding your best friend's lifeless body was on a whole other level.

I can still remember Beth in the water the day I found her. For as much as I dream about what happened, I sometimes forget that when I found her she wasn't wearing the gold friendship pendant. That's only a cruel joke my brain makes.

I never knew what happened to her pendant. I assumed it was in her bedroom. I asked her mom if they could place it in her coffin for burial, but Linda said she couldn't find it.

It had to have been there, though, I'm sure. Where else could it have been? I wanted to search their house myself to try to find it. It only seemed right that she'd wear it even in death, or at least have it near her. I settled for a picture of us instead. It was the same photo she'd used for the pendant.

I thought about burying my necklace with Beth, but couldn't let go of it. I struggled with the idea for a long time. I couldn't even tell you where the necklace is today.

Soon after Beth's death, I left Muskoka and moved to Toronto. I enrolled at the University of Toronto to study social work. I never had an interest in social work before, but I felt like I owed it to Beth to continue what she would have wanted to do.

I thought after years of therapy, I would be able to let go of the emotions I had about it all. I guess going to therapy doesn't stop you from having emotions, only lessen the impact they have. I think of the conveyor belt exercise that Dr. Albee taught me. We practiced picking up the package of Beth's death many times. It was only after taking medications that it didn't impact me as much.

I put a hand on my belly, and another on the tombstone. "I wish you could see me right now," I say with a thin smile. "I wish you could see my baby. I wish you were here. We could have had babies around the same age. Our children would have known each other well. Maybe even be best friends, like us." I lower my head, another tear forming.

I laugh. "You'd find it funny to know that Kelly is now my neighbour." Somehow pretending I'm talking to Beth as if she's there makes it feel better. "When she was your neighbour, you guys became friends. Now she's mine, and I wish I could move again, far, far away." I laugh again.

I think about what Allison told me today at the children's store. Ryan McDermott killed himself. Kelly found him.

Just like I found Beth.

I let out a breath. "I guess Kelly and I have something in common, don't we?" I say to the tombstone.

I wonder what Beth would say back to me, had she actually been with me at the moment. She always hated how much I didn't like Kelly. She wished the two of us would get along. She hoped we would have. She probably wished the three of us would be the best of friends.

I thought of Kelly again. Somehow, knowing that the death of someone she loved impacted her as well made me empathize with her.

Kelly wasn't a bad person after all, no matter what I made up in my head about her. I may not have gotten along with her when we were younger. I may have been jealous, for stupid reasons, but she was never directly mean to me. Even now, as adults, she has been nothing but welcoming.

I think of Dr. Albee and the therapy I did. The work I put into myself. It felt like it was all for nothing if I couldn't learn from my past. It was my insecurities that got the better of me when I was a teenager. I was jealous of Kelly. Her looks. Her relationship with Beth. Even the fact that Ryan McDermott chose her.

None of that made me less of a person, but for some reason I compared myself to her, and felt small.

Now, as an adult, I'm doing the same.

I say my goodbye to Beth's tombstone and leave the cemetery. The whole way home, I think of Kelly. Usually this would raise my blood pressure, but not now.

Now, I realize I shouldn't avoid my new neighbour. I need to embrace her.

That's what Beth would have wanted.

I park in my driveway and look over at her house. I lower my head, working myself up. I finally move my feet toward Kelly's home until I'm at her front door. I ring the bell and wait patiently. Her dog, Lady starts barking and for a moment, I think of turning around until I hear the door unlock and open.

Kelly looks at me, confused.

"Hey," I say to her. I look past her at a small

table. I immediately spot a picture of Ryan and Kelly, along with a vase. He's older in the picture. His hair is much shorter than I remember it being, but his face is still as handsome as it was in high school.

"Hey, Nora," Kelly says. "Can I help you?"

I nod, taking in a moment to find the right words. I look at the beautiful marble floor and large white kitchen in the back, with the numerous plants scattered around the open concept room.

"I love how you decorated your home," I say. I consider making up an excuse and leaving immediately, but tell myself to stay.

Kelly looks behind her and back at me with a wide smile. "Thanks."

I can feel my nerves jitter, but I manage to ask her, "You mentioned having tea tonight. I would love it if you came by after dinner to my house. I would love to catch up with you."

Kelly's smile widens.

CHAPTER 22

Kelly

This is perfect. I was struggling with how I would get back into the Bowmans' home and Nora knocked on my door with an invitation.

Not only do I need to play secret agent again and grab the listening devices, but I also now have my new master plan.

I'm not good at creating one solid plan from the get-go. It's apparent to me now. I need to think on the fly, which so far has worked out great.

The plan is straightforward, but complex. I imagine myself talking in a room full of different parts of my personality, showcasing the plan like a military general.

This is the objective. This is the outcome. Here are the tactical ways we will complete this operation. A hand swings up in the front of the class from the part of me that represents empathy.

"What if you're wrong about everything?"

Military general me ignores that personality. Sure, I've wondered throughout what I'm doing, and what I have left to do if it's the right thing, the moral thing to do.

I know it is.

Nora deserves everything she has coming.

Empathy me raises her hand again. "She's also pregnant."

I ignore myself again. That doesn't matter to me. It should be irrelevant.

I stare at Lady, sitting at my feet, as if she can give me an answer on what I should do. Now was her chance to speak up and veto my stupid plans. Now was her chance to stop me from going through with it and avoiding the terrible outcomes that could result. Lady raises her head at me for a moment, before blinking and lowering it back down and going back to her nap.

A lot of help you are, I think.

I continue to break down the plan in my head. The personality representing the scared shitless side of me screams in terror, "What happens if we get caught?"

It could happen. If I don't think I can follow through with the plan tonight, I can back out at any time.

I can ensure I grab the listening devices, run back to my house, which in my daydream is now called HQ. I can think of a new plan. Something safer.

Nora isn't leaving anytime soon. There could be other ways to do this. Ways that will ensure I won't rot in jail somewhere.

I've been so consumed with Nora that I haven't sat and thought about what will happen if everything comes out. What if I'm discovered? I haven't done anything too bad yet. Unless you consider bugging someone's house to be breaking the law.

Shit.

Scared me has strong points that are hard to ignore. I can pretend the caring, empathetic me does not exist, but getting caught will ruin everything.

I can imagine Nora laughing at me as I'm placed in handcuffs by police, and dragged into a cruiser. I imagine myself kicking and screaming, while the few neighbours on the block gather around to watch the crazy widowed lady be taken away.

If things aren't going well tonight, I'll bail on the plan entirely. I'll do what I need to clean up the terrible things I've already done and get the hell out.

Maybe I'll get out of town while I'm at it, too. If nothing happens to Nora, I know I can't live beside her for the rest of my life. It would be unbearable.

I would rather kill myself than live anywhere near Nora in Muskoka. That's an intense thought. A bit too much.

I breathe out. I can't help but think of Ryan. I try to get the image out of my mind.

If I get caught while attempting to fulfil what I want to do with Nora, it could call into question everything that happened with my husband.

If they discover the truth, my life will be over.

I continue to get ready for teatime with Nora Bowman. I dress down for the event, wearing a white t-shirt and jeans. I didn't put on much make-up, going for a more natural look. I want to connect with Nora, or at least make her feel connected to me, so I can do what I have to do.

I head into my walk-in closet. The size of the room is ridiculous. My closet is bigger than the bedroom I had growing up. Ryan's clothes still take up half of it. I can't bring myself to donate them yet, but don't know why. I know it's time to move on.

I finger through his suits to a small shelf where I've kept the package I ordered. I already read the instructions carefully several times, but do so again. Knowing me, I'll make a mistake, and everything will be ruined.

I put a lot of thought into this plan. I just have to get through tonight. I have to find a way to complete what I need to do.

"I won't get caught," I say out loud. I take a

deep breath in, thinking about it.

I look at the clock in my bedroom. It's almost time. I put the small package in my purse. I typically wear little purses, but today I need something bigger.

I had to buy one because none of my purses would fit everything I need to bring. Straight after Nora knocked on my door with an invitation to her home, I enthusiastically ran out and bought a purse and tea since I have none in the house.

There's a local store in town that has a great selection. I asked which was the bestseller she had for people who are pregnant. The cashier pointed out several, and I got them all. I sigh, alone in my room. Even when I'm planning the demise of someone, I have to buy the best tea in town, of course. They also had some amazing biscuits that were out for sample that would pair well with their products. I bought a few bags of those as well.

After coming back home from buying what I needed and reading the instructions on the package many times over, I listened to what was happening inside Nora's home. I must have sat in my office for hours, taking in any conversation I could.

Nothing was useful. Nora mentioned teatime with me to her husband. Jameson said he was happy that she was attempting to reconnect with an old friend.

Old friend? I nearly laughed out loud when he said that. What followed almost made me belly laugh harder.

"Well, we weren't very close," Nora admitted to her husband, "but people change. I should get to know Kelly better."

I shook my head in disbelief.

CHAPTER 23

Kelly

I knock on the door nervously. When I hear footsteps coming towards me, I shake off feelings about what I'm doing and plaster on a fake smile.

Nora opens the door, and for a change, shares a smile of her own. She's smiled at me before, but this one seems authentic.

"Hey, beautiful!" I say enthusiastically. I step inside and give her a hug. "I'm so happy you invited me over." I wave the bag in front of her. "I got special tea from this cute store in town. You're going to love this place. It's right on Main Street."

"Thanks!" Nora says with enthusiasm I wasn't expecting. "Come on in."

I do, commenting on how nice their home is looking.

"It's all Nora," Jameson says, coming down the hallway.

"Hello again," I say to him. He gestures for a handshake, and I wave him away. "After the third time I meet someone, I'm on hugging terms." We embrace quickly. Even in the fleeting moment we touch, I can feel his rock-hard body. Nora's a lucky girl. Jameson laughs.

I can't help but notice he's wearing a non-flannel navy blue dress shirt for a change with a nice pair of grey slacks. The outfit suits his tan skin nicely. A long cigar sat in his shirt pocket.

"Going somewhere?" I ask him. Please say yes. Please, pretty please. It's enough having to figure out how the hell I'm actually going to do what I need to do today without getting caught, but if the man of the house is away, I may have more opportunities.

"Just hanging around tonight, but don't worry, I won't get in the way of your girl time," he says playfully. "I'm not much of a tea guy. I plan on having a beer and sitting outside. Let you girls catch up."

Damn.

"That's great," I say with a smile. "Such a lovely backyard to relax in. You know, though, if you're looking for a great brewhouse in town, there's this place called Schmitt's. Sounds funny, but everyone loves their beer. The raspberry flavoured one is my personal fave."

"Thanks," he says. He goes to the fridge and grabs a bottle, raising it to us. "To tea and beer." He opens the patio door and walks outside to sit on a beach chair by the pool.

Nora stands beside me, shaking her head.

"I used to love the smell of his Cuban cigars, but I can't stand it since I've been pregnant. Do you still smoke?"

I shake my head. "Not really. Ryan and I quit together a few years ago. He was a big cigar guy too... Our husbands would have gotten along, probably."

Even though I would have hated the idea, it's likely true. Ryan was an easy-going person. He was a sociable man. Despite his antics in high school, a lot of people liked him as he aged out of his dumb teenage stage, even some who hated him before.

"Here, I'll take that," Nora says, grabbing my purse. I make a face at first until she pulls lightly again. "I'll just put it in the front closet for you."

Already my plan is going to hell. "Thanks so much."

If I were to call a meeting inside my mind again, the multiple personalities would be executing a revolution instead of my plan.

"Did you unpack a teapot?" I ask. "I can run back and grab mine?" Part of me might want to stay home if I do though. It's much safer in my house. I'm in enemy territory at the moment and feeling a bit overwhelmed.

"No, that's okay," Nora says with a smile. She walks over to the kitchen, bends down to some lower cabinets and grabs a teapot. She puts in some water from the tap and puts it on the stove.

I almost cry when I see the tap water. I love to use purified water for all my drinks. Town water seems so... yucky. Usually, I would say something, but tonight I'm trying my best not to piss her off or make her uncomfortable.

"Guess who I ran into?" Nora asks. She waits a moment before answering. "Allison Graham."

"Beth's sister," I say with a smile. "I don't really talk to her much these days, but I see her in town from time to time. I noticed that she's like you, with one in the oven." I laugh.

Nora smiles. "Yes, it's a girl, she tells me." She sits at the counter and gestures for me to join her.

Part of me is taken aback. I don't think Nora was ever this welcoming to me. She was never friendly. I had assumed she hated me from the first day I met her. There was this tension in the air whenever I was near her.

"You'll have a baby buddy, I guess," I say with a smile. "It'll be nice to have someone you know with a newborn."

She nods. "I was worried at first, since, you know, she's Beth's sister. I almost feel guilty making plans to see her."

I bet you did, I think.

"There's nothing wrong with catching up

with her, though," I say.

She nods again. "I'm sure Beth would be happy if she could see us. I visited the cemetery today too. To visit Beth. It's weird calling it a visit. I haven't seen her tombstone in long time."

"How did that go?" I am genuinely interested in what she has to say.

"Difficult," she says, lowering her head. "Difficult. It's weird being back in town. It's serendipitous, us being neighbours. Me connecting with Allison again. Reconnecting with you. It's... I don't know. Part of me is happy being back, but it stirs a lot of emotions."

I nod. It certainly stirred my emotions when I found out Nora was my new neighbour as well. I lost plenty of sleep over it. It consumed me. My hatred for the woman in front of me has become an obsession in the unhealthiest of ways. I'm here tonight to ruin her, and she has no clue, and despite that, I'm having tea with her, pretending to be best of friends.

Despite my grave ill will towards this woman, I'm surprised how my feelings change as the night continues. I still dislike her, but my anger softens. I actually start to enjoy our conversation.

We talk endlessly about the changes in town while Nora was living in Toronto. I spill the tea, as the saying goes, on everything that's been happening. I enjoy watching Nora's expressions as I tell her all about the people we knew from high school and what they're up to today.

Who's married, who has kids, who divorced, whose spouse cheated on them, and, who's currently cheating on them. Nora ate it up. She's hanging onto every word.

Before I know it, we've been talking for over two hours and it's pitch dark outside. I can barely see Jameson now in the backyard, unless he draws on his cigar, and I catch a glimpse of red smoke. He's come inside several times to get a fresh beer. He's likely on his fifth or sixth now. I wonder how impatient he is, waiting for me to leave, although he does seem content with his cigar and cell phone.

"This tea really is fantastic, by the way," Nora says, finishing her cup. I offer to pour her more and she readily accepts.

"I'll bring you to shop in town sometime," I say. "Maybe we can stop by that Boot and Mittens store while we're there. I have to get baby something." I smile and she does so back.

Suddenly, I feel a wave of guilt hit me. I was authentic in wanting to buy something for the baby inside her. Pretending to be friends for so long has made me believe we were. If only she had any idea what I have planned.

I question how terrible of a person I have truly become.

"What ever happened to Sandy?" Nora

asks. "You remember her? Sandra Tallie? I don't even remember the last time I saw her."

"Well," I say with a smile, "she's literally the law now." I laugh.

"What, a police officer?"

I nod. "That's right. She's been an police officer for a long time now. She's stationed right downtown on Main Street, too. The uniform looks so right on her. The stab-proof vest and the gun at her side. It seems so natural on her. It's as if she was born to be a cop."

Nora nods. "I can't believe it. All these things have happened in town since I left. My mom would tell me things here and there. She doesn't have her finger on the pulse of Muskoka like you do, though."

"I try not to know everyone's business, but it just happens." That was true. I know a lot. I could open a gossip magazine in town if I wanted. I could write novels with what I knew.

Jameson opens the patio door and walks inside. He stumbles over his feet and smiles at us. "You ladies partied all night," he says with a laugh. He looks at the stove timer. "Nearly ten."

I laugh. "Looks like you've had dozen beers as well there."

Nora shoots him a look, and I can immediately tell what she's thinking. "Stop drinking!"

That doesn't work for me. I'd rather

encourage him to keep going.

"Nora," he says, slurring his words, "I got the perfect name." Nora grins at me before looking back at her husband with a patient smile. "If it's a boy, we call him Todd."

"Todd?" she repeats with a laugh. "Too plain for me."

"I knew you would say that. Okay, you'll be proud to know I have a girl's name as well to present to you. Bella!"

Nora squints. "Well, it's pretty, but we're not Italian."

I laugh. "You two are too cute."

Jameson scoffs and gives up. "Who wants a sandwich?" he asks us, stepping into the kitchen. "I make a killer baloney and cheese." Nora and I share a look and I can tell immediately we're both not interested. "No takers, okay." He opens the fridge and starts taking out items. He sighs loudly. "And... no baloney. Honey—"

"I'll grab you some tomorrow," Nora says, smiling at me. "What grown man loves baloney sandwiches?" I laugh.

Jameson does too. "I elevate mine with mayo, lettuce and onions, though." He makes a chef's kiss gesture.

"Gordon Ramsay would be impressed," I say. The three of us laugh.

Jameson pulls out a Ziploc bag and opens it on the counter behind Nora. "Only sliced chicken breast. Will have to do I guess." He opens the pack and flaps a thin piece in his hand. "Are you sure you ladies don't want a healthy chicken sandwich?"

Nora suddenly covers her mouth, and without saying a word, runs down the hall.

Jameson immediately slumps his shoulders. "Oh, crap."

"What happened?" I ask.

"Ugh," Jameson says, mostly to himself. He takes a sip of beer before answering me. "Chicken."

"Chicken?"

"For whatever reason, she gets a bad pregnancy reaction with any kind of chicken. Of course, I love chicken. I can't believe I did that. I only use it when she's out of the house, knowing what happens to her." Jameson opens a cabinet behind him, grabbing a glass. He fills it with water and walks down the hall. "I'll be right back."

I can hear the faint sounds of regurgitation echoing down the hall. It's almost sweet watching him care for his wife in that way.

It would likely be a better gesture had he used purified water, though. Maybe I'll give him that tip when he comes back.

I wonder how Ryan would have reacted had it been me. Would he have run after me, water in hand, to make me feel better?

I immediately snap out of my thoughts

and realize the opportunity I have and remember why I'm here. I quickly go to the front closet and grab my purse. I peer down the hall and can still hear Nora in the bathroom. I can almost imagine the terrible sounds I would be hearing if I was at home, listening to the bathroom bug.

I quickly go back into the kitchen and sit at the table, rummaging my hands under it. I can't find the listening device, though. I freak out inside.

I'm certain I put it on this side of the table. Am I wrong? I'm about to get on my hands and knees to look underneath when I hear footsteps from the hallway.

"She's okay," Jameson says with a smile. "Sorry for ruining the tea date." He looks down at the plate of biscuits that Nora and I had and grabs one. He takes a bite, and his eyes widen. "These are amazing!"

"They're from town," I say with a laugh. I try to maintain solid eye contact with Jameson as my fingers feel around below the table.

Where is it? Did it fall? Is it on the floor somewhere?

"Nora is a little out of it now," Jameson says. "She feels terrible, but sometimes after a puke session like this, she wants to rest. I think she's embarrassed to come back out here, since I'm sure you heard everything she just did inside the bathroom."

I panic inside. I haven't gotten any devices back or dealt with the package in my purse. I can't leave yet.

Maybe this is a sign. A warning for me to stop everything I planned. Go home. Put up a sale sign and move out of town. I would be much happier somewhere else.

I smile suddenly as my hand touches something small and round. I know instantly I've found the device. I grab my purse and open it, plopping it inside, and grabbing some Chap Stick. I apply it to my lips and put it back inside, zipping it up.

"So very understandable," I say. "I hope she feels better." I'm about to stand up to leave when Jameson sits across from me at the table.

"So," he says, only slightly slurring his words, "you knew Nora pretty well in high school."

I nod. "We were friends in senior year, yeah."

He nods back. "So you must have known her friend, Beth? Beth Graham?"

The smile on my face vanishes. "I did. We were close."

He nods again. "Apparently, she and Nora were, too."

"They were."

"I'm worried about her. Being back in town where the… accident happened."

I sit up in my chair. "What exactly did she tell you about what happened?"

His eyebrows rise for a moment. "It sounded terrible. Her friend, Beth, killed herself. She found her body in the lake. She seems to be taking things well. She hasn't said anything to me about it since being back in town. I just, you know, worry."

"Right," I say. If only he knew the truth.

"Apparently, she killed herself because of some boy."

I grit my teeth but present a smile. "What was the boy's name?"

"I feel terrible. The number of times Nora has told me what happened. I should remember every detail... I don't though."

"Did she tell you much about me?"

"No, not really." Jameson smiles. "Well, I'm sorry again for ruining tonight. Despite us being neighbours, there's a bit of distance between our front doors. It's pretty dark out there. Do you want me to walk you home?"

I smile. "Well, to be honest, I'd rather you pour me a beer, or something harder if you have it." I smile at him. He doesn't answer me. "Pour us both a shot and I'll tell you all about what Nora was like in high school."

CHAPTER 24

Nora

I feel terrible. The night is ruined. It's all because of chicken.

Thinking of the word makes my stomach roil. I put my hand on my tummy, soothing my baby inside me. Don't worry, I say. The terrible chicken is away from us.

I can't believe the intolerance my body has to poultry. There was a time where I loved it. Chicken thighs could be so juicy. Wings were amazing.

Ugh.

I don't need an ultrasound right now to know that the little thing inside me is going crazy at the thought of any chicken dish.

The night with Kelly was going so well, too.

I've never spoken to her alone for so long. I never understood what Beth saw in her until tonight. There's something enigmatic about her. You want to hear what she's going to say next because it will either be funny or appalling.

The amount of gossip I've learned in one night with Kelly is astonishing. I feel like I know what everyone is up to in town.

After rescuing myself from the thoughts and smells of chicken, I hide out in my bedroom. Jameson stands nearby, water in hand, to comfort me. When I start to feel better, I accept his offering and climb into bed. I just need rest. It's not exactly late, but I'm not used to staying up past ten most nights, anyway.

I used to be a night owl when I was a teenager. Beth and I would stay up late talking on the phone.

I imagine what Kelly must think of me. Am I lame for going to bed this early? Maybe she doesn't think that way, though. I'm sure she has friends who have kids. She must realize the changes a body can go through when there's a baby growing inside, even if she hasn't experienced it herself.

I'm tempted to talk to her about her husband, Ryan. Here she is spouting off everyone else's gossip when I know something about her life that she hasn't shared with me.

Her husband killed himself. She found his body.

What a terrible thing to happen. She comes off so friendly and full of life, meanwhile her soulmate ended his own.

If something happened to Jameson, I wouldn't have any pep in my step like Kelly. I'd more than likely curl into a ball of tears and snot for the remainder of my miserable life.

She didn't even require years of therapy to get to a place of peace, like me. No medications either.

I shouldn't assume that.

For all I know, she sees a therapist weekly and gives them regular wicker baskets as presents for payment.

I tell Jameson to let Kelly know I'll be resting for the rest of the night. I can't go back out there after the devastation that came out of me. Jameson points out some of the mess that's stained my shirt.

It's embarrassing. I just want to rest.

The bed's so large and soft, too. It's easy to relax on it, and I can already feel my eyes start to drift away to sleep land.

Laughter from down the hall makes me open my eyes. I'm not sure how long I've been resting for, but I assume it was for a while.

Kelly must be finishing her last bit of tea.

I think of Jameson laughing with her. Usually, the idea of my husband alone with Kelly would be enough to make me jump out of bed and run down the hall frantically.

Tonight, things feel different. I've got to know Kelly better. I've got to see what Beth saw in her all those years ago, and it wasn't bad.

All the resentment I had for her seems to be lifting. Could it be the beginning of an actual friendship? Beth had wanted me to get close with Kelly. It wasn't until she was gone that I could muster up the courage to try to. I think of Allison. I know it's a weird thought, but I wonder what it would be like to be close friends with Allison and Kelly. Perhaps the three of us could be great friends together.

Allison wouldn't be a proper substitute for her sister, Beth, but it would be ironic.

What a day, I think.

After coming back from Boots and Mittens, Jameson and I made up, too. He immediately apologized for the fight. I apologized as well.

I held his hand as I guided him to the new nursery room where we talked for a long time. I showed him the dresser and crib. He loved them both.

I kissed him, and he accepted my apology.

I accepted his kisses, which turned to wandering hands, which turned into much, much more. It was a weird place to have sex for the first time in our new home. Soon this would be our baby's room, but today we christened it.

I suppose it isn't too weird. After all, sex is how our baby was conceived. The love Jameson and I share is the whole reason it exists inside me.

It's also the reason that I feel incredibly

sick most of the time as well. I put a hand to my mouth and consider running to the bathroom again. The urge to vomit stops, thankfully. I'm not even sure what made me feel that way.

Being pregnant makes no sense at times.

I hear laughter again from down the hall. Kelly is certainly taking her time finishing her tea.

I close my eyes and try to relax.

Suddenly I think of Beth. I think of the beach where I found her. I manage to calm my mind. The last thing I want is another nightmare. I take several deep breaths and imagine myself next to a long conveyor belt. A green light buzzes above me, and the belt moves. I see the first box coming down.

It's labelled "Father". I leave that package without looking at it. Some packages are not worth picking up.

The next one coming down reads "Kelly Van Patten". As it gets closer, the usual feelings of jealousy and anger aren't present. I pick up the box and let myself feel some new emotions I've attached to it. Feelings of a possible friendship. I place the box back on the belt and watch it leave.

I turn and see another box coming towards me. Elizabeth Graham.

I breathe heavily, calming myself. I pick up the box and stare at it for some time. Other boxes pass. "Fear of being a bad mother", one reads. It passes me as I continue to look at Beth's. "Does Jameson really love me?" is another box.

The only thing I can see is Beth's package.

I'm not sure how, but sleep overcomes me. I feel at peace. Baby is resting inside me. It must be tired from putting its mom through hell. Finally, my body is at ease. Both mom and baby are peacefully resting.

That's until a hard sensation comes down my throat. I nearly gag and sit up immediately, coughing. I turn and puke on the mattress.

Ugh. What have I done? I've never regurgitated like this while sleeping. Is this going to be a new normal for me? Worse was, I vomited on Jameson's side of the bed.

A noise in the dark room makes me turn my head. I hear the door creak, and a gust of wind, followed by quick footsteps.

The back of my throat aches. I've vomited many times in the past few weeks, but nothing had the sensation I have now.

"Jameson?" I call out.

There's no answer. I look at the nightstand. Sometimes Jameson leaves a cup for me there. Did he come into the room to bring me another one? There's only the half-drunk one from before.

"Jameson?" I call out again. When there's no answer, I stand up slowly, making a face at the mess I've made on the bed. I'll need to clean it up immediately to avoid the stomach acid staining the mattress.

I open the bedroom door and stare down the dark hall. I think I hear a thud at the end of it.

Suddenly I feel like a woman in a horror movie. Why does my throat hurt so much? Why is my husband not in the bed? I mean, thankfully, he wasn't. He would not have been too happy being woken up by what I would've done to him.

Did he sleep on the couch again? Why? We more than kissed and made up today.

I go down the hallway, into the foyer. The front door is closed, but the door unlocked. How very unlike my husband. He lived in downtown Toronto nearly his whole adult life. He was the kind of person who locked his doors during the daytime. He was surprised when I said it was not uncommon for people in Muskoka to never lock their doors at all.

Crime isn't a factor here. It's something the townsfolk read about in newspapers, but never experience in their day-to-day lives.

I lock the door and call out for my husband again. I go to the kitchen and turn on the light. Jameson puts a hand up in protest.

"Please turn that off," he manages. He raises his head and looks at me. "Hey, are you feeling better?" He burps and pounds his chest with his fist.

I look at the table and there's an empty cup and shot glass beside him, as well as a half-emptied bottle of Jack Daniels. Across the table is a second cup and shot glass.

I look back at the front door, and at my husband. "Were you drinking with Kelly?" He looks at me, confused. I can feel my blood pressure rising. I invite her to come over for tea, and when I'm sick in bed, she switches to hard liquor with my husband.

I remember the laughter the two shared when I was trying to sleep.

"What did you two—" I calm myself, trying not to let my anger get the best of me. I remember the feeling I had when I woke up in bed. I thought someone was in the room with me. I assumed it was Jameson, but in his state he's barely able to put a few words together in a meaningful way.

"Did you come into our bedroom just now?" I ask him anyway, trying to understand.

He breathes in deep. "I think... I've been out here."

"When did Kelly leave?"

He looks around the room as if to say he thought she was still there.

"Why were you drinking alone with her?" I ask.

He makes a face as if to say, not this again. I don't dig into him. There's no point. He's obviously drunk.

"I'm going to bed," he says in a raspy voice. He stands up and slowly makes his way down the hall.

I walk over to the side window near the entrance. I peek between the blinds, staring at Kelly's house.

I can see a light on inside, near the front of her home. I look around the sidewalk and the streetlights illuminating the road and sidewalk outside, but see nothing. Suddenly, the light turns off inside Kelly's home.

"Uh, honey!" Jameson calls out from down the hall.

CHAPTER 25

Kelly

I did it. Somehow, I pulled it off.

I'm out of breath by the time I get inside my house and shut the door behind me. I didn't know what to expect when I went into her room. For some reason, I thought she would keep sleeping even with my hand down her throat, as naïve as I am.

I don't think she saw me. I pray she didn't.

Maybe I *didn't* get away as clean as I thought.

Nora could be calling the police right now. What would I say to an officer if they knocked on my door?

Nothing is probably the best option. Talk to my lawyer? It's not as if I have one for criminal purposes. I probably should have been proactive on that. I don't think the estate lawyer I used for Ryan's will would be of much use. He could potentially point me in the right direction, though.

I try to calm myself and realize with fear that my foyer light is still on. I quickly turn off the lights. I wait in the darkness, standing by the table with Ryan's vase.

I did it, I tell myself.

Not only did I complete my main goal, but I grabbed the listening devices as well. At the moment, I'm a little upset about that. I would love to be able to listen in to what's happening inside Nora's house right now. Is she up? Does she suspect something?

I peek out the window at her home and thankfully the lights inside are all still off. I count my blessings.

I may just have gotten away with everything. Me.

Time to apply to become a spy. I literally have experience now.

The whole night went impossibly smooth. I have Jameson to thank for a lot of it. Thank goodness for morning sickness as well!

A few slices of deli meat took care of Nora. She ran to her bedroom and was out of commission for the rest of the night.

I didn't know how to handle Jameson. How could I get around the house without him suspecting something. I wasn't sure what to do. With him already tipsy, I asked for a drink. I wasn't sure how getting liquored up would help my situation. I just didn't want him to ask me to leave.

Thankfully, he accepted my request. I told stories from St. Joe's High for nearly an hour. I had his complete attention as I talked about some memories I had with Nora. I do admit that I lied to him a wee bit. I may have told more stories of Beth and I and replaced her with Nora in my retellings. After all, I didn't have too many of just Nora and me.

It didn't matter. Jameson loved hearing everything I had to say and was willing to drink more and more as I told him.

I wondered if he would come on to me. A few times, I caught his boozy eyes lowering to my chest level. Just as quickly, though, he would look back at my eyes and ask another question about what his teenage wife was like back in the day.

After he took out the Jack Daniels, things got harder. Not only for him, but me. I had way too much as well. My stories got even sloppier, and I may have begun making things up entirely. I'm sure Jameson doesn't exactly remember every word I said, though.

At some point I left, saying I had to go to the bathroom. The hallway is thankfully out of sight from the kitchen area. It's a weird layout for a large bungalow. I nearly jogged down the hall. The plan was to grab the listening device from the bathroom first, then figure out how to deal with Nora.

I nearly kicked myself when I realized I didn't bring my large purse with me. I jetted back to the kitchen. Jameson looked tired and beat from all the drinks I'd been encouraging him to down. He gave me an uneven smile.

"Forgot my purse," I said with a smile back.

He laughed. "Girls and freshening up, huh?"

I ran back down the hall but stopped when I heard the faint sound of snoring coming from the main bedroom. The door was ajar. I peeked inside and, sure enough, Nora was sound asleep.

This plan couldn't have come together any better.

First, I grabbed the device behind the bedframe. After, I took out everything I needed from my purse. When I was close to her, I softly put the swab inside her mouth, and she immediately made a noise, and turned over, waking up.

I didn't wait for her to open her eyes. Instead, I nearly ran out of her room and quickly went back down the hall. Jameson had his head on the kitchen table.

I wasn't sure if Nora was actually waking up. With any luck, she just went back to sleep.

"Goodnight," I said to my new drinking buddy. Jameson didn't flinch. I turned off the kitchen light and quickly put my shoes on. I quietly closed the front door behind me as I left.

I'm a runner. I love it. I enjoy the feeling my lungs have when I push it to the limit. I never felt my heart beat faster than when I made my getaway from the Bowmans' home, though. I felt like I could have had a heart attack as I closed and locked my front door.

I didn't even look back at Nora's house until I was inside on my own.

That's when it hits me. The bathroom listening device. I smack the side of my head.

How stupid could I be?

How many drinks have I had tonight? I thought I was setting up Jameson, but I got myself in trouble, too.

Ugh, I can't believe I forgot the stupid bathroom bug. Of course, the most useless of them was the one I forgot to grab.

How would I be able to get back inside their house to get it now?

I didn't want to. I wanted to be far away from Nora now until everything comes out. Until I get the results back.

I look inside my purse and pull out the Ziploc bag where I kept the swab in the cup the company provided me.

"Family Genes", the package read. It was a medium-sized DNA company from Toronto.

I have to give it to Nora for giving me the idea through the listening devices. I would never have thought of it had it not been for her.

So ironic.

For years she's got away with what she did. I raise the Ziploc bag in my hand to look at the sample I took tonight.

Now I have all the evidence I need to prove what I always knew.

Nora killed Beth.

CHAPTER 26

Kelly
Before
The first day of school

Why can't my parents just divorce, like everyone else?

It's a terrible thought but as I eat my Cheerios, listening to them fight in the morning before I go to school, I can't stop thinking about it.

My first morning in Muskoka Lake is just like most mornings when I lived in Toronto, filled with raised voices and tension between my parents.

I have no clue what they are bickering about today. Something to do with the move to this town. Something to do with the older house they bought, and how renovations will cost more than they expected.

With my headphones on, everything they say sounds like Charlie Brown teacher sounds. Only they're more animated with rage than a cartoon and there's a lot more four-letter words they can't say on television.

The use of the pointer finger is especially heavy by my mother.

Hadn't we moved to this town for a more relaxing life? That was the crap they sold me when they told me we were moving.

I'm nearly graduating high school, with only a little over a month left, and they pick up and move? How did the school even accept me as a student this late in the year?

It likely has something to do with my dad's money. Money can make things easier, no matter how hard they seem.

I guess he forgot to budget enough for renos at the new house. Even though dad has plenty of money, everything needs to fit into his budget.

Ugh. I can't wait to leave home this morning just to get away from them.

Today will be my first day at St. Joseph's Catholic High School. I hate it already. I hate coming from a public school to a Catholic one. I have to wear a school uniform. I have to dress a certain way, I'm told. At least that's what the principal said at our meeting last week when he explained to me what the school was all about.

Integrity, and honour, and blah, blah. It's a month left of school, can you please just let me graduate so I can move on with life?

My dad stomps his feet, something that

always annoys me when he gets angry. I almost picture a toddler not getting the sucker he wanted from the grocery store when he does it.

I realize school will be starting soon, even though we haven't hung up a clock to confirm it or set the stove timer properly. I also realize that there's little chance I'm getting a ride there. I don't bother asking.

My mom has her arms folded, nodding to something my dad is saying to her. I lower my headphones for a moment.

"Bye, Mom. Bye, Dad."

Just as quickly as their faces were full of anger and rage, they switch to loving parent mode when they look at me.

"Bye, sweetheart," Dad calls out.

"Have a good first day," Mom says.

How can they be so fake? There's a terrible saying that someday, we all become our parents. What a nightmare that would be!

I throw my backpack over my shoulder as their loud voices become louder. I walk outside my new home and shut the door behind me. Even from outside, I can still hear them barking at each other. I smile at my elderly next-door neighbour who's cutting his grass. He looks at me strangely as if to ask, what the heck is going on in your home?

Even this senior citizen at his age can hear my parents argue.

I smile back and wish him a happy morning.

I begin to walk down the street towards the school. The day before, my dad took me around the town. It's pretty easy not to get lost here. A big city like Toronto, it can easily happen.

Not here.

The town has a downtown area with only a few stores, a police department and a small, pitiful mall. The school's only a few blocks away from home, and I can spot the roofline of the large building from my block.

I turn around and notice a brunette girl walking the same way as me. She's wearing the same uniform as well. She looks about my age, with large blue eyes. They're not as blue as mine, though.

She waves at me. I smile back but turn quickly and keep walking. She likely heard World War Three happening inside my home as well. It's just so embarrassing.

Why did my family move here? Why did I agree to come with them?

I'm eighteen. I could have stayed in Toronto. I asked my parents if I could live with a friend until the end of high school, but they outright refused me.

I guess my parents don't trust me, and I can't exactly blame them. I've never been great at following their rules.

The no boyfriend rule was continuously broken. My dad had wanted me to focus on my academics. I wasn't a bad student but wasn't good either. I wasn't dumb. I could likely have done well, had I applied myself, but I rarely did.

I applied myself towards good-looking boys, though. That was definitely more fun than a textbook.

That was something else I left behind in Toronto, a boyfriend. We had only been dating a few months, but for me, that was a record. Tom was his name. Tom Enthrone. I speak like he doesn't exist anymore. He may as well not, though. I told him I would call him, but during the move out here, I feel like I lost interest.

A long-distance relationship is not something I have in mind.

It's not like anything happened between us that was special. Something my parents would be happy to know about, if I ever told them, was I still had my V card.

It would probably surprise many people who knew me to find out I'm a virgin, though. I've had strong feelings for boys, but nothing special. I'm not sure what I'm waiting for, but it wasn't Tom Enthrone.

When I get to school, I go straight to the principal's office. I was told that with such little time left in the school year they had to figure out what homeroom to give me. I found out it would be English.

When I get to class, a teacher named Mr. Johnson introduces me. It's awkward as hell facing a bunch of students like this, being presented by a teacher.

The boys in the back of the class almost look like a pack of lions, and I'm a piece of fresh meat. One boy in particular catches my attention. I assume he's on some type of sports team because of the varsity jacket he's wearing. I give him a thin smile and he immediately smiles back.

Maybe Muskoka Lake won't be so bad after all.

When Mr. Johnson tells me to find a seat, I look around the room. I'm tempted to sit near the boys until I see the same girl I saw just a little while ago walking down the street behind me.

I sit beside her, and she introduces herself. Beth's her name. While she's introducing herself, I feel a finger dig into my back. For a moment, I think it's one of the boys trying to annoy me.

When I turn around, I'm surprised to see another girl.

"Hi, I'm Nora," she says. I smile back at her and introduce myself, although can still feel pain in my back from where she touched me.

The rest of the day is uneventful. I spot the same boy from English class walking down the hallway. Our eyes meet again, and I can feel myself blushing.

Poor Tom Enthrone. I seem to have already forgotten about him entirely.

After school, I see Beth walking down the street ahead of me.

"Hey," I call out to her. She stops and waits for me to catch up. "Beth, right?"

She nods. "That's right. So, how do you like Muskoka so far?"

I let out a sigh. "I mean, the scenery is beautiful, but doesn't seem like a lot happens here."

Beth laughs. "Seems like you already have a good idea of what living in Muskoka Lake is like already but, I'd be happy to help you get to know the town better," Beth offers.

Right away, I can tell Beth Graham is a sweetheart. A kind person. The type of girl someone who could easily befriend.

I smile and nod. "Thanks, I'd love that."

CHAPTER 27

Kelly
Present
The plan

I toss and turn in bed nearly all night.

I can barely contain myself as I think about everything that happened this evening.

I literally swabbed Nora's mouth as she slept. I collected her DNA. Tomorrow, I have a bit of a drive to Toronto to get it to the lab. I already have everything set up ahead of time.

I spoke with the company and paid an exorbitant fee to expedite the results. Typically, it would take up to a month, but I spoke with the manager of the lab, made up some crazy reason why I needed it done early, and offered him triple the price to have it done as soon as possible.

Money can solve any problem. The manager happily accepted the offer so that I could have my DNA ancestry results ready for my big family reunion next week, which, of course, wasn't real.

Once Family Genes' lab tests Nora's sample, it will be used to map out her whole history. She'll find out her ancestral heritage, understand what her ethnicity is, and link up her family tree with others.

Only these DNA databases are so much more than that. I read that recently a serial killer was caught because of DNA taken from a family member on a database matched with DNA found at a murder.

The Golden State Killer had racked thirteen murders, and over fifty rapes in the 1970s and 80s, and for the most part got away with them until 2018 when an elderly man named Joseph James DeAngelo was arrested for the crimes. He was an ex-cop and above suspicion.

It was likely assumed that the Golden State Killer would never be caught until a company called 23andMe, a DNA ancestry business, took a DNA sample of a relative of DeAngelo. With this DNA registered, police were able to link it to the DNA found at his crime scenes, and the Golden State Killer was brought to justice.

He's rotting in a jail cell until he dies now.

It's too bad it took decades to discover the truth. By now, the killer was a senior citizen.

Nora wasn't going to enjoy her golden years as much as Joseph James DeAngelo had. Once her DNA was confirmed and matched to the skin found under Beth's fingernails, she would have plenty of jail time left to serve ahead of her.

I was going to solve the murder of my friend. Beth's family was going to find peace in knowing what really happened to their daughter.

Beth drowning was not an accident.

I can't believe the nerve of Nora. She actually talked to Allison Graham today. How can the woman live with herself?

I smiled, imagining Sandy Tallie arresting Nora at her home.

Who would have thought Officer Tallie would be such an important part in my plan? After researching more about the Golden State Killer, I went to the police station and talked to her privately. I even brought a thank-you basket to sweeten her.

That part of my plan didn't work out well. When we were alone in her office, Sandy confirmed she couldn't accept my basket, and asked that I take it back home with me. I agreed, but sat down in front of her desk and was ready to talk to her more about what I really wanted.

She asked what she could do to help me today, and I got right to the point.

"Elizabeth Graham's murder. The case is still cold, right? No new developments?" I asked.

Sandy raised an eyebrow at me. "It's not considered cold. It wasn't considered a murder, but an accidental drowning, and her case is closed." She shuffled in her chair and examined me. I almost felt like I was suddenly in an interrogation room with her. "Why do you ask?"

I shrugged. "You remember Nora Cameron, I'm sure?" I didn't wait for her to answer me. I was certain she remembered who Nora was. "Well, now she goes by Nora Bowman."

"Okay," Sandy said with an eyebrow raised.

"She moved next door to me."

"I see." She moved some paperwork to the corner of her desk. "Well, what does that have to do with Beth? Can you just tell me what you're really here for?"

I put a hand to my chest. I had prepared this elaborate speech, and the tone with which I would present it. I would build up my case like a PowerPoint presentation as to why I felt the way I did, but Officer Tallie was making that hard.

"You think Nora murdered her best friend?" Sandy said, getting straight to the point. I sigh. She's taking all the fun out of my sleuthing. "Why?"

I leaned back in my chair. "Beth's body was found in that hidden part of the beach, a place only she and Beth visited."

"I was sure you went, too," Sandy said. "At least, that's what the reporting says. I'm well read on the case, as you may imagine. It's one that bothered me for a long time."

Me too.

"That's true. Just once— well, once with

Beth and Nora, and another time with Ryan. I took him there for some alone time. That was before everything happened, though. My point is, Beth had no reason to kill herself."

"And Nora had no reason to kill her."

I raised a hand. "That's true, as far as I know, but isn't it odd that it was Nora who found her?"

"It is, sure, but that's not enough to assume she killed Beth."

I sighed. This wasn't going how I imagined it would.

Sandy leaned forward in her chair. "One of the first things I did when I became a constable in town was read Beth's investigation. I know all the details. Just like you, it bothered me. I shouldn't say this to you, but it never sat right with me either, how they called it an accidental death, and even implied it was a suicide to her family."

"You saw my report to the police as well, didn't you?" I asked.

She nodded. "I did."

"You know what I said about Beth being scared of Nora."

"It's not enough to—"

"Okay, okay. Well, if I remember right, there was DNA evidence found under Beth's fingernails, right?"

"That's right, the fingers on her right hand, but again, Nora didn't have any marks on her face."

"Did the police examine Nora's body in full? What if Beth scraped Nora's skin somewhere else besides her face? Her abdomen? Legs? If Nora was drowning Beth, she could have scraped skin from anywhere."

Officer Tallie sighed. "No physical examination of Nora was completed. I don't know why. The reporting suggested that she was hysterical when police arrived. They must have empathized with her."

"That's my point," I said, feeling like I am making strides in my reasoning. "Nora was above suspicion that day, just like Joseph James DeAngelo was for decades. You've heard of the Golden State Killer?"

"Of course."

"Well, the whole reason he got caught was because a relative of his submitted their DNA to one of those ancestry sites, and voila! I remember the story when it broke years ago. Who would have guessed that something like that would lead to the arrest of a serial killer? Unimaginable! I had bought Ryan an ancestry test from 23andMe as a gift for our anniversary last year, too." From the look on Sandy's face, I could tell I was getting her attention. "Let's not allow Beth's murderer to live a full life. Let's not allow Nora to get away with what she's done for much longer. The DNA found under Beth's fingernails, what are the chances that it's still usable?"

"High," Sandy said confidently. "You want me to run the DNA database to see if there's any matches in the ancestry companies' registry?"

"Exactly!" I nearly jumped out of my seat now that we were on the same page.

"I've done that," she said coldly. "Two years ago. I requested our Major Crimes Unit run the DNA evidence. They spent a lot of money developing a DNA profile and ran it against the DNA databases, and... nothing."

"Okay," I said, feeling only slightly defeated. "But they didn't have Nora's DNA."

"Are you saying Nora took a DNA test for one of those ancestry sites?"

I breathed heavily. "Not yet, but she will."

Officer Tallie stood up from her desk. "Well, let's say Nora murdered Beth. You honestly think she's going to willingly give her DNA to you? If you heard about the arrest of the Golden State Killer stemming from ancestral DNA checks, there's a good chance Nora has as well. Why would she want to give a sample?"

That was something I didn't have an answer for at the time. "She will do the test, I guarantee it."

"What does that mean?" she asked, raising an eyebrow. "Kelly, you can't force someone to take a test."

"I didn't say that," I said, raising my hands

in the air as if to say, hey don't arrest me.

"Then how do you expect Nora to agree?"

I paused, and didn't answer her question. It was better for both of us that I didn't. Nora wouldn't be sending in her DNA for ancestry analysis. I would do that on her behalf. Only, it wouldn't be under her name. It would be mine. I'd set a profile for me, but complete a test using Nora's DNA.

"Let's just say DNA will be available in the database soon," I finally answered. "Now, what can we do to expedite what's needed on your end for this? Once the DNA is available, how long will it take?"

Sandy sighed. "I need to request funding, and that's not easy right now. I already have the DNA profile from before, though, so that makes things easier. I'll need to involve the Major Crimes Unit. There's also a cost for—"

I took out my cheque book from my purse aggressively. "How much?"

She covered her head in frustration. "Kelly, it's not-"

"Give me a number, please. Consider it a charitable donation." When she didn't answer, I felt my pulse quicken. "This is Beth we're talking about. You said it yourself; something doesn't feel right about her death being ruled an accident. If I'm wrong, you can use it against me for the rest of my life, but I need to see this through. *We* need to see this through for our friend."

Sandy let out a heavy breath. "We'll figure out a way to expedite this. The most expensive aspect of this is already done. A DNA profile was made from what we found under Beth's fingernails. The hard part is... whatever you're planning."

I sit up in my bed and laugh.

I thought swabbing Nora's mouth was going to be hard. I was determined to make it work. I had to.

Beth had meant so much to me in the short time I knew her. She had an impact that was hard to explain.

And she was murdered. Nora did it. It's time this town finds out how much of a monster Nora really is.

CHAPTER 28

Nora
Present

I'm not going crazy.

I'm certain Kelly was in my room last night.

When it's morning, I lie in bed thinking about what I remember.

I know she stayed in my home after I fell asleep. When I woke up and went to the front door, I saw Kelly's light on at her house and suddenly turn off. I know that she was at least awake. Unless she has a timer for her lights?

When I woke up Jameson at the kitchen table last night, he had a confused look on his face when I asked where Kelly was.

That was something else I tried not to think about. She drank with my husband.

What did the two of them talk about when they were alone? They were laughing several times throughout the night. I could easily hear them from the bedroom. What could have made

Jameson laugh that hard?

What else did they do?

They were drunk. She's beautiful. I strike the side of my head, trying to get the thoughts out of it. I hit a little too hard though and can feel actual pain. I cover the side of my face and feel a tear forming.

Jameson is acting like nothing out of the ordinary happened last night. I can hear him whistling some stupid tune from the kitchen as he makes breakfast.

My husband is usually a happy man. I'm more known for being the moody one. He's also a morning person, which I'm not.

After drinking so heavily, though, how can he be so happy this morning? We're not that young anymore. Drinking and waking up early don't tend to go well.

It's seven o'clock, I realize. What time was it when he came to the bedroom last night?

I slip out of bed and put on a robe. I open the bedroom door and can hear him whistling. It sounds like a familiar song, but with his terrible skills it's hard to know which. When I get to the kitchen, he stops and gives me a concerned look.

"You okay?" he asks. "You look rougher than I do."

"I'm just pregnant," I say pointedly. "Aren't you feeling at all hungover?"

He raises a finger. "Water! It's the trick

that's always helped me not feel like garbage the next day. Drink a lot of water before bed. Liquor dehydrates you, and if you don't get any liquids before you sleep, you feel worse the day after."

I nod and give a thin smile. "Thanks for the lesson." It's one he's told me before, but years ago. We don't drink that often. I was surprised last night when Jameson had several beers by himself. "How was it with Kelly, after I fell asleep?"

"Good," he says with a wide smile. Part of me wants to shake him and demand why drinking with Kelly would be so great.

"How long were you two drinking for?"

Jameson puts down the spatula and looks at me. "Are you upset? Why?"

"You never answered the question," I say.

He shrugs. "I don't really know. I wasn't looking at my watch or anything."

"What did you do for such a long time? What did you even talk about?"

He breathes in deep. "What are you really asking? What are you trying to say?"

"Nothing," I say innocently. "I want to know why, when I went to sleep because I felt sick because of our baby that's inside me, you drank with our hot neighbour until God knows when."

He turns off the stove. "Nothing even remotely happened, Nora. I can't believe you would even say something like that. When have I ever given you a reason to think that way?

When?"

"What were you two laughing so much about? I heard you two giggling like schoolgirls."

He laughs again. His reaction almost feels smug, like he's putting me down for feeling this way.

"We talked mostly about you," he says. "She told me some stories of what you were like, back in the day, or the pre-Jameson era, as I call it."

"What? What did she tell you?"

He tilts his head. "I'm having some memory problems, I guess. I don't exactly remember what she said to be honest, but I remember it was funny."

What's happening? Is Jameson covering up for what they did last night?

"I need to go to Toronto today," he says, turning the oven back on. "I'll be back a little late."

"Why?"

Is he really going to Toronto? Is he already making up lies to be somewhere else, with *someone* else?

What do you do if you suspect your husband is lying? There are people you can hire. Follow what they do. I feel my stomach roiling. I'm not sure if it's the baby or the gut-wrenching feeling that my husband isn't telling me the truth.

"My bank," he says, piling his eggs on his plate. "Are you sure you don't want some? I didn't think you would wake up so early. I can make you something, but I know with scrambled eggs, the texture bothers you right now."

I ignore his attempt to redirect me. "Why do you have to talk to your bank in person?"

"Do you really want me to explain it?" he asks. I hate it when he talks to me with that tone. He pretends I'm stupid. Just because I don't understand financing well, or how he does his job. "It's financing. I want to get a better interest rate. The banks are trying to hike the rate on my business loan. And—"

"Are we in trouble financially?"

He looks at me oddly for a moment. "No, not at all. I just want to fight to keep a better rate. Going in person makes that easier."

"Why didn't you tell me you were going to leave today? You just decided this morning?"

He sits at the table. At the same spot he sat last night with Kelly. Only now the bottle and glasses have been cleared away, as if it never happened.

Jameson nods. "Well, sort of. I only just found out about the rate hike the other day." He eats a large bite of scrambled eggs and takes a sip of coffee. When I don't say anything, he puts his fork down and gives me a look. "What? Why are you looking at me like that? Why are you like this?"

"Like what?"

"You're like a helicopter around me right

now."

"Okay," I say. "I'm just asking questions. You never told me about any of this."

He continues to eat.

How do I really know he's going to Toronto? How can I trust anything he says? I picture Kelly sitting at the table last night. I imagine their friendly drinks turn into something more romantic. It wouldn't take much. An awkward pause in the conversation. Their gazes meet. Jameson could easily fall for her, looking into blue eyes. He'd melt like butter.

"Why was Kelly in my room last night?" I ask him straight out.

He turns to me with a questionable stare. "She wasn't. What is your problem with this woman? I thought you two were friends. You had tea, or whatever, last night."

"That's right, and afterwards you two had much more fun, didn't you?"

Jameson stands up abruptly. "I'm going to grab something to eat on the road. I'm leaving. I'll be back tonight. When I come back, I want you to stop whatever stupid thoughts you have running in your mind right now." He breathes out, calming himself. "Maybe you should call Dr. Albee? Have you spoken to her? Is *this* all because of your friend, the one who... Is that why you're like this?"

"No!" I shout. He takes a step back.

"Okay. We haven't talked about that, though. The move's been so busy, and you haven't brought up Beth. Now, with how you're reacting, I worry."

"How am I acting? You're the one who's drinking all night with our bombshell of a blonde neighbour. I know how you *like* blondes! You told me when we first started dating that I was the only brunette you'd been with. I wasn't your usual type."

Jameson lowers his head. "Nora, we're married. Why are you like this? This... jealousy? Where does it come from? I love you, Nora. *You!*"

I don't say anything. I walk back down the hall and close the bedroom door behind me.

I'm not crazy. Kelly was in my room last night. Something is going on with her and Jameson. I can feel it.

I lay in bed again, staring at the ceiling. Eventually Jameson comes in and gathers a few things for the trip. I don't talk to him.

Something is happening. Kelly is up to something. What, though?

She wants my husband, that much is confirmed. She's playing him. Maybe he doesn't know it yet. Maybe he's telling the truth. It wouldn't take long for a woman like Kelly to turn my husband against me.

She did it to Beth, and now she's working on my husband.

What if he's really spending time with Kelly instead of going to Toronto? I quickly get out of bed and run down the hall, moving the blinds just enough to see Jameson drive down the road. He passes Kelly's home, thankfully.

What did I expect? Would my husband be stupid enough to stop at the neighbour's house to pick her up before leaving together? If something was happening, they would have a meet-up place. Kelly could already be there right now.

I look at her home, and for a change, her pink Porsche is nowhere in sight. Has she parked in the garage? She never does that, though, as far as I can tell.

I breathe in deeply. Kelly was in my room last night. I know it. It happened. What was she doing there when I was sleeping? Was she watching me?

I suddenly don't feel safe in my own home. I take out my cellphone from my robe pocket and notice a text from Jameson saying he'll see me tonight and we can talk more. Out of anger, I don't respond.

I should, but I'm so focused on Kelly instead. My mind is racing. All of my thoughts are bad. From Jameson and Kelly, and what they may be up to, to whatever Kelly was doing in my room last night.

Is it all in my head? What if it is?

I shrug off the feeling of insanity and search

for what I want. A security company near me with same day quote and installation. I click on the first result.

CHAPTER 29

Nora

I've called him several times, and he hasn't picked up his cell. Yes, he's probably still driving, but he has Bluetooth in his car. He could pick up safely and tell me where he is, or who he's with, for that matter.

I've been peeking out the windows, looking at Kelly's home. I haven't seen her out for a run. I haven't seen her watering her flowers. I haven't seen her, period.

Since moving into this house, I haven't been able to get away from her presence. She was always outside, haunting me if I wanted to leave. Today, of course, is different. She's nowhere in sight.

I should be more trusting of my husband, I know. I try to calm myself, like I've been attempting to do all day.

Jameson's right. He hasn't given me any reasons not to trust him in our marriage. Despite that, I feel like I'm breaking down.

Calming myself worked, multiple times today, until intrusive images of Kelly and Jameson making out at my kitchen table last night while I slept in the bedroom overwhelm me.

I curse myself.

I wish I knew what happened. I'm sure there's a logical reason why Kelly isn't home, and at the same time my husband is gone as well. People leave their houses!

I can't stand the dread inside me. I feel like I'm going crazy.

My cell phone buzzes in my pocket, and it's Jameson. I immediately pick it up. It's nearly one in the afternoon. He should be well on his way back from the bank meeting he had.

"Hey!" I say, a little overly enthusiastically.

"Hey, hun," he says with a laugh. "Everything okay? I saw that you called."

"I just wanted to call and say I'm sorry that you left the way you had before we could talk more. I hate not resolving things before you leave."

"I understand, me too. The bank meeting went well, though!" he says enthusiastically back.

"Hell yeah, it did," another voice calls out. Jameson shushes the mystery person.

"Who's that?" I ask.

"You remember Trevor?" he says. "Trevor Beaton? He used to work at TD with me. Since I was in town, I asked to meet up with him."

"When are you coming home?"

"After lunch, well, late lunch, I guess."

I take in a deep breath, trying to relieve my worries. It's working until I hear a woman laugh in the background.

"Who else is with you?" I ask, confused.

"I'll be heading back in thirty minutes or so," Jameson says, ignoring my question. "Listen, I need to go. I want to catch up a bit before we leave."

"We?" I ask, confused.

He sighs. "Everything's okay, Nora. I'll talk to you when I get home." He ends the call with more laughter in the background. I notice the woman laughs the hardest.

Jameson said he was catching up with Trevor, so who was the woman? He said "we" had to leave. Who was he referring to?

I continue to pace around my home, every so often running to the window when I hear a car passing by, hoping it's either Jameson or Kelly. Time moves by at a snail's pace. My anxiety only increases with each minute.

I call Jameson again after an hour, hoping to catch him in the car.

Why is he not picking up? Is someone else in the car with him?

It's nearly two in the afternoon now, and both still aren't home. I peek outside my side window and stare at Kelly's house.

She has a garage, one that could likely fit three cars, and yet she always parks her Porsche outside, at least for the past few days.

Maybe she's been home the whole time?

She hasn't come outside though, which isn't like her.

She could be sick. She could be having an off day. It could be one of those days where you eat junk food and watch Netflix all day. Somehow, I know Kelly isn't that type.

I wish I had binoculars or something to look into her home. I need to know if she's there or not. I think of the woman's laughter during the phone conversation with Jameson and cringe. It feels like they were laughing at me. It's silly I know.

He's just catching up with friends, or is he?

I open my front door, putting on my sandals. I walk quickly down the block towards her home, slowing as I get near her property.

I peer through her large windows, looking for a light on, or movement, or Kelly herself. Of course, I'm not that lucky.

I walk up to the front door, taking my time to try to come up with a story of why I'm there. I knock, still completely lost for what to say if she answers.

After several knocks, I realize she's not home. I don't even hear her small dog.

I'm not sure why, but I try to open her door. I click on the handle and push, but it doesn't budge.

Many people in this town don't lock their doors. It's not uncommon.

What troubles me is why I was trying to break into her home to begin with. What am I planning on doing once inside?

What further troubles me is the determination I still have to get into her home.

What do I think I'll find? A picture of Jameson and her on a date, kissing? Some evidence of something terrible happening? Something to validate why I feel so terrible inside?

I walk around the house, taking a moment to stare around the neighbourhood. The benefit of living on a street with so few neighbours is being able to sneak around with little suspicion.

When I get to the backyard, I spot the back patio door near her pool.

I feel my pulse quicken when I see the pristine blue water. Wasn't the pool under repair? What was the reason she gave Jameson for swimming at our home? She needed to fix the liner.

I stand above the water, take my sandal off, and dip my toe inside. The pool is immaculate. It's been skimmed of any bugs and looks crystal clear.

I imagine I could jump in right now and not notice anything wrong.

Why was she using my pool then? I feel lightheaded thinking of how Jameson watched her swim. He said he wasn't looking at her. Was he lying too? How long have the two of them been lying to me?

I can't believe I thought a woman like Kelly had changed. She's even worse than I remember.

She's up to something. What is it, though?

Is this all for her to steal my husband? Make him fall for her? Has it already worked? Did he bring her to Toronto, making up excuses for why he had to travel?

How many other things has Kelly been lying to me about?

I quickly make my way to her patio door, trying with all my might to open it and failing miserably.

I look at the many windows. There's a good chance one of them is unlocked. I could sneak inside.

The sounds of movement inside her home break my thoughts. From her back patio, I peer inside and can see the front door open. Kelly walks in with several shopping bags in her hands. Her dog runs up quickly to the back door, barking at me. I quickly get out of view and hide behind the brick wall.

Did she see me? She had dark sunglasses on. I think she looked in my direction, though, but I can't be certain.

What excuse will I give if she did see me?

Who cares? I have questions of my own.

Why is her pool suddenly working fine? Why was she in my pool the other day? Why was she up late drinking at my house with my husband? Why did she sneak into my room last night?

I turn back to the patio door and face her. I'm about to pound on the glass door and demand she answer my questions when I see her put the bags on the kitchen table. My mouth suddenly opens wide, and I have to cover my mouth to stop myself from screaming.

The shopping bags are from the Eaton Mall. The largest mall in Toronto.

My husband lied to me.

I know it now.

Kelly was with him.

I turn away from the patio door, walking slowly back towards my yard. I take my time going up the steps to my home, and as I do, I realize I haven't looked back at Kelly's. She could have spotted me, and yet none of that matters.

Part of me wants to go back to her home and pound on her door until I can confront her, but I don't have the energy.

My husband is cheating on me. Jameson lied.

Kelly's trying to destroy my life. It's just like with Beth. Kelly Van Patten has a way of finding out what you love and tries to take it away from you.

She's vindictive. Evil.

I walk inside my home and take out my cell phone. At first, I think of calling Jameson, but quickly change my mind. What would I even say to him?

I open the contact for Dr. Albee. I decide against that too. I cover my mouth, walking to the bathroom. I feel nauseous and lightheaded.

I dial the number for my mom. It rings, and she quickly picks up.

"Hey, dear," she says. "I was thinking of you. I wanted to see if you wanted to have lunch together tomorrow?"

"He's cheating on me," I answer.

"What?" she asks, concerned. "Jameson?" I begin crying uncontrollably. "Dear, what do you mean? What did he do?"

What did he do? It's a good question. I imagine Kelly and him, laughing together at some fancy restaurant in Toronto.

Laughing at me.

"He—" My cell phone drops, banging hard on the tiled floor. I worry it's broken and breathe a sigh of relief when I notice it's fine. Bent over, I look up and see a small, round, black item stuck between the edge of my bathroom counter and the cabinets beneath.

"Nora?" my mom's voice calls out to me. I don't answer, as I reach out and grab the black ball. I look at it carefully, wondering what it could be, until it hits me.

My mom frantically calls out again. "Nora! Answer me!"

CHAPTER 30

Kelly

An eventful day.

I left early this morning for Toronto. I could have paid to expedite the shipping of the DNA sample to the lab, but was too worried.

What if it didn't get there and was delivered to the wrong location? Or worse, what if it got completely lost in the mail? These things can happen. Packages can be mishandled or broken while in transit, and I couldn't chance it.

I risked a lot to get that sample, and needed to ensure it got to where it was needed, so I had to deliver it myself to the lab to make sure.

I'm not going to lie; I enjoyed my road trip to Toronto with Lady. I felt like I was bringing Nora Bowman to justice myself.

I imagine there will be a lot of backlash over what I've done, but if Beth Graham's killer is finally brought to justice, it will all be worth it. Her reported drowning has plagued her family. It tarnished the small town.

After the discovery of Beth's body, the police investigated me. I was questioned for hours. I agreed to answer all of their questions, even without a lawyer. I was eighteen, and knew I had done nothing wrong, so why shouldn't I?

I had never felt so grilled in my life. The officers would ask questions, and move, and ask the same questions and knit-pick any differences I made when answering. I almost felt like I had committed a crime by the time I was finished. Then I would get called back to the station just to be asked the same questions over again. It was nauseating.

I wondered why they were so obsessed with talking to me. Somehow, I knew Nora was involved in that, too.

I told the police my side of the story, and what I knew.

I wondered why Nora wasn't already handcuffed for murder. I spotted her coming into the police station as I left the interview room. She was a complete mess. Snot was literally running down into her mouth.

A great act, I knew. Nora didn't even acknowledge me as we passed each other. Police escorted her into the interview room, and I left the station.

Looking back, I wish I had never agreed to let the officers question me. They felt strongly that I was a suspect. What if I had told them something that could incriminate me in some inadvertent way?

I've seen documentaries like *Making a Murderer* on Netflix as an adult. I know that even without strong evidence confirming you killed someone, you can be tried and found guilty of murder.

It was for that reason that when the police wanted to question me about what happened with Ryan, I absolutely refused until I had a lawyer with me. I hated the optics of what people would think, but that was better than saying the wrong thing.

I had, after all, lied to the police about what happened to my husband.

After dropping off the sample to the lab and confirming the results would be completed within a week, I indulged myself.

A quick shopping adventure was required to celebrate everything I had done.

I rarely find myself in Toronto, so could you blame me for wanting to shop at nicer stores? Muskoka doesn't have some of the ones I love. I only allowed myself two hours of shopping time at the mall before leaving, which for me was a miracle.

Despite the short time I had, it was a solid shopping trip. I bought a few bras, a nice summer dress, and likely solved a murder. How many people can say that? I had to reward myself.

I drove back into town as quickly as I could. I had one last stop before this long day could end.

It was as if everything I'd done today was meant to be. I got everything sorted at the lab so quickly. I had a very successful shopping trip, and now the parking spot right in front of the police station is available.

Everything's going perfectly. I step inside the police station and request to speak with Constable Tallie. Continuing with the day's luck, she immediately comes. I ask to speak in private again, and she brings me to a back-office area.

She sits behind a desk and gestures for me to join her. I sit with a wide smile on my face, unable to hide my happiness.

"It's done," I say, 'barely able to contain myself. "The results will be available in a week. Now, are you able to confirm what you need to do on your end?"

She shakes her head. "How did you— Never mind. Maybe it's better that I don't know what exactly you did here. So, Nora's DNA will be in the database in a week's time?"

I nod.

"Well," she says, sitting up in her chair, "things are moving quickly. I spoke with the Major Crimes Unit, and we're willing to spend the money to retest the DNA database again. I explained to the department why I thought it was a good idea, and they agreed. Once the DNA is available, we should be able to use the pre-existing DNA profile we have and run it through the database and get results within a week ourselves."

I nearly laugh with excitement. Sandy smiles back.

"Now," she says, changing her demeanour, "we need to talk about what happens if this doesn't go the way you think it will. If Nora's test is negative, this stops."

"If I'm wrong, then I'm wrong," I say confidently. "If Nora had nothing to do with Beth, then I will let this go."

"That's right," Sandy says. "I'm not going to listen to you if you come in next week with a new suspect you want me to check out. That's not how this works."

"I understand," I say. And I do. If it's not Nora, then I'm likely wrong about many things. Perhaps the police were right all along. Beth could have drowned, as hard as that was to believe.

I thank Constable Tallie again for her time and tell her I'll be in touch once I confirm the results are back from the lab.

On the way back home, I think about what Sandy said.

If I'm wrong, all the things I've done were for nothing.

Beth was intoxicated when she was found dead. She was drunk, and I know who gave her the bottle that caused her to be that way.

It was me.

I gave her one of my mom's vodka bottles. She asked me for one. I didn't want to say no. I didn't know what harm it would cause.

If Nora didn't kill Beth, then does that mean I'm to blame for her death? If I refused to give her a bottle, would she still be alive?

When I arrive home, I grab my bags and go inside, the terrible thoughts ruminating inside me.

I notice movement on my backyard patio, and Lady barks. Walking towards it, I look around and see nothing outside.

I'm getting paranoid now. I look at the cold blue water of my pool. I think of jumping in, knowing I can't given the lies I told Nora.

I think of Beth. What would it have been like to find her body at the beach that day? A young woman dead.

Beth Graham was a good person.

I pray that when the results from Officer Tallie come back, it shows what I believe to be true. If it's not, I don't think I can face the reality of what happened.

The thought sits with me for some time. I change into my workout clothes. I can always think more clearly after a run.

Lady looks like she needs one. She's been following me around the home since I've returned with a concerned look. Maybe I'm just reading into things, though.

"Run, girl?" I ask enthusiastically, and she wags her tail in response.

When I step outside, a large square van drives past me and parks in front of Nora's home.

"Cottage Country Security", the side of the van reads.

I spot Nora coming out of her home to greet the security company representatives. I put in my AirPods and connected to my playlist and put Lady on her leash.

As I run past Nora's home, I watch her talking to the men from the corner of my eye.

Security in Muskoka is a rare concern for most. I don't know anyone in town with a security system. Most never even lock their doors. If it wasn't for what I did the night before, I wouldn't think twice about it.

I *did* do something, though. I snuck into Nora's room and collected her DNA while she slept. I thought I got out of her home without arousing suspicion. Was I wrong?

I pass Nora and the two security representatives without looking at her. I look back at them and, to my surprise, Nora is staring straight at me with a wide smile.

CHAPTER 31

Nora

The security company installs everything I requested that same day.

I was worried that I was overreacting this morning when I called them. I felt so strongly that something happened last night in my bedroom.

When I found out what was in my bathroom, I knew I was right.

A Series Six Tech Listening Device.

It took some time for me to figure out what kind it was. There was no text on it to tell me, of course. When I found an image on Amazon that matched, it only upset me more.

Wireless, with a range of up to two miles, it can store and transmit live audio for up to forty-eight hours.

I wasn't dumb enough not to know who put it in my home. Instantly, I thought of Kelly.

What is she up to? It's now the only thing I can think about. She has some sort of plan. I was nearly having a meltdown with my mom when I found the device. I was able to calm myself and tell her I was overreacting. She made me promise to call Dr. Albee. Of course, I haven't. There's been no time, too. The security company came soon after I got off the phone.

After installation, the salesperson and installer show me how to use the system. We have a doorbell cam, a backyard cam, and other cameras on the sides of my home and above the garage. If any of them detect movement, they'll instantly start recording, and will stop if there's no further movement for over ten minutes.

I've installed multiple motion-sensitive cameras inside our home, too, including the hallway leading to my bedroom. Several glass break devices are placed near windows. Any loud noises will instantly set off the alarm, and a member of the security team will call me directly. If I don't pick up, the police will be notified immediately.

If someone is inside my home, or trying to break in, I'll know.

It makes me feel better knowing my home is impenetrable now.

What was even better was seeing Kelly's face as she ran by me, speaking to the company. I hope she realized everything I'm doing is because of her.

I'm on to her now.

Whatever she has planned, she won't get away with it.

When the company leaves, I Google Kelly's name, hoping the web can give me an answer or some ideas on what's happening. Instead, articles about her husband load on the screen.

The first one speaks of his multiple businesses in town. Ryan McDermott became successful after I left Muskoka. He owned a local Pizza Hut, Taco Bell, and Mr. Sub. When I Google the businesses in town, it seems most are now out of business except Pizza Hut.

I click back and scroll down the page until a headline catches my attention. "Resident found dead inside home". I click on the page and read the article. I know Ryan killed himself and Kelly found him. It isn't new information. What is, though, is that the article implied it wasn't suicide. It suggests foul play was involved.

At the bottom of the article, it says if you have any information on this situation to call a number. This didn't sound anything like what Allison had told me. She said it was a suicide, but evidently there was more to the story.

Ryan died from a shotgun blast. The firearm was registered to him. There was no mention in the article if anything was stolen. If it was a robbery gone wrong, wouldn't the intruders try to take something before leaving? If it was a robbery, why would they kill him with his own shotgun?

It doesn't make any sense.

In the centre of the article is a picture of Ryan smiling in a business suit. He's heavier in the face than I remember from high school, but he's still attractive.

Somehow, I knew that whatever happened to Ryan, Kelly had some hand in it.

If police suspected foul play, and Ryan was killed with his own firearm, who could have killed him? The only logical answer was Kelly. She would have easy access to the weapon.

It makes me nervous knowing that Kelly may still have access to a gun, but so do I.

I smile.

Jameson and I have fought many times over the rifle he keeps in a gun safe. I've asked him to keep it at a rented locker away from our house, but he's always refused.

The man never hunts or goes to a gun range. When I ask why he owns a gun, he refuses to say, but I know why.

Living in Toronto his whole life, I knew what he wanted a gun for. In Canada, you can't use a gun to protect yourself or your property. It isn't allowed. That doesn't stop many from owning them or using them, at times questionably against others.

I know the code to open Jameson's locker.

Kelly may have a gun, but so do I.

I can feel my anxiety growing at the thought of having to use it. Kelly may still have listening devices in my home, or worse, cameras. She could be watching me right now. I haven't been able to find any more devices so far, but that doesn't mean there aren't more here somewhere.

A shooting pain in my abdomen makes me curl over a moment. Thankfully the sensation fades quickly. My thoughts of Kelly help me not think of it.

She's trying to torment me, I know. She wants me to break. A few times I think about calling the police, but I know that's something she wants me to do.

She wants me to break. She wants to ruin my life. She wants to take my husband. She wants the baby inside me. She wants my life, and maybe to take it.

I won't let her win, not again. This time I'll fight back.

I go back to the bathroom and pick up the device. What does she have planned for me?

CHAPTER 32

Kelly

When I get back home from my run, it's starting to get dark. The security van in front of Nora's has left. She must be quite worried about her security, since her home is now loaded with cameras. I spotted one on each side of her home and another on the front of her garage when running.

A bright light pops on, casting shadows from my partially opened blinds on the floor and wall. It was so bright it felt like an alien spacecraft was landing outside my home. I peer through and see a large floodlight on the side of Nora's home that faces mine.

I breathe in deep and start to worry.

She must have seen me.

If she had, wouldn't she have contacted the police? Wouldn't they be breaking down my door with a search warrant to see what other things I've done?

What's the punishment for planting

listening devices inside someone's home?

I take a shower, attempting to calm myself.

I just have to wait for two weeks, and then I will know if this was all for something or not.

One week for the lab to process the DNA sample. Another for Sandy to check it against the profile they have from the DNA found under Beth's fingernails.

I can wait two weeks, can't I?

I'll back off now. I can avoid Nora for two weeks if I need to. I'll hunker down inside my home. I have a gym membership. Instead of running outside, I can go on the treadmill, or find a nice trail somewhere nearby.

I get changed into more comfy clothes. Today feels like a nice cozy sweater while blasting the air conditioning kind of night.

I'll watch something on television. A comedy. Something light and fluffy. No true crime or thrillers. Even though I love anything suspenseful, my life feels intense enough.

I go into my office and turn on my desk light. Lady follows me into the room, going to her favourite corner and sitting. She must think I have another night of spying ahead of me, but that's far from the truth.

Time to go back to a normal, much more boring life. Fat-free popcorn and Netflix is what's in store for me tonight.

The binoculars are on my desk. I quickly put

them away in the closet. No more of that.

I'm retiring from espionage. No more sneaking around. Officer Tallie is right. I need to wait for the results and to see if I'm right. I also need to prepare for what to do if I'm wrong.

"I'm a bad person."

The voice startles me. At first, I feel like it's coming from my own head. My conscience is finally speaking out about the terrible things I've done to get to the truth about what happened to Beth. When I hear the voice again, I know I'm wrong.

"God, help me," the woman's voice says. I hear crying. I look down at my desk and it's the receiver for the listening device. The headphones are disconnected, and the machine is actively recording Nora.

It must be coming from her bathroom. The only device I failed to get from her home.

"What should I do?" Nora asks. "What do I need to do to get you to stop?"

I hold my breath for a moment. I look out at Nora's home. The lights are all off.

"I see you," Nora's voice says with an eerie tone.

I panic and turn off the office light. I turn back to the window, attempting to see where Nora is.

"I know you're listening," her voice says coldly. "I know you're watching me. I know what you've done with my husband."

Maybe she's talking on the phone? After her last comment, I breathe a sigh of relief. She must be talking to someone else. Who, though? How does it involve Jameson?

"Kelly," Nora's voice says in a whisper. "How many of these little devices do you have in my home?"

I start to panic again, looking out at her house. My heart is beating out of my chest. With the sun nearly set, I can barely see anything inside. There's an eerie sense as I look into her dark rooms. All the blinds are open for a change, but I don't see her.

Is she going to call the police? What is she planning?

Suddenly, I see movement in the main bedroom. Shadows moving in the dark catch my attention. I open my closet door and grab the binoculars, peering into the room.

I hold my breath again when I see her shadow in the room. She's sitting on her bed, staring at the window. Staring at me.

"You want to ruin me?" she says coldly. "You want my husband, my life. You want my baby? I finally have what you don't, and you want it."

I can see something long and narrow in her hand. I nearly scream out loud when I realize what it is.

Nora places the rifle on her lap, as she

continues to stare out through her window, towards my home.

"I hope you are listening right now," she says, nodding. "You're not going to take what's mine. I won't let you this time."

Another shadow enters the room behind her.

"Nora, what are you doing?" Jameson says to her.

CHAPTER 33

Nora

"Put my gun down," Jameson says in a soft voice. "Please."

I drop the listening device on the bed and sit up, the rifle still in my hand. Tears are streaming down my face.

"Where were you?" I ask, barely able to say the words between breaths.

"What are you doing?" he asks, confused. "Nora, you need to stop, please. Just put it down."

"You were with her, weren't you?" Before he can respond, I answer my own question for him so he can stop playing dumb. "Kelly. You were with her today."

"No," he says again, confused. "I told you: I went to Toronto for work. I wanted to hang out with my friend. That woman, she was Trevor's wife. We went out, the three of us." He stares at me blankly, and at the rifle. "Are you going to hurt me?" he asks plainly. "Are you going to hurt yourself?"

I take a moment to answer him, taking in the gravity of the situation. "I... don't know anymore."

He lowers his head. "Nora, please, on our baby, I'm not doing anything with another woman, certainly not with Kelly. You have to believe me. I didn't get home until late because of traffic. It was rush hour in Toronto; you remember what that's like. Now put it down, so we can talk. You're scaring me."

"I'm scaring myself," I say. I place the rifle on the bed carefully. "It's not loaded. I just wanted to scare her."

"Who?" he says, looking around the room.

"Kelly!" I raise my voice, not understanding why he's not getting this. She's the reason for all of my troubles. She's behind everything. She's been manipulating us.

"What are you talking about?"

"Her pool—it's perfectly fine," I say with a laugh. I feel a pain in my abdomen, and cover my stomach, wincing in pain. "Don't you see? She just wanted to use her pool as an excuse to get closer to you."

"Okay," Jameson says after a moment. "Even if that's the case, it doesn't matter."

"Doesn't matter!" I repeat. "She'll find a way to get to you! That's her game." I take the black device from the bed. "Do you see this?"

"What is it?" he asks, confused again.

"A listening device. I Googled it. She put this in our home!"

"I'm sure there's a reasonable explain—"

"It's Kelly!" I scream. "She wants to be in our life so she can ruin it. It's what she does!"

"What if it was there from... the previous owner?" he asks, trying to offer an alternative I already know is false.

I shake my head. "Who knows how many more she put in our home, or when?" I look at Jameson, confused as ever. He's been gone all day, and he comes back home offering me no kisses or hugs. All he does is stare at me like I'm the monster when it's Kelly!

"You don't believe me?" I say quietly. "You don't love me anymore, do you?"

"Nora," he says calmly, "let's talk to Dr. Albee together. I can get her on the phone. I mean... I come home, and you have my rifle in your hand. There's a floodlight on the side of our house, and cameras everywhere. You're... not well. We need to talk to Dr.—"

"I'm not talking to her," I shout.

"Your mother, Dorothy. I'll call her and ask her to come over."

"I don't need her right now. I just need you to believe me!" I look at my husband and his cold eyes stare blankly at me. I've seen this look before, when I was unwell. He thinks I'm making this up. "She killed her husband!"

"Kelly?" he asks.

I nod. "Of course. She killed him and got his life insurance money. That's how she can afford to do nothing all day. That's how she has all the time in the world to figure out how to ruin our marriage." Another stabbing pain in my abdomen hits me. I let out a moan and take a step back.

"Nora!" Jameson calls and holds me close. I calm my breathing, taking in a moment to smell his woody cologne. His touch comforts me. He wraps his arms around me firmly.

"You're going to be okay," he whispers. "Let's go to the hospital."

"For what!" I shout.

He pats my backs and puts his hand on the side of my face. He looks at me concerningly. "You need help," he says. "Think of our baby." He lets out a deep breath. "I shouldn't have left today. I shouldn't have. I'm sorry, Nora. I love you, but my god I'm sorry."

Another pain hits my abdomen, and suddenly I think of my baby, growing inside me. My upper thighs feel sticky. I place my hand between my legs and feel dampness. When I raise my fingers, I see the faint colour of blood.

Jameson's eyes widen. "I'm calling 911."

Soon after, paramedics arrive, as well as my old 'friend', Officer Sandra Tallie.

CHAPTER 34

Kelly

I can hear the knock on the door from all the way upstairs. I know who it is. I've been listening the whole time.

I can already feel the dread about what will happen next. It's also starting to hit me how much of a bad person I've become.

Another firm knock quickens my step and I open the front door.

Officer Tallie stares at me blankly. "There's no easy way to ask this, so I'm going to just say it, no matter how ridiculous this is... Did you plant listening devices in Nora's home?" I stare back at her in response. After another moment, she curses under her breath. "What the hell— what's wrong with you, Kelly?"

I lower my head. "I... don't know."

"Do you know how much trouble you're in?"

I quickly raise my head. "I never admitted to anything," I say defensively.

"Right," she says, crossing her arms. "I let you stroll into my office with your little basket and listened to you about your theory. I didn't think our talk would encourage you to take it this far, but I thought wrong. I should have kicked you out of my office right away when you started inferring you would get her DNA without her permission."

I panic. "Are you not going to look at the DNA now?"

She doesn't answer and uncrosses her arms. "What you're doing to these people is wrong."

An ambulance drives off down the street. Inside, I know, is Nora. I ask the question anyway, to make it look more innocent. "What happened?"

"Nora had to be taken. You know she's pregnant, right? Paramedics are worried about the baby. She's going straight to ER. The paramedics believe she's having issues because of stress... What else have you been doing to her?"

I don't answer again. You have the right to remain silent. I remember the words Ryan told me. He coached me on what to say to the police, and I won't go against his advice now that I need it more than ever.

"Fine," she says, "have it your way. It's not going to take much investigation to find out what happened here, Kelly." She looks at me sternly.

"There's that spy store on Main Street. What's the chance if I ask the clerk on duty, they'll say a pretty blonde girl bought a bunch of listening devices from their location recently?"

She has another point. Something I never thought about when I quickly schemed about how to expose Nora for what she's done.

I don't answer Officer Tallie. "I won't bother them," I agree. "I mean, I never have. But I will stay away from them now. Looks like Nora's going through a lot." Sandy looks at me coldly. "Is the baby okay?"

"You better hope so," she says. "You also better keep your word. If I find out you've done anything else to instigate anything with Nora or her husband, I'll arrest you myself. Do you understand?" When I don't say a word, she repeats herself louder.

"I understand," I say finally. I nod repeatedly. I was already planning on doing that before she knocked on my door tonight, but I wouldn't tell her. I never wanted anything to happen to her child. I just wanted to find out the truth. Now, all my plans were crumbling, and I've been the one exposed.

"You will review the DNA, though?" I ask again.

This time it's her who doesn't answer. "Stay the hell away from them, Kelly."

I let out a breath. "Why did you go along

with what I was planning? I told you what I was going to do, even if I didn't spell it out."

She gasps. "I never said you should spy on them! Or go into her room and swab her." She looks at me with a raised eyebrow. "That's what you did, didn't you? She told me she thought you went into her room the other night, and today you come to my office saying you got what you needed. What did you do?"

"She did it. She killed Beth! When the truth is out, you'll know I was in the right for what I did. That's why you didn't try and stop me when I came to your office. She killed our friend! Just because she's pregnant doesn't mean she should get away with it!"

Officer Tallie smiles at me. "Well, at least that's something you two have in common now. She thinks you killed someone, too. She went on raving about how you killed Ryan. Now both of you think each other are murderers." She shakes her head and laughs. "And you live next door to each other. I knew you two didn't get along back in school, but this is something else."

I take a few steps back. Part of me worries if Nora's ravings get the attention of the insurance company and the authorities? Will I have to go through another investigation myself?

Officer Tallie points a finger at me. "Remember what I said. Leave them alone, or else."

CHAPTER 35

Kelly

I lie in bed, having trouble sleeping again.

This time, it's not from excitement.

Nora is still at the hospital. I had heard from the device that she was bleeding. I wondered how badly. After the paramedics came, I had to stop listening. I was worried I would hear about the baby passing away.

I couldn't listen to that.

Nora was right about me. I'm a terrible person.

I've always known that I can be manipulative and callous. I never thought I would become what I am now.

Vindictive.

I made myself believe what I did was necessary to find out the truth about what happened to Beth. I made myself believe I was the good person in this situation.

How could I be so stupid?

Now Nora is at the hospital. God knows

what will happen to her baby. If it's harmed, I plan to tell the police everything that I did. I will be completely honest. I will take everything that I deserve.

It won't stop at what I did to Nora. I'll tell the police what happened with Ryan, too.

I pet Lady, who lies on the bed beside me. She's completely knocked out from our run and breathing heavily, asleep. I'm envious of her ability to rest.

I wish I had been honest about everything with the police from the start.

I turn onto my side in bed, trying to get the image of my husband out of my mind.

When I came home the day I found him months ago, there was something eerily quiet when I walked into the house. Ryan's truck was in the driveway, which in itself was a surprise.

He was usually out and about at that time of day, not coming home until six or later. He would be making the rounds, as he called it. He would travel to his numerous businesses, reviewing finances, or talking to managers. Usually he brought home something to eat, even though I tended not to eat any of the fast food he presented to me.

I cooked my own meals instead of eating what his restaurants made. He had easily gained thirty pounds since owning his first fast-food franchise.

I closed the front door and called out for him, but there was only that deafening silence.

I expected to hear the television on in the living room and to find Ryan sitting in his favourite recliner watching the sports channel.

"Ryan?" I called out again. I threw my keys on the side table near the entrance and saw a folded letter.

"READ THIS. DON'T CALL THE POLICE."

I picked up the note and examined it. I knew instantly it was Ryan's writing, but didn't understand. That's when I saw his arm dangling from the side of the leather recliner facing the television. The back of the chair faced me, and I had no idea what would be in store for me when I walked around to look.

I wish I hadn't.

I could still see my husband, what was left of him, in the chair. A gaping hole in his chest.

I quickly covered my face and went back to the side table, opening the letter.

"*I'm sorry*," was the first sentence he wrote. I breathed out and tried to calm myself. Even though my mind raced, I continued to read his last written words to me.

Don't go into the living room. Don't call the police either, not yet. Read this letter several times until you remember what you need to do.

I haven't been honest with you about many things.

I'm a bad person. A bad husband.

I've cheated on you. I think you suspected it, but never said anything to me. It's no one you know. Thankfully, I had enough common sense not to do that to you. There was more than one woman.

I'm sorry. I hope someday you can forgive me for the things I've done. If there's a God, I hope I can be forgiven.

I never deserved someone as beautiful as you. I hope you find someone worthy of your love.

I lied to you about our finances. We're broke. My businesses are crumbling, and I'm in the process of filing for bankruptcy. I couldn't tell you. I didn't want to break the only thing I did right for you, which was to provide our lifestyle.

The truth is, you deserve better. So much better.

I've told you so many lies that it's hard to keep track of.

I told you that I went to the doctor and they said my sperm was perfectly fine. That's not true as well. I was never going to be able to give you a child, and you deserve one.

I'm so sorry. Know that as I write this, I finally figured out how terrible a person I truly am.

I failed you as a husband. I failed to give you a baby. I failed to provide for you, but maybe there's one last act I can do that's not selfish.

The way I did it, it will look like a suicide, and if that's what the police report, then you won't be able to get a penny from my life insurance. So do not tell the police I killed myself. Do not tell the police anything. Call my lawyer instead. Have him help you. There will be an investigation not only by the police but the insurance company, too.

I positioned myself and the gun in a way to make what happened look like an accident. An accidental firing from a weapon that wasn't properly taken care of. That's what will come out of the official investigation if you play your role correctly.

With the help of my lawyer, that's what will happen. You won't ever have to worry about money again.

It's more than enough to start a new life. A life you deserve, with a person who deserves it more than me.

I hope you're not too angry with me. I did this for you. To give you everything you deserve, that I selfishly took away.

No matter what happens, and what gets discovered during the investigation, always remember that the best part of me loved you.

Burn this note before the police come."

I stare at the ceiling in my room as I lie in bed. The bed I once shared with my husband. Now it's only Lady.

Sure, I got the insurance money after a long battle.

Apparently, committing suicide to leave money to beneficiaries is a thing that happens often. I wish Ryan had told me what he had planned. He didn't understand that I'd rather have him.

Our marriage was not at all perfect.

I had in fact no clue that he cheated on me either, until the day I found him and his letter.

I could have forgiven him. I like to think I would have, knowing what the alternative would have been.

Despite him not being able to have a child with me, we could have looked at other options. Or who knows, we could have gotten lucky and conceived, anyway.

His restaurants may have been failing, but even if bankruptcy was the final option, we could have survived elsewhere. He had a great business mind. A company could have used his skills. He could have found work as an executive or some upper management position.

He didn't have to do what he did. Leave me for good.

Nora called me a terrible person today. I shake my head, thinking about what Ryan must have thought on his last day.

For what it's worth, I feel like the worst person on earth. I pray Nora's baby is okay. No matter what the truth behind Beth's death is, it's not the baby's fault.

The things I did to Nora were unforgivable.

I cringe now when I think of the lie I told

about the Miller family losing a child in the home they now live in. That wasn't necessary. None of what I did was necessary.

Ryan and I deserved each other. He was a self-proclaimed bad person, and now I realize I'm no better.

As I stare at the ceiling, I wonder, was I always this way?

I reach for the gold pendant necklace on the nightstand and open it. I gaze for a while at the picture of Nora and Beth. I hope I did the right thing. I pray I'm not wrong.

CHAPTER 36

Nora

I've been at the hospital for nearly an entire week. When I first arrived in the emergency room, they checked on the baby.

Thankfully, there were no issues. She was healthy as could be. Despite the blood, the doctors told me not to worry about baby.

I, however, was not okay.

After being medically discharged, I was sent to the psych unit for the harmful behaviour I exhibited when paramedics arrived. Jameson didn't hold back. He told them all of his concerns.

He was right to be worried. I wasn't in a good place.

I felt silly as the psychiatrist at the hospital reviewed my history. This was not my first time being admitted to a ward for self-harm. When I first moved to Toronto, I made some bad choices. I had too many pills.

My roommate in university found me and called an ambulance, and I was okay after a brief hospitalization. Afterwards, I took therapy more seriously. It took me some time to find the right psychologist. Then I met Jameson and things got even better for me.

After finding the right medication, my mood stabilized. When my depression subsided, I finally felt more like myself again.

The psychiatrist at the Muskoka hospital was kind but stern with me. He asked why I stopped my medication when I knew I could continue with them. He asked why I didn't reach out for help when I knew I needed it.

After listening to the terrible excuses I came up with, he gently told me how some patients who get to a point of stability forget about what it took to get them there. They do things like not take their medications, or not follow the safety plans that helped bring them to stability.

I agreed to start taking my medications again and had began on them after my third day at the ward. We agreed to a safety plan if I felt unwell again. First, I would speak to Jameson. If he was not available, or if it was him I was having issues with, I would speak with Mom or Dr. Albee.

Since being admitted, Jameson has visited me every chance he can. He removed the rifle from the house permanently. At least something good came out of this. Looks like I got my way in the end.

The psychiatrist and I even made a plan for Kelly McDermott.

I was going to avoid her like the plague after discharge. Jameson would speak with her if she tried anything else.

I sit in the visitors' room, waiting for Jameson to arrive. I'm still not sure when I will be able to leave, but I've been told it could be soon.

The hospital staff worried about my fixation on my neighbour. I explained everything to them, and they were more sympathetic given what I shared with them about my past history with Kelly. They knew about Beth.

The psychiatrist understood why I was so distraught. Finding the body of your best friend could change you. It certainly had for me. I wasn't the same after what happened.

The doctors listened to my ravings about Kelly killing her husband, her spying on me, and the games she played.

They helped me see that since I was wrong about Jameson and Kelly, that I could be wrong about other things as well.

I tried this exercise a lot, but it still didn't change the fact that I'd found the listening device, and the lie about the pool. I still feel strongly that something is happening. Kelly is playing a game with me.

Usually thinking this way would work me up, but not today.

The reason I feel at peace with it is I don't have to join her games. She can play on her own. Jameson is looking into a restraining order and talking to a lawyer. He says he'll be talking to Officer Tallie once things are better.

Jameson walks into the room, a large visitor's sticker on his t-shirt. He smiles at me when he spots me on the couch. He immediately sits beside me and grabs my hand.

"You're going to be leaving tomorrow," he says.

I smile back, not understanding. "I was told I didn't have a date."

"I just spoke with Dr. Lee, your psychiatrist, in the hall just now. He tells me you're doing so well. Much better than before."

I lower my head and hug him. "I can't wait to be home with you."

"I can't wait either," he says. "About that other stuff, with... you know who. I spoke with the police. You're right about that Officer Tallie. I feel like she's not listening. You said Kelly and her were friends in high school?"

I think about the wicker basket that Kelly carried when I spotted her leaving the police station. "I think they're close."

He nods. "I worry about that too. I may file an official complaint." He looks at me with concern. "Don't worry. You don't worry about any of this. I'll take care of everything. You just rest."

He puts a hand on my belly and smiles again. "You need extra rest for the both of you... I spoke with your mom today, too. She's going to be even more excited when I tell her when you're leaving."

"Did she do the squealing thing that she does?"

Jameson puts up his hands and attempts to make the sound my mom is famous for. "Eeeeeeee! Does that sound about right?"

"It does," I say with a laugh. "Did my dad say anything?"

"He did," Jameson says with a frown. "I hope you're not upset."

"What? What did my dad say?"

"He wanted to visit you the first night you got here."

My face stiffens. "He did?"

"I was worried, given how you were, that it wasn't a good time for you two to meet that way. He's... actually with me today. He's outside in the car. He wants to see you, if that's okay."

I can feel tears welling in my eye. "I understand why you didn't tell me." We've had a rocky relationship ever since I could talk back to him. "I'd like for him to see me now, though."

Jameson explains he'll be back soon. I sit in the room and wait for my father to arrive. I hate the idea of him seeing me this way. I felt broken.

Now my dad wants to see me? He can be such a cold-hearted man. I can almost picture him looking at me with disgust. Looking at the psych ward in disgust. He wasn't the type to feel emotions. People who thought about hurting themselves were weak.

I've been in town for how long now? He could have visited anytime.

I'm worried that when he walks through the door, I'll shout at him, "This is your fault!" or something equally hurtful. I can feel the rage boiling inside of me.

When the door finally opens and my father walks through, my anger leaves my body immediately. His stern face has softened. Tears of his own are in his eyes and down his cheeks.

He raises his arms as he approaches. He's so much older than I remembered. I quickly get up and walk to him. He closes his arms around me gently at first, squeezing once he has a grip.

Both our tears are falling freely now.

"My little girl," he says softly. "It's going to be okay, my sweet girl."

CHAPTER 37

Kelly

I kept my promise not only to Sandy Tallie but to myself as well. I didn't bother Nora or Jameson Bowman any further.

It was easy to do when Nora was at the hospital.

I assume she spent some time at the psych ward after what happened the night she left.

A few days ago, though, she returned home. This is going to be a challenge, I thought. How do you avoid your next-door neighbour? I keep to myself entirely. I barely leave my home. I keep my car in my garage for a change; that way if I need to go out, I can do so without seeing her.

I'm sure that's the last thing either of us wants.

I worry about what will happen next, though.

Any time now, Sandy will be contacting me with the results. Once I had confirmation that the DNA ancestry record was ready, I contacted

Officer Tallie, who agreed to continue with comparing it to the DNA evidence.

I was worried that after our last exchange she would ignore me completely. She must still have her own strong opinions about Nora being involved.

It's been six days since the ancestry test was completed. A call can come any minute. I know Sandy will be confused when the results show the name.

The profile I created was for me, not Nora. This is going to be another terrible conversation I'll have to have with Officer Tallie.

If the test is positive, though, it will certainly make things much easier. I can say whatever I need to. So what, I swabbed someone's throat without their permission to get DNA evidence—they killed someone! I'm sure it will be easy enough to not get into too much trouble for it. After all, because of my actions, the murder of a teenage girl will be solved. Sure, I'll have some explaining to do when it shows my name as a match, but once I give my own DNA test, I'll be free and cleared of any wrongdoing.

There is, of course, the question of what Nora and her husband will do in the meantime. So far, I haven't been arrested or questioned about the listening devices. Officer Tallie did say that Jameson visited her at her office and was quite upset. Threats of lawyers were made.

I try not to think about what that could mean for me. I need to stay positive. I also need to be careful and cautious of my actions now.

A few days after Nora went to the hospital, I got rid of the "evidence". I destroyed the audio receivers and tossed them in a commercial garbage bin near my home. I got rid of any notes I took when researching what to do about Nora.

I even deleted my history on my computer.

Okay, so I was a little paranoid.

I'm supposed to be the one having someone else arrested, and I was worried I'll be the one in handcuffs soon.

Since Nora returned home, I've seen a lot more activity next door. No, I'm not spying anymore. It's hard not to notice.

I've never seen Nora leave the house. I assume Jameson is taking care of everything for her. Nora's mother visits frequently, sometimes twice a day. Today I saw an elderly man visiting who I didn't recognize. An older man with a stoic face. He looked like the epitome of a geezer who'd yell at children to get off his lawn.

I wonder if it was her father, but he appeared much older than her mom.

Sitting at my dining room table, I get a call. I picked up when I see it's from Shannon Manning, my real estate friend who sold the house to Nora.

"So," she says, after exchanging a few

pleasantries, "have you thought about what you want to do?"

I nod, even though she wasn't in the room. "Yes, I've been thinking about it a lot since you gave me the appraisal. Let's put my house on the market."

I look at my living room, where Ryan's favourite recliner used to be. Where I found my husband.

It's time to leave. After what happened in this house, and what's been happening with Nora, I need to leave Muskoka forever. Whether she's guilty of Beth's murder or not, I can't stay in this house, or town, any longer.

I fidget in my chair. "When can we put the sale sign up?"

She tells me we can do it soon, given the incredible condition it's currently in. I end the call with Shannon and lower my head.

The anticipation of the results coming soon is getting to me. I've been so focused on visualizing what it will be like when I find out Nora was behind Beth's death, I've barely spent time thinking what the opposite would be like.

It's either she drowned by accident, or Nora did it.

CHAPTER 38

Kelly
Before
The day Beth went missing.

All I want to do for the rest of my life is kiss Ryan McDermott's lips.

At the end of the school day, Ryan has me up against his locker, and he's all over me.

This must be what heaven feels like.

I know he feels just as excited from how close he holds me. I've never kissed a boy who could read me as well as Ryan.

For a moment, I completely forget where I was at school, in the hallway in front of others-everyone.

I would have kept letting Ryan have his way with me, but then I hear Beth shouting from down the hall. Between kisses, I open an eye and see her walk past me, scowling at us.

"What's up with her?" Ryan asks, taking a moment to breathe.

I know about Beth's crush. She told me

about it soon after Ryan and I started hooking up. She said she was okay with us being together. When I heard Ryan wanted to ask me out officially, I immediately went to Beth and asked how she felt about it.

I could tell she wasn't in love with the idea of her friend dating the boy she's had a crush on since forever, but she agreed.

I thought we were okay.

Is it about prom? She's been telling me about her mom's obsession with her daughter going. Beth doesn't want to go, almost on principle, to get back at her mom.

She said none of the boys wanted her at school. That was a dirty lie.

I know I'm pretty. Sometimes I take that knowledge a little too far. On the other end of the spectrum are girls like Beth. Gorgeous as hell, but can't see it when they look in the mirror.

I demanded that she admit she was pretty. One night at my house, I forced her to say it in front of a mirror in my room. At the time, we both thought it was funny and awkward, but laughed as we continued to chant "I'm pretty", getting louder and louder until my dad knocked on the door to ask what we were doing.

I told her that even Ryan thought she was good looking. Now that was a little white lie. Ryan never really talked about her. I thought if she knew a boy like Ryan saw her as beautiful, she would feel that way more about herself.

She must be having a bad day today.

Even as she storms down the hallway, all I can see is how beautiful she is, and I'm upset she can't see it.

I kiss Ryan. "I don't know what's wrong, but I should talk to her."

Ryan shakes his head. "Not right now. You're all mine. You're not going anywhere."

I smile and begin kissing him again, and his touch intensifies. I notice Nora standing in the hallway watching us, and suddenly feel uneasy. She has her arms folded as if giving a disapproving mom look at our display of affection.

I take Ryan's hand and guide him down the hall. "Let's go somewhere more private," I say playfully, and he readily agrees.

"I know exactly where to go." He brings me to a smaller, windowless room beside the gymnasium. I open it and see blue matts scattered all over the room. The smell of feet instantly hits me.

"We had wrestling practice today," Ryan says. He shuts the door behind him and locks it. "We can't get any more private than here. Plus," he says, bringing me closer, and lowering me to the nearest mat, "I think I can take you."

I laugh and let him kiss me more, his hands getting more touchy. Things are escalating as he brushes against my breasts and I start to tense up.

I think of a way to redirect him. I know I wanted more privacy, but I just wanted to keep doing what we were doing in the hallway. "I should really talk to Beth."

"In a while," Ryan demands. "We're not done yet."

Ryan and I have only been together a few weeks. Although we kiss a lot, we haven't done much else, to Ryan's displeasure.

I've made up many reasons why I have to leave or stop him when things are getting too far. I'm scared to tell him the truth.

I'm not ready. I certainly don't want this room to be where I have my first time. Isn't it supposed to be more romantic? I've been worried about how Ryan will react if I tell him I'm a virgin.

Why can't we just keep kissing? Why does he want to go much further so aggressively? As he kisses the side of my neck, I realize he's trying to hit a home run—in this stinky-ass room.

I turn my head, first because of the pleasure of his kiss, followed by the smell of teenagers' feet on this mat. Does anyone who uses this room wash their feet? Have these mats ever been sanitized?

I put a hand on Ryan's chest, pushing him gently back. "Beth's been having a hard time lately. I need to check on her."

Ryan scoffs. "You act like you're best

friends. What does that goody-two-shoes have to be so upset about?"

I sigh. "Us. She's... had this thing for you since forever. I think her seeing us in the hall upset her."

"She had a thing for me?" he asks playfully. "I had no clue."

I roll my eyes. Most girls at school had a thing for him.

"Off," I say, playfully. "I'm on friend duty right now. Besides, this is the worst place to have sex."

Ryan gets off me, sitting up, visibly frustrated. "You're such a tease, you know that?" he says in a harsh tone. "Any time I try to, you know, you push back, or leave. What's your problem?"

"Nothing. I just want to—"

"Go find your upset friend? Or do you need to get home early? Or the excuse I loved the night at that beach area you took me to: 'I have homework'? You don't want me?"

I let out a sigh. "Of course I do."

"I bet I could have gotten more action from that Beth girl. Goody-two-shoes is probably a freak in the sheets, but instead I'm stuck with you."

I let out a gasp. "What did you say? Get off me!" I shove him and stand up quickly.

"Are you a virgin?" he asks. He laughs when

I don't answer him immediately. "Oh, man. You're really something. You pretend to be this perfect girl. You pretend you want to bang, like you've done it many times before, but it's all lies. We're done. Through!"

I watch as Ryan storms out the door, leaving me in the stinky room alone.

CHAPTER 39

Nora
Present

Mom and Dad visit me at home nearly all day. It's Dad's first time at our house, and Jameson enjoys showing it off.

Dad doesn't show much expression during the visit, but he smiles faintly when we show him the future nursery.

"This is going to be the room, Grandpa," I say with a smile.

He nods with satisfaction. He looks at Jameson and pats him on the back. "You've done well, providing for my daughter. You two will make great parents to my future grandchild. Now, which room will be mine and your Mom's for when we want to stay over and help out with the baby?" He smiles at me, this time authentically happy.

It's weird, but I can't remember a time my father has ever looked so genuinely enthused. For a moment I wonder if he's putting on a show for me, to make me feel better: my unstable daughter has just come back home from the psych ward after a freak out; I best be careful around her.

I shake the thought when my dad kisses my cheek. "When do you find out if it's a boy or girl?"

I smile. "Next month."

His face sours. "You're not going to do one of those parties, will you? What are they called? Gender parties? You know, that's how a huge fire started in Alberta a few years ago. A couple had one of those dumb parties and caught the entire woods around them on fire with their stupid blue or pink fireworks."

Thankfully, we aren't planning on having one, and I reassure my dad. With that remark, I'm finally free of worry he might be being delicate around me.

We walk out to our driveway, waving at my parents as they get into their old car.

"You have a beautiful home," my father calls.

"Eeeeee!" my mom cries out with joy, which I translate to, 'I'm so happy Dad came.'

I'm happy he came, too.

Jameson walks back inside, but I watch them as they drive down the road and can't help but stare into Kelly's yard. I haven't seen her since returning home from the hospital. I'd worried about what it would be like when I was forced to see her again. I expected to see her run by in her skimpy clothing every day.

My hard work at trying to avoid my neighbour has paid off.

Inside her yard is Shannon Manning, the real estate woman who sold us our home. She's using a rubber mallet to knock a pole into the ground. The bright white sign that stands in Kelly's yard puts a smile on my face.

"For Sale."

I never thought I would be so happy.

Kelly's yard is so large that Shannon's put up multiple signs. She's close enough for me to yell at.

When she looks up, she smiles at me and waves. "Hey, Nora!" she cries out. She walks up to the white picket fence on the edge of Kelly's property. I walk up to greet her, my smile wider than humanly possible. "How are you two settling in?" she asks.

"Great," I say curtly. "Is Kelly putting her house up for sale?"

It's a stupid question. Houses that are for sale typically have a sign like the multiple ones in Kelly's yard. I need to hear Shannon say it, though.

"She is!" she says with a laugh. "I know, too bad for you. You guys were friends back in high school. I'm sure you were starting to get close again."

"Something like that," I say with a thin smile. "When does it officially go on the market?"

"Tomorrow," she answers. I can barely control my excitement.

"That's so fast."

"Well, it's just her in this big house with her cute little dog, plus..." She looks back at the house and at me. "After what happened to—"

"Her husband, right," I say.

"When I explained to her that it won't hurt the sale price, that was all the reassurance she needed to put up the home officially. The house is already in good repair. It's move-in ready. Kelly keeps it looking like a show home inside. I don't even need to prepare it for sale at all."

I nod, but what she said about the resale value of the home after her husband's death sticks with me. "I know that Jameson paid full price for our home, even after what happened with the Millers."

"What do you mean?" she says, confused.

"The Millers, who used to live in my house," I say.

"Right, but what do you mean 'what happened to them'?"

"They lost a child. That's why they moved so quickly."

She laughs. "Where did you hear that? That old couple? They haven't had kids in their home since... well, I can't even imagine when.

I know they have adult children. Maybe one of them lost a child, or maybe when the Millers were younger, at the turn of the century, something terrible happened."

I feel a chill run down my spine. Another lie.

I wonder if there's anything genuine about Kelly. I end the conversation with Shannon quickly and walk back to my house, trying to control my anger.

Why would Kelly make up such a terrible story?

The answer seemed obvious. She wanted me to think about dead babies. She wanted me to ruminate on it. She wanted me to have that image in my mind.

Jameson and I changed the nursery because of what she said since I was so paranoid.

I feel rage boil inside me like a teapot left on the stove for too long. I could shout loudly.

As I walk closer to my home, I see Jameson, standing by the window, a smile on his face, only he's not looking at me.

That's when I see her, running by innocently as if she hasn't done anything to ruin my life over the past few days. Jameson continues to watch her as she jogs.

Kelly McDermott and her little dog slow down as she nears me, nearly stopping completely. She looks at the front window. I turn my head and I see Jameson still staring at her. More like gawking at her.

She's wearing her bright pink sports bra and tight shorts. Nothing is left to the imagination about how beautiful she would look if those articles of clothing were to suddenly be removed.

I stare at my husband in rage. I look back at Kelly, who starts to jog faster, past my home. I watch her as she runs all the way up her steps and closes the door quickly behind her.

I open my own front door and stare at my husband. He turns to me and smiles. "That was a nice visit," he says innocently. "Glad your dad came finally."

I shake my head. "She lied to me again."

"What?"

"The Millers never had a child who died of SIDS."

Jameson looks at me, confused. "How did you find that out?"

"I just spoke with the real estate agent. Kelly's home is up for sale. She told me just now when I asked her about it." He looks confused. "You didn't see the real estate lady there, did you? You were too busy checking out Kelly as she ran by, practically naked."

His smile fades, quickly.

I try to tell myself to think about the reasons why my suspicions of infidelity are wrong, but I struggle to calm myself. Jameson just stares at me, not knowing how to respond.

"You can't even deny it now, can you?" I yell. "Kelly's been lying to me, and so have you!" I run into the kitchen and grab the keys. I storm out the front door and Jameson quickly follows me.

"Where are you going?" he cries.

"Away from you!"

CHAPTER 40

Kelly
Present

When I get home from my run, I let out an extra heavy breath.

I hadn't seen Nora in days, and then I ran past her. Part of me was waiting for her to freak out. Scream at me. Yell or make a scene.

She did nothing.

That made it worse. Her stare pierced through me like a knife. She didn't even have to say anything at all for me to feel what she wanted to tell me.

Shannon Manning waved at me as I ran into my home. I ignored her completely as I escaped inside.

I thought that when Nora saw that sale sign in my yard, she would feel happy. Overcome with joy. Since making the decision to move I know I've been feeling much better.

It's only when I took a step back from what I was doing with Nora that I realized how *obsessed*

I was. I let my feelings of guilt and shame around Beth's death overcome my reason.

I know I can be ferocious when I want something, but I also know I've gone too far. I crossed the line of reasonable actions a long time ago.

The image of Nora staring at me as I ran past her comes back to me. Worse was the look she gave her husband.

I've noticed his glances, which can sometimes turn into longer observations.

It's not uncommon for me to attract attention.

Did he have to do it in front of his wife?

Some men are pigs, truly disgusting. I think of Ryan. He wasn't much better. The multiple acts of infidelity he committed and never told me about.

I grab a towel from my linen closet and turn on the shower. Before I can get inside, a loud knock at my door interrupts me.

Nora. It has to be her.

Part of me is nervous, scared even. All the things I've done to her have been exposed. She knows. I think about calling the police for my own protection. I suddenly wish I had my own security alarm system. I would arm it immediately and stay inside.

The knock gets louder.

I grab my phone, dial 911, but don't call the

number. If I have to, I can quickly close the door if things go wrong, then call the police.

Nora has a right to be angry with me, to confront me. I never thought she was the type to do that. Had our situations been reversed, I would be pummelling down her door, demanding she answer. I wouldn't let up until the police put me in handcuffs.

I put the towel around my neck and open the door, ready to hear Nora give me my just desserts.

I'm shocked when it's Jameson. He's in a tight fitted workout shirt, revealing his bulging muscles beneath. He looks at me with the usual intrigue I've come to expect from him.

Struck by the situation, or that it isn't Nora, I drop my phone accidentally. Worried that it dialled 911, I bend down to grab it. Jameson does the same, and our hands touch. He grabs my phone and when we both stand up, our bodies are closer. He hands it to me.

Is this really happening? Is he doing what I think?

Suddenly, the look on his face sours into a scowl.

"What kind of person are you?" he asks, his demeanour now totally changed. When I don't answer, he asks me again.

"I'm sorry?" I ask, confused, even though I shouldn't be.

"You lied about the Miller family having a baby with SIDS. You told Nora and me that's why they moved out of our house. That's a lie. I just confirmed it with the real estate lady."

I peek outside and see Shannon staring at me with a look of concern. I wave at her to let her know I'm okay.

I'm speechless.

"A dead baby is, what, funny to you? You think that's a funny thing to lie about, to my pregnant wife?"

"I..." I lower my head, unsure of how to defend myself against what's indefensible.

"You put listening devices in my home?" he says, raising his voice. "Who the hell does that? What kind of a *freak* are you?"

"I think that Nora—"

"Don't you dare say my wife's name," he says. "You pretended to be her friend. I don't know what your game is here, but it ends now. I spoke with that tiny store downtown, Sam's Spy Store. I know you bought the devices. I'm having my home searched for anything else you may have put there. What the hell were you trying to do? It makes no sense at all!" He raises his hand. "My wife, she's pregnant. You understand that, don't you? There's a baby growing inside her, and you put my wife in the hospital! God help you if something were to happen to my child." He points a finger at me and lets out a breath. "That's not a threat. That is a *legal* threat, though. I've contacted my lawyer. I've filed a complaint with the police so that we can get a restraining order against you. You're done messing with my wife! Do you hear me?" He waits for me to respond.

"I... hear you. I won't bother you two. I'm sor —"

"You will be sorry. It's a good thing you're leaving this house. I'm sick of seeing you around mine. Every day I see you it makes me sick to my stomach, what you've done. You run around this neighbourhood and everyone probably sees how pretty you are. Nobody knows how ugly you really are underneath it all. I do."

I let out a breath. "I can explain what happened. Why I did everything."

"Not interested! Sell your home. Move far away. Leave my family alone!" Jameson starts walking back down the path towards his house. After a few steps, he turns back, his eyes still full of rage. "Nora was right about you. You really are a bit—" He stops himself before finishing, even though I know where it was going.

I deserved the end of that sentence.

CHAPTER 41

Kelly
Before
The day Beth went missing.

Ryan won't return my calls. I've called him three times now, and he never picked up or called back. When I realize it's nearly nine at night, I come to understand he won't be calling me.

Where is he?

I visualize him kissing another girl in front of me, a girl who's willing to go all the way with him. I hate myself.

I should have just let him do what he wanted. Sure, it's not how I envisioned my first time, but from what I hear, nobody's first time is that great. I may as well do it with a boy I at least really like.

If Ryan calls me back, I'll tell him that. I'll tell him I'll do whatever he wants. Just don't leave me.

Even worse, I couldn't find Beth after. I knocked on her door and her mom said she had just left. I assumed she was with Nora somewhere. The two were probably talking about how terrible I am.

I lie on the bed in my room, thinking about how nobody likes me.

I came to this new town and soon after, the hottest boy at school was dating me, and I had already made a good friend with Beth, and now I've lost them both.

It sounds petty, but I thought with Ryan being who he was, and us going to prom, that we could even be Prom King and Queen.

I know that doesn't matter. It's just a stupid title. It doesn't make me royalty in real life. It does make me *feel* important.

I hear the shouts of my parents from outside my bedroom, and cover my face with a pillow. I want to scream into it to stop hearing them bicker.

Sometimes I wonder what's the point of love. I'm sure my parents were infatuated with each other at some point. Now they're at each other's throats on a daily basis.

Maybe Ryan did me a favour breaking it off with me.

Maybe I'm better off being single forever. I can go stag to prom, or even better, go with Beth.

I sigh, thinking how even Nora has a date.

A bang on my window startles me. I look and standing outside is Beth, who waves at me awkwardly.

I open the window, and she puts out a hand. I grab it and help her come into my room.

"Why didn't you knock on the front door?" I laugh.

"And go through your parents? No thanks," Beth says with a thin smile. She's changed out of her school uniform into a flowy white dress. Again, I want to tell her how beautiful she looks, but know it's not the time.

I also feel a sting of anger for a moment, wondering if Beth will be happy that Ryan and I broke up.

"Is everything okay?" she asks.

"Not really, but I should probably be asking you the same. What happened at school today?"

She lowers her head. "I need a drink. Have any more vodka?"

"If I bring a bottle, you have to tell me what's wrong with you, and I'll tell you my story." She nods. I smile at her, but instead of smiling back, her eyes water. "Oh, beautiful," I say, putting a hand on her shoulder, "what's wrong? What happened?"

"Don't call me that," she says.

"Okay, I'll grab a bottle and be right back. Drinking makes everything better," I say playfully. I quietly leave my bedroom and make my way to my mom's stash, grabbing a bottle as my parents continue to argue. Thankfully, neither of them notice me.

I quietly go back inside my room and shut the door. Beth walks over to me and grabs the bottle, opens it, and takes a quick sip. She passes it to me.

I take a long drink and tell her what happened. "Ryan, he broke it off with me today," I say, taking another sip.

Beth's eyes water again. She grabs the bottle from me and takes a much longer drink. "I never wanted any of this to happen."

"What's wrong, beautiful?" I ask.

"Stop!" she demands. "Just stop calling me that."

I put up my hand and gesture for her to quiet a little. "I don't want my mom catching us," I tell her. She nods back. "What's wrong? Can you just tell me?"

She sits on my bed and takes another sip from the bottle. "I was upset about you and him. Then I was upset about prom. Then upset at what I did."

"What did you do?" I ask, confused.

She shakes her head. "We're friends, right?"

"Of course," I answer.

"Why?"

"You're a great person, easy to talk to. A loyal friend. The best kind of friend, really."

Beth's eyes water. "Had the situation been

reversed, had it been you who had a crush on Ryan, and me who strolled into school and took him, what would you have done?"

I put a hand on my chest, not knowing what to say or why she was asking. "You told me you were okay with us being together—not that it matters anymore."

"I… don't know what I want anymore. I thought I knew, but I don't." She takes another sip and wipes her lips. She starts to cry again.

"Just talk to me," I say. "I'm here."

Beth stands up. "I need to go."

"Why can't you talk to me?" I ask. "Don't leave. You're, like, all distraught. It scares me. Stay. We can call Nora. The three of us can talk together."

She scoffs. "She's another one." She takes a long sip and touches the pendant around her neck. "I'm not sure who's worse, her or me." She looks me in the eyes intensely. "Sometimes she freaks me out."

"Nora?"

Beth nods. "She can be so controlling. I hate it. She scares me. She holds resentments and grudges against everyone. I'm basically her only friend. When I talk about leaving Muskoka for university, she gets worse. Recently she told me she thought of killing herself after I leave. She phrased it as if it was a joke, but it wasn't funny. I worry she'll do it. I worry- ugh, I'm so fed up with her." Beth yanks her necklace forcefully from her neckline, leaving a red mark. She tosses it across my room.

Beth walks back to the window, the bottle still in her hand. "I don't deserve you as a friend. I don't deserve anything good." She leaves my room quickly. I run to my window and call out to her to come back.

She ignores me and continues to storm down the block. What's come over her? I don't know Beth as well as I like to think, but she's not acting like herself.

I put a leg out my window, but before I can go after her, a knock on my door stops me.

"Kelly," my mom shouts, "Ryan's on the phone."

I put my leg back inside my room, stare at Beth one more time, and open my bedroom door, taking the phone.

My dad stares at me harshly. "And who's Ryan?"

CHAPTER 42

Kelly
Present

Even from a young age, I knew I was pretty. As I got older, I knew I was stunning. Gorgeous. Any adjective you could think of to describe beauty.

Tonight is the first time I've felt ugly.

Jameson's words really stung me deeply.

I deserved all of it for what I put him through.

Even though I know what I did to Nora was wrong, I still felt so strongly about what I knew she had done.

She killed Beth. I know it in my heart to be true.

Even if I prove it, will it change how terrible I've become?

Is there any absolution for me if I'm right?

I imagine what it will be like for Jameson when he finds out that his pregnant wife killed someone.

How do you handle that? How can you even comprehend it? Imagine you try building a family with someone and find out they're a complete monster.

I think of Ryan.

He wasn't close to Beth, but knew her. After she was found in the lake, I spoke about her often. A lot at first. Ryan was always there to listen. It was weird. The night Beth died, it brought Ryan and me closer together.

I thought he wanted to end our relationship. After the news broke, many people didn't go to school.

I went because what else could I do? I couldn't sulk in my room. I was surprised when Ryan didn't show up. Plenty of students didn't go to school for the rest of that week. Even prom was cancelled. Still, I didn't know how it impacted Ryan. He wasn't the only guy on the varsity team who didn't show up to school either.

The principal basically gave all students permission not to attend. Trauma therapists were made available for any students or staff who wanted to talk to someone.

I walk over to the table beside the front door and look at the picture frame of Ryan and me on our vacations. I stare at the one in Fiji for a while. We made so many great memories on that trip. I pick up the vase with his remains.

"I wish you were here," I say, alone in my

large home.

The real estate lady messaged me an hour ago. She said she already had a few interested people who want to see the house immediately. She literally put the signs up only a few hours ago and already people were calling her.

A loud knock on my door startles me.

Not again, I think. Jameson reamed me out good. I don't think I can take anything else tonight.

Was it now Nora's turn to take a dig at me?

If it is her, I'll tell her what I've done. No point in hiding anything now.

I open the door and Officer Tallie is there.

"Hey, Kelly," she says softly. "I'm sorry to bother you. I know it's getting late."

I look outside and see the sun has already set. I've been decompressing after my visit from Jameson for longer than I thought. I didn't even realize what time it is.

"No, that's okay," I say. "Is everything alright?"

"We got the results," she says. I smile, but Sandy doesn't reciprocate. I mean, how could she? She's going to have to arrest Nora. They were friends at one point. "Can I come inside?"

I wave her in, and she walks past me. She takes a moment to stare at the picture frames of Ryan and I before looking back up at me.

"I have hard news for you," she says.

"What do you mean?"

"We took the DNA profile from what we found on Beth's body and we compared it to the database. This time there was a confirmed match. It's at a high rate of accuracy... Your last name immediately came up as a positive."

I let out a breath. Of course, my name popped up. The test was under my name. I feel my body shaking with happiness. I knew it. I knew Nora killed Beth. The DNA test proves it. A wave of relief comes over me. All the terrible things I've done were worth it.

The guilt and shame I carried with me for all those years can finally be let go.

"I know," I say with a smile. "I didn't tell you, because, well, I'm not sure what I was supposed to say. When I sent Nora's sample to the lab, I did it under my name. I... it's a long story, but I need to tell you everything now."

Sandy lets out a breath. "No, you don't understand. It was a match to Ryan's DNA."

I feel the air suck out of me. I can't breathe for a moment.

"Ryan?" I say, confused.

She nods. "I had my suspicions for a long time. It was only when I joined the force that I read everything about the case. Did you know that Ryan was questioned?"

I take a step back and look at the photos of us. I look at Ryan, smiling back at me.

"No, he never told me that," I answer.

"He was. He even had bruising on his face that looked like it could be from someone scratching him. He didn't talk to the police. His family got a lawyer. His story was that he was injured at practice. The gym teacher corroborated the story that he hurt his face that day. Another one of his friends told a similar story. The police backed off after the coroner said she died from drowning. No bruising was found on her body to suggest someone killed her."

"I don't understand," I say. "Ryan?"

She puts a hand on my shoulder and squeezes it gently before continuing. "When you came to my office and told me your plan with the DNA and you mentioned Ryan had completed a test, I saw an opportunity. I have to tell you, I've always suspected him. I couldn't tell you, of course."

I nod, understanding her position. "I see. What if... but how could..." I stumble on my words, not knowing what to say.

"I'm sorry," Sandy says. "I can't imagine what you're thinking. I can arrange for a social worker to come by. You can talk to them. I know this is hard."

I look at the framed picture of us. Anger hits me now. I could scream. If he wasn't already dead, I don't know what I would do. I could break his vase right now and toss what was left of him in the garbage.

"What happens now?" I ask.

"I spoke with the Major Crimes Unit," she says. "They will be formally declaring Ryan as the likely murderer of Beth. Her parents will be informed soon."

I feel dizzy. My world is completely spinning. It's almost like I'm drunk with confusion. I try my best to meet her gaze.

"I'll need you to come by the station tomorrow morning," she says. "Is that okay?"

I laugh hysterically for a moment. My grand plan was supposed to have found justice for Beth's murder, only Officer Tallie had her own. "I'll bring a thank-you basket for solving a murder." I laugh again.

"Kelly," she says sympathetically. "None of this is your fault."

I bite my lip, trying to keep myself from breaking down in front of her. "I know... thanks. You should have said something to me before." She's about to respond when I wave my hand. "Never mind. That's okay. I'm sorry for everything."

I confirm a time to meet her at the police station tomorrow before she leaves. When I close my door, I watch her from inside my house as she gets back into her cruiser and leaves.

In an instant, my life has changed.

I looked one last time at the picture of Ryan

and me. I put my hand gently on the top of it, and then smash the picture into the table. Glass flies across the table and onto the floor. Lady jumps up from her bed and barks hysterically.

I try to calm my nerves. I need another run. I need to think about this. Thank god my house is for sale. I can't stay another night here. I'll go to a hotel if I have to. My stomach turns at the idea that I've shared my life with a man who killed my friend.

I look out my window at Nora's home.

I blamed another friend for killing Beth. I've done terrible things. Jameson won't need to investigate what I've done. I'll tell him and Nora everything.

I'll expose every crappy detail of the things I've done. How could I have been so stupid?

I look at Lady and try to calm her. I pet her head to let her know it's okay, even though everything is going to hell. "I need to make this right," I say to her. I smoosh my dog's face and give her a kiss. I'm about to leave when I notice the glass on the floor. Instead of cleaning it up, I take Lady to my bedroom and close the door. I can sweep up later.

Before leaving, I blow a kiss to Lady. "Mommy needs to fix this," I say to her as I close the door.

In a fit of anger and guilt, I put on my shoes and leave my home. I quickly walk up to Nora's house and knock.

Jameson quickly answers the door, immediately scowling when he sees me.

"What are you doing?" he demands. "Did I not just tell you to—"

"I'm sorry!" I shout over him. "I'm sorry for everything I've done to you and Nora. I'm a piece of shit. I know it. I planted listening devices in your home. I lied to you about the Miller baby. I even watched you from my home... It sounds crazy, and it is. I thought... Nora had done something terrible to a friend. Well, I was wrong. I just found out. I need to tell Nora how terribly sorry I am." He folds his arms in response. "You can sue me. Take every penny you can from me. Criminally charge me. I'll tell you and Nora everything that I've done. I'm selling my house and moving far away from you guys now. Hell, I'm thinking of staying at a hotel tonight, even... From the bottom of my heart, I'm sorry. I need to tell Nora this. I have to come clean. You can stand beside her when I do it. You can record my words. I deserve it. I'm a terrible person. I am. But I need to do this. Now, can you please get Nora?"

He unfolds his arms. "She's not here. She left hours ago."

"She's not picking up her phone?"

"She didn't take her phone," Jameson says, a look of worry on his face. "She's not at her mother's. I called the police, but they told me to stay home and wait. She could come back."

"Do they know she was recently discharged from the hospital?" I ask. "Do they not know about her self-harm concerns?"

He gazes at me sternly. "They know. I told them. I told them about how you harassed her. The weird things you've been doing. The police know."

"I can help you find her," I pleaded. "I know the town."

"You've done enough," Jameson says, slamming the door in my face.

I lower my head. This is my fault. What if Nora does something to herself? What if she tries to hurt herself again, but this time she's successful at ending her life?

I curse under my breath, thinking of my husband. This is all *his* fault.

I curse at myself as well. Ryan may have killed Beth, but whatever happens to Nora is my fault.

I need to find her. I have a few ideas where she could be.

I first drive by the cemetery. The gate is shut and locked. I look inside, trying to spot Beth's tombstone. It's been years since I've been here to visit, but I know the area. Even though I can't spot her grave, I don't see anyone living in there.

I get back in my car, and go where I feel deep down she really is. I park at the trail that Beth showed me years ago. I get out of the car, and it's pitch dark outside. I think about going back home until I open the flashlight app on my phone and start illuminating the trail.

I haven't been to the beach since Beth was found dead there.

Murdered, I remind myself. She didn't drown. She was killed, not by Nora, but by my husband. I try my best not to think of that right now. It'll do no good to beat myself up. There will be plenty of time to do that after I find Nora.

When I see a weirdly shaped rock on the side of the trail, I know I'm close.

"Nora!" I cry out into the darkness. "Nora! Are you there?"

Silence and a strong gust of wind answer my calls. What if Nora has done the unspeakable? What if she did it where she found Beth?

I shine my cell phone flashlight into the dark brush as I make my way through it. I continue to call out for Nora but get no response. I stop suddenly when I hear a branch break.

In the darkness, I finally remember I'm not the only thing out here. Bears and other animals could be nearby and I'm in their home tonight, uninvited. I'm about to turn around and go back when I spot dark waves ahead of me.

I see the lake.

I'm close. I know it.

I continue to walk into the thick trees,

ducking under a branch when I see a clearing. Even though it's dark, I know I've arrived.

I shine my light around the beachfront, trying to find Nora. I can barely see anything. I stand closer to the beach, the rocks beneath my feet. I shine the light into the water, worried I will find her floating.

I hear another branch crack and quickly turn.

Nora, sitting on a large rock, is facing me. She covers her face against the light.

CHAPTER 43

Nora
Before
The night Beth died.

After dinner, I go to Beth's home, wanting to clear the air with her. I'm worried about how she was at school. I know a lot of that was because of Ryan and Kelly.

I'm surprised when Linda says she left a few hours ago and hasn't seen her daughter since. She assumed she was with me. I thank her and walk down the block towards Kelly's home. I touch the pendant around my neck, hoping that Beth will be there.

There's a good chance that as she isn't with me, she'll be at her supposed other *friend's* house.

As I get closer, I can hear people arguing inside. I reluctantly knock on the door and the voices stop.

A woman opens the door, her large pink press-on nails shining under the light inside. Her strong perfume makes me nearly gag.

"Can I help you?" she asks.

"Hi, I'm looking for Beth," I say and realize how silly that sounds, "and Kelly?"

"Oh, you must be one of her new friends from school," she says with a wide smile. "Let me get her for you." Her voice is nearly as enthusiastic as her daughter's. I can see where Kelly gets her personality from.

A few moments later, Kelly comes to the door. "Hey, Nora," she says, her usual fake enthusiasm not present for a change.

"Is Beth here?" I ask. "I went to her house, but her mom said she was out."

Kelly looks at me for a moment before answering. "I thought she was with you. She came by about an hour ago. She left and was pretty emotional. If she's not home, I'm not sure where she'd be."

I nod. Why would Beth come to be consoled by Kelly? I was her actual friend. Kelly was the root of her issues.

"Was she okay when you saw her?" I ask.

Kelly shakes her head. "No, she was upset, but she wouldn't tell me why."

How can Kelly not know why? It's obvious.

"Well, if you see her, tell her I came by," I say. I turn to leave and Kelly calls out to me.

"Did anything ever happen between Beth and Ryan before we dated?"

I turn to her with a look of surprise. "No.

She was scared to even talk to him. I don't think he ever noticed her, to be honest. Not the way he noticed you." I let my words sting her.

Beth was upset, and it was because of Kelly. Now, her new friend is suddenly worried about Beth's feelings? She would have stayed away from Ryan McDermott had she truly cared.

Kelly scoffs. "Nora, you don't always have to act like such a bit—" She stops herself from finishing her sentence, even though the damage is done.

I roll my eyes at her and leave her front porch. Even if she and Beth reconcile their issues, I'm done with the New Girl. Kelly is out of my life forever.

Linda and Kelly may not know where Beth is, but I have a good idea. The sun is setting. I start a light jog to the hiking trail by the lake.

As it starts to get dark, I worry that I'm wrong.

Why would Beth come to the beach at night alone? That isn't like her. Then again, she hasn't acted like herself all day. I'm completely out of breath when I get to the mushroom-shaped rock and start heading north towards the lake.

When I get to our spot, I'm nearly frantic when I don't see her. Then again, I can't see much anymore. The woods are silent except for the sounds of the waves on the lake. I'm worried I made a terrible mistake coming out here with no flashlight.

"Nora?" her voice calls to me. When I turn my head, Beth's sitting on a rock, cross-legged, wearing a flowing white dress.

I walk closer to her. "I knew you'd be here."

She sighs. "I guess I'm easy to figure out." She unscrews the cap of a vodka bottle that she kept in her lap and takes a long sip. "Want a taste? There's not much left, sorry."

I shake my head. "What are you doing out here drinking, alone?"

Beth finishes the bottle and throws it into the woods behind her. "I'm not alone now, am I?" She laughs a little too loudly. I can tell she's had way too much.

Beth lowers her head. "I had sex with him."

I look at her, surprised. "Who?"

She let out a heavy breath, and burps. "Ryan... Our first time was a few days ago. We've been talking more since Kelly started dating him." She looks up at me. "I didn't do it on purpose. Ryan and I started talking after school one day and... ugh, he's so gorgeous. Handsome. He looked at me like no one had ever done before. And we kissed. Then... you know. He said he was going to break it off with Kelly. He told me she wasn't for him. I was more genuine, he said. He could relate to me better." Beth laughs. "We had sex again that day after he said those sweet words to me."

I sit on the rock beside her. I had no clue how to react. Beth and Ryan? How did I not see it?

"Does Kelly know?" I ask.

Beth lets out another breath. "I was going to tell her, but I couldn't. And when Ryan didn't break things off with Kelly, and I saw them in the hall today, I just broke down." She sighs. "And then I met up with him after school today at our spot, behind the tennis courts. He told me he did actually break it off. I didn't believe him, especially after what I saw in the hallway."

I lower my head. "He doesn't deserve a girl like you, Beth. There's so much better out there. You—"

"We had sex again," she sighs. "I'm so stupid. I wanted him, though. I've always wanted him since I met him. I never saw how shitty he was until he was on top of me. Even while when we were doing it, I knew how stupid I was. He was playing me and Kelly both. I told him to stop, but he didn't listen. I screamed for him to, and when he didn't respond right away, I clawed his stupid face. Then he listened. He told me to never talk to him again. He called me a whore."

"What a scumbag," I say under my breath. "He and Kelly deserve each other."

"No, she doesn't," Beth says. "I'm much worse than Kelly. I had sex with my friend's boyfriend. What kind of a terrible person does that make me? I never thought a boy like Ryan would like me, let alone want to be with me. Kelly did nothing wrong, and I screwed her over."

"Kelly is—"

"Stop!" Beth shouts. "Enough with your weird issues you have with her. She's pretty! Hot! You feel inferior. I get it. You don't like that we're friends. I get it. You act so damn weird about it, though."

"What?" I had heard every word she said, however, even if she stammered on them.

Beth lowers her head. "You get so *protective* over me, like I'm some child or something. Like I'm some... thing you own. I can be friends with *who* I want. I can smoke if I want and drink if I want."

I scoff at her. "And have sex with whoever you want, too."

"Shut up!" Beth shouts, pointing a finger at me. "You act like you're morally above everyone else, but you don't think I noticed you flirting with Ryan, right in front of me? You would have hooked up with him eventually, I know it. At least Kelly had the decency to ask me first."

I put a hand to my chest in defence. "I would have never done anything with him!"

"You would have don—" Beth stands up as if to shout more and suddenly hunches over, puking on the stony beach. She steps near the water and spits out what's left.

"Are you okay?" I ask, getting up and

standing beside her. I touch her shoulder and she shrugs me off.

"Don't touch me! Kelly is a better friend than you," she says, catching her breath.

"Don't say that!" I yell, her words piercing my soul. I grab the gold pendant on my neck and notice Beth's not wearing hers.

"She's a better person than you," Beth continues. "Better looking. More fun to be around. Just better. I'm glad I made friends with someone like her, not that I deserve her after what I did. I'm glad you're not coming to Toronto with me either! I'm sick of you. You're like a leech, sucking the life out of me. You—"

In a fit of rage, I react to her cruel words. Beth's too drunk to fight back.

It's almost like someone else is controlling my body. I'd do anything to stop what's happening. Someone else shoves Beth's head under the water. It's someone else who keeps her head there until she stops moving.

CHAPTER 44

Nora
Present

I sit at the beach, staring off into the water. It's as if I can see Beth's body still floating there. I have the same expression on my face now as she did on the night she died.

I wonder what it was like for my friend in the last few moments of her life. What fear did she have? Was she in pain?

Would I feel any pain if the same happened to me? It would be a fitting end.

I place a hand on my belly, a tear forming in my eye. "I'm sorry you're stuck with me. You deserve a better mommy."

I've been sitting on this rock contemplating what to do. I only want the pain to end. The suffering to go away. The thoughts of what I've done to leave me. I know what I've done never will. It's been easier to live life pretending other people were to blame for what I did.

That's when I hear her voice.

"Nora!"

My sad face turns into a scowl.

Why is she here? I breathe in a sigh of relief when I don't hear her voice again. It's as if Kelly's voice was just a nightmare, haunting me before I entered the water.

"Nora!"

No, no, please.

When I see a slender silhouette reach the beach, I know it's Kelly. I close my eyes and wish her to leave. Perhaps if I do it enough, the world will give me what I need, one where Kelly is far away from me at this moment.

A light flashes in my eyes and I cover my face.

"Nora, oh thank god."

I don't answer. I can feel my anger boiling inside me. She's been manipulating me, lying to me, and trying to make me go mad. She wants me to kill myself. She wants me to break.

Well, now I'm broken. She's won.

I bend down and grab a large rock, gripping it tightly.

"It's your fault!" I shout. Before I know it, the rock in my hand has struck Kelly on the side of her pretty face. The light in her hand and her body drop to the ground simultaneously.

In my anger, I don't realize what I'm doing until Kelly's body is halfway under water, and I'm pushing her down further.

She kicks, and bubbles fly to the surface rapidly.

For a moment I have clarity about what I'm doing. Kelly stops fighting me. The light from her cell illuminates us in the darkness. I see Kelly's blue eyes, nearly the same colour as the water in daylight, stare at me with fear.

I've seen this look before.

My hands begin to go limp. Kelly's mouth reaches the surface, and she coughs hysterically. Blood stains the water around us.

What am I doing?

What have I done?

Kelly's arm reaches out and finds my cheek. She digs into the side of my face with her nails.

I scream in pain and push down on her chest, forcing her deeper into the water. The rapid bubbles continue to the surface until they stop entirely.

CHAPTER 45

Nora
Two weeks later

I'm not a terrible person.

I've continued to remind myself of that for the past few weeks. It can be hard to remember the good I've done in this world.

When I worked as a social worker dealing with seniors, I helped many of them. Beth would have loved a career in social work. She, like me, always wanted to help others. I thought of her a lot when I completed my degree.

Sometimes too often.

I would lose track of the good I wanted to do in this world and focus heavily on the bad I've committed.

What happened to Beth was a tragedy. I never wanted it to happen. It wasn't something I intended. I only wanted her to stop talking.

She didn't listen, though.

Beth could be so stubborn.

I sit in the waiting room of the ultrasound

clinic, Jameson beside me. He's on his phone as usual, checking out details of stocks he's interested in.

I'm staring off, looking at the wall, unable to control my thoughts. Perhaps it's because we're at this clinic to see the life inside me that I can't stop thinking of the death I've caused.

I touch my belly. There's a lot more good I will be bringing into this world.

They say one good deed can erase a lifetime of bad ones.

I plan to be the best mother I can. I will teach my child, and someday children, to treat others how you would like to be treated. Be kind. Be loving. Be a good listener.

I will teach them that making bad decisions doesn't define you. There's always a path to redemption.

Sometimes I think of what happened to Kelly.

We both made bad choices. Kelly wanted to bring me down. She wanted to ruin me. She wanted to come between Jameson and me. Break my family apart before it even started.

I could never let that happen.

I'm happy to say that I'm feeling better these days. I'm leaning on my support network. Jameson, of course, is my rock. My mother supports me no matter what, and even my father is more involved in my life now.

I'm not skipping on my medication either. It took some time but I'm feeling the effects of my Prozac now. My emotions are muted. The feelings of dread about what I've done don't upset me.

I don't have to use the conveyor belt strategy Dr. Albee taught me to feel at peace. The packages labelled Kelly's and Beth's murder pass by me without me feeling anything.

What happened to Kelly was a tragedy. Had she focused on her own life, she would still be here.

Sometimes we make poor decisions and have to pay for them.

I worry about mine. Beth's death was ruled an accident many years ago.

Kelly may be a problem someday, but not right now. I learned from my mistake with Beth.

No body, no murder.

I enjoy true crime stories. I've heard that saying somewhere; I can't be sure from where, though.

Jameson told police that Kelly McDermott was distraught the night she went missing. She told Jameson herself that she was planning on staying at a hotel. Police would check her credit cards and cell phone records. They couldn't find anything, of course.

After I took care of the loose ends of my actions, I had a car accident. Not really an accident, since it was on purpose, but it would explain the marks on my face, and why I didn't come home until late.

A nurse breaks my attention and calls us into a small, dimly lit room. I lie down on the examination table. We've had ultrasounds before. I know what to expect. They glob this jelly on my bare belly, and push this handheld wand into my stomach.

The nurse makes some notes throughout the assessment and finally turns to us. "I understand you want to know the sex today?" she asks.

Jameson pops his head up. "Yes, we do." He stands beside me, holding my hand tightly.

He smiles at me, squeezing my fingers. He's so giddy, he could be a child himself right now.

The nurse raises the sound on a speaker, and we hear the baby's heartbeat. I feel a tear welling in my eye. Jameson is also nearly weeping at the sound of our child.

The nurse clicks a button on her console. "Okay, you ready?" she says with a huge smile. We wait with anticipation for her next words.

The moment she says it's a girl Jameson and I are both tearful, still holding hands.

"This is really happening," Jameson says between breaths. "Papa's little girl. Our baby girl."

I lower my head, taking in a deep breath. "I know her name, too." Jameson looks at me, a new tear forming. "I know you may not like it, but it feels right."

"What do you want to call her?" he asks, caressing my hand.

"Elizabeth."

EPILOGUE

Constable Sandra Tallie
One month later

Nobody reported Kelly McDermott missing for three days from the last day anyone saw her. It was her real estate agent, Shannon Manning, who did. She had been trying to contact her about organizing showings of Kelly's home but had no response.

I knew something was wrong when Kelly didn't show up at my office like she promised she would. I had even gone to her house. When I knocked on her door, all I could hear was her dog barking. I left that day, and the next, when I came back to knock on her door again and nobody answered.

Something didn't feel right. I assumed it was because of us officially accusing her husband of the murder of Beth Graham.

When Shannon called to report her concerns, I knew something was wrong.

When I went back to Kelly's home on the

third day, I brought a locksmith with me. I could still hear her small poodle inside Kelly's bedroom. The poor thing must have been starving and thirsty. I made sure she was well fed and watered before the Humane Society was called.

Later in the investigation, a gold pendant was found on the nightstand beside Kelly's bed. Inside the pendant was a picture of Nora and Beth from high school.

Kelly was not in her house. Her car was not in her garage.

After interviewing everyone I could think of, the person who last seemed to talk to her was Jameson Bowman. Jameson admitted the last conversation they had was heated, but said she left his home that night. Footage from their doorbell camera and the front and side of the Bowman home showed Kelly leaving the property safely. It also showed Kelly getting into her pink Porsche and taking off.

Nora Bowman returned home later that night. Camera footage caught her coming back past midnight. Police reports confirmed that Nora was in a car accident with minor injuries. She admitted she was suicidal, but nothing else. She was immediately brought back to the hospital and was released after two days.

Nora reported to me that the last time she saw Kelly alive was when she ran past her outside her home. That was confirmed through their security footage as well.

I, of course, did not believe a word of that.

After Kelly was reported missing and I found out the last thing she had wanted to do was find Nora, I searched all the places I thought Kelly would have looked for her, or places that I remember us going to as kids.

I even checked out the old bowling lanes. It had been closed for over a decade and never reopened. At times there were squatters who lived there, but I knew who they were and knew they weren't dangerous people. Troubled, yes, but not the type to murder a woman.

Then I went to the beach where Beth Graham's body was found. I felt strongly I would find a trace that Kelly had been there, but found nothing.

It could have been the days in between us learning of her disappearance or the severe rainy weather that concealed the evidence of what really happened the night Kelly disappeared.

I was beginning to hope that the story of Kelly hightailing it out of town was true, but suspected it wasn't. She didn't take out any money from her bank account. Her walk-in closet was packed full of clothes, some still in shopping bags.

Then everything changed.

We found the remains of Kelly McDermott. It took weeks to do so. Despite the search parties I had organized in town. Despite the dogs not picking up her sent. Despite the terrible thunderstorms we had this summer. Her body was found.

Off-trail hikers, visiting from Sweden, found a shallow grave with some branches and moss piled on top of her.

Her body was badly decomposed, but from the clothes she was last reported wearing, there was no doubt it was her. Forensics discovered a major clue. Underneath Kelly's fingernails were traces of skin. From those, forensics was able to secure a DNA profile that we could compare with the registry.

Obviously, Nora Bowman was the prime suspect. Her husband, wanting to protect his pregnant wife from the stress of dealing with authorities, got his lawyer involved. She refused to provide any DNA evidence for us.

I didn't need it, though. The victim herself, Kelly, had done all the work for me already.

I waited patiently for the results to come back. I prayed that I would get the call soon from Major Crimes, who'd promised to keep me involved in the case.

Any day now, it could come.

I sit at my desk, reading the small crime reports from Muskoka Lake. New phallic graffiti under the bridge by Main Street. A physical altercation between a pair of drunk men at a local bar. It's all typical.

It's all a distraction until I can find out what happened to Kelly.

My phone rings, and I immediately pick it up. I can feel my pulse quicken when the investigator from Major Crimes greets me.

She tells me the results. I write down the name quickly. A match has been confirmed. The investigator is confused though by the results, but I immediately understood.

Nora would not get away with what she had done.

Before explaining what happened, I take a moment to read the name I wrote, and smile.

Kelly McDermott.

❋ ❋ ❋

Download My Free Book

If you would like to receive a FREE copy of my psychological thriller, The Affair, please email me at jamescaineauthor@gmail.com.

Alice Ruffalo is on the run from her violent husband. She believes she found safety in a rundown motel in a small town.

The handsome motel clerk helps take her mind off her fears, until she starts to hear weird sounds outside her motel room and sees shadowy figures near her door.

Alice finds out the hard way that she shouldn't have stopped in this small town. Her husband knows exactly where she is.

⋆⋆⋆⋆⋆ *"This is such a thrilling read." Goodreads reviewer*

⋆⋆⋆⋆⋆ "A brilliant read. " Goodreads reviewer

❋ ❋ ❋

I truly hope you enjoyed reading my story as much as I did creating it. As an indie author, what you think of my book is all I care about.

If you enjoyed my story, please take a moment to leave your review on the Amazon store. It would mean the world to me.

Thank you for reading, and I hope you join me next time.

Sincerely,
James

I'm always happy to receive
emails from readers at
jamescaineauthor@gmail.com.

* * *

Now, please enjoy a sample of my book, The Family Cabin.

The Family Cabin

There's a young woman tied up in the basement of our cabin.

It was supposed to be a fun weekend at our family cabin. I was going to surprise my husband, Mike, with a small get together for his 40th birthday.

Something is wrong though. Mike isn't himself lately. He goes out often, and by himself, leaving me and our young son. Our happy marriage is fading away and I don't know why.

This weekend is just what's needed to cheer him up. It's what we need for us.

When I get to the cabin and set up, I hear sounds coming from the basement. That's when I see her. A young woman tied up and scared.

She cries out for me to help her. Before I can, Mike comes to the cabin early.

Who is she? Why is she here?

What has my husband done?

Please enjoy this sample
of the Family Cabin:

CHAPTER 1

Amber

My head throbbed with pain. I slowly looked around the room, seeing double. A light above me burned my eyes while I tried to make sense of where I was. The room had cement walls with a matching floor.

I knew I was in a basement but couldn't remember how I got there. I attempted to lift my hands to rub my forehead but felt strong resistance.

My hands were handcuffed behind my back. I began to realize my situation. I leaned forward and nearly fell off the metal chair. The pain in my head was immense, and I winced.

I saw no windows, only a wooden door. A large metal table was against one wall. The room was bare, except for me, the table and the chair.

I let out a sigh of relief when I saw my feet were not tied. I stood up immediately and walked towards the door, but stopped a few feet from it. I looked behind me and found a chain connected to the handcuffs kept me from moving further. I wiggled my hands and watched the chain move. It was connected to a metal hook cemented into the back wall.

A tear formed in my eye as I realized with fear that I had been taken.

"Help!" I cried. "Please! Someone help me!"

I took in a deep breath, trying to calm myself and collect my thoughts. What happened to me? Why couldn't I remember? I attempted to retrace my steps before waking up in this basement, the pain in my head making it more difficult.

I was studying late in the university campus library. I had a midterm exam the next day and wanted to do a cram session. Criminal law. It was a basic course to introduce new law students to the fundamentals we would need to know moving forward.

I had been there most of the day, and night. The library held extended hours during exam times. I sat in a cubicle on the fourth floor, facing a window. It was my favourite spot to study.

I tried not to be superstitious, but I had studied for all my examinations in my undergraduate degree in the same cubicle. The one time I hadn't and pulled an all-nighter in my room the night before, I got a B-, which was truly horrific for me at the time. I promised myself I would always ensure I had a long study session at my fourth-floor cubicle after that.

If I ever got to the library and someone was sitting in my spot, I would politely ask how long they planned on being there for and would sometimes wait nearby waiting to pounce as soon as they made any signs they were leaving. I couldn't focus right if I wasn't in my cubicle.

It was my special place. My study spot somehow gave me superpowers to remember course materials and ace any test.

The sound of the footsteps above me broke my fantasy and reminded me where I was. I shuddered. They echoed across the ceiling. Whose basement was this? How did I get here?

It had been close to midnight at the library. When I felt comfortable I knew what would be required for my test, I gathered my things to leave. After packing away my laptop, I tossed my oversized University of Calgary sweater on. Although it was a typical cold February day in Alberta, the fourth-floor campus library was always boiling hot.

The footsteps continued above me as I moved around the room as much as the chain allowed. I stood above the table, which was unusually low. I let out an audible gasp as I noticed a dark red stain on one corner.

I looked down. I was still wearing my white campus sweater but saw drops of red marking my shoulder.

My eyes widened as I remembered now. I left the library, waving at the campus police officer who sat at a table near the entrance.

I winced in pain, thinking of my walk to the parking lot where I had parked my beat-up Volkswagen. All I had wanted that night was to grab some McDonald's drive-through, go home, and if my roommate was still up, watch a movie with her.

The university campus was quiet at night, unlike the usual hustle of students during the daytime. The buildings were dark now, with only a few dim lights illuminating the pathways. The grassy lawns were empty.

I remembered feeling uneasy. I thought about turning back to the library. Campus guards had offered to walk me to my car when I studied late. If only I'd taken them up on that offer.

My phone rang loudly, breaking the silence of the night. I jumped and took my cell out of my pants. It was my mom. I rolled my eyes. It was past midnight; what could she want? I knew the answer though and didn't have time to deal with her. I needed sleep. The test was early the next day, and my brain was fried. A late-night argument with my mother was not what I needed. I slipped my phone back into my pocket and could now see the empty parking lot, and my car.

As I neared my vehicle, I took out my keys and unlocked it. That was when I felt the pressure to the back of my head, and then... nothing.

Until I woke up.

I knew I had to find a way out before it was too late. I pulled on the chain, trying to loosen the metal hook from the wall. I screamed for help, hoping someone would hear me. But as the minutes ticked by, I knew I had to come up with a plan on my own. My only hope was to keep my wits about me and find a way to escape from this nightmare.

That's when I heard the footsteps above me move again. They went across the room, and stopped. I took a deep breath realizing the person hadn't stopped moving, but the sound they made had changed.

The thud the person made was soft and muffled, with a rhythmic tapping sound as the heel of the shoe hit each step.

I stared wide-eyed at the wooden door, waiting. I wanted to scream, but my body wouldn't allow me. It was as if someone had taken the batteries out of me and I was stuck in mid-motion, staring at the door.

Even when there was a loud thud on it, I wasn't able to react in any way, besides watch as the door slowly opened. When the person walked into the room, I managed to open my mouth.

He was tall, wearing a red flannel shirt with

the sleeves rolled up exposing his thick forearms. He carried a bucket in one hand, placing it on the floor once inside.

I felt my hands behind my back tremble. The face that stared back at me was one I recognized.

The dead red eyes stared back. Its mouth was open, revealing all of its white, menacing teeth. Its ears were pointed backwards. The mask of the wolf's head that the man wore looked as if it was about to attack me.

"You're awake," the man said, the mask muffling his deep voice. "This is for you." He lowered the bucket to the floor, nudging it with his foot towards me. "Step back," he demanded suddenly. I continued to stare at the menacing mask, not comprehending what he asked. "Step back!" he yelled. I did what was asked this time, moving closer to the chair. "Sit!" his deep voice boomed. I sat on the chair and did not take my eyes off the man with the wolf mask. "Good girl." The man stepped outside the room momentarily and re-entered with two large metal bowls. He placed them near the table. Water splashed from one of the bowls onto the cement floor as he did. I stared at the other bowl. It almost resembled cereal until the smell struck my nose.

Dog food.

"Eat," the man said. "Drink." He turned his head to the bucket. "Alleviate yourself."

"Please," I said, tears streaming down my

face. "Please, let me—"

"This is your home," the man interrupted. "Be a good girl, and I won't... put you down." I screamed. The man raised his shoulders and turned his face towards the door. "Stop that! Stop that, now!" He grabbed the metal bucket and slammed it against the wall, denting it.

I took a deep breath. I looked at the red eyes of the wolf again. It took me a moment to see two holes below them, where I saw the dark brown eyes of the man staring back at me.

"Don't hurt me," I pleaded, staring at the man's eyes now. "My name is Amber Townsin. My mother is very wealthy," I lied. "Let me go, and I'll make sure you're compensated." The man with the wolf mask shook his head. "She will!" I yelled. "Just... please let me go and—"

"Stop!" the man barked. "That's not your name, anymore. Your name is... 'girl' now." I raised my head and stared at him. "You can be a bad girl or a good girl, that's up to you. Good girls can stay with a master. Bad girls get put down. What will you be?"

I breathed in, my mouth gaping open.

He shook his head again. "You have a lot to learn, girl. Rule one, no screaming. If you do, I'll put you down like a dog right away. The second, do as I say. The last rule, and this is important... Call me 'Master'."

CHAPTER 2

Dawn

"Thank you so much for helping me today. Dawn, was it?" the caller asked.

I smiled, sitting in my cubicle with my headset on. "That's right. I'm glad we were able to resolve your concerns today. Are you happy with our resolution?"

"It's not what I wanted," the man muttered, "but you've been great. What was your last name again? I want to write a good review for you."

"Dawn Nelson, and thank you for your kind words. Have a great rest of your day." I waited for the man to say the same and ended the call, taking off my headset. I took a deep breath, noticing on my computer screen the other twenty-one calls in the queue.

The calls never end. A customer is never truly happy. These were facts of working at a customer service call center that handled complaints. All day I dealt with conflict but did it exceptionally well.

The call that had just ended for example. The man started yelling and swearing almost immediately after I asked him what his name was. Most customer service reps would have hung up, but I managed to turn the call around.

Practically all of the callers were upset because they felt wronged in some way and needed to feel understood. Listening and understanding were the key skills. And when I couldn't manage to empathize with them, I pretended, which was something else I did really well as an actress.

I put on my headset, ready for the next caller, when my friend Sarah Bendry wrapped her arm around my shoulder.

"How do you do that?" she asked.

"What?" I said, adjusting my headset.

"Smiling after a call like that?" She shook her head. "I heard that grumpy old man from across the room complaining about his toaster, and how it broke a week after purchasing it. You tell him it's not covered under warranty, and still somehow manage to smile at the end of the call, and he wants to write you a good review?"

I laughed. "The man shoved a fork into his toaster, fishing out his burnt toast, breaking it. He's lucky he didn't hurt himself, but of course it's not covered. He knew that before he called." I shook my head. "My acting coach told me if you want to pretend to be happy, smiling is the first step. It helps get you in the right state of mind when you need to act the part. Sometimes I even say or think the word 'smile' just to help set the mood. It's the same for all emotions when I act."

Sarah shook her head again. "This job is getting to me. I can't wait to find a new one someday."

Serendipitously, our manager, Ronald walked by as Sarah expressed her dreams of escaping.

"Break, Sarah?" he asked with his usual crappy tone.

Sarah perked up. She plastered a fake smile on her face. "Hey, Ron! Of course I'm on a break. A coffee break... with Dawn." Ronald nodded and continued to walk past us, watching other customer service representatives in their cubicles.

"You're right," Sarah said. "Smiling at Ron makes me not want to choke him with my mouse cord."

"Dark! I like it. What time are you and Vic coming tonight?" I stood up from my desk and tucked in my chair. A coffee break did sound good.

"That's why I popped by," Sarah said with a pout.

"You can't come?" I asked, concerned. It would ruin my surprise party if nobody was there. Sarah and Victor were the only two invited.

"No, of course I'm still coming. Victor was told he has to stay late at work. Only a few hours, though. So we'll be there before eight for sure. We're excited! Can't believe old man Mike is turning the big four zero."

"Please don't call him 'old man Mike'. Something tells me he'd hate it."

Sarah raised an eyebrow. "Mike? Upset? He's a Zen master. I don't think I've seen that man angry the whole time I've known him."

I could agree to that. Being married to him for over thirteen years, though, I knew when he wasn't himself. The past six months I had noticed changes in his mood, and behaviour. It was almost as if he was never truly present with me. He appeared deep in thought and whatever he was thinking about didn't seem to involve me or our son.

Mid-life crisis, I was told. I never thought Mike would be a victim of one, though.
"He is still the Zen master, or whatever you called him, but lately I think it's bothering him. His age. Everyone he knows is younger than him."

Everyone he knows, I repeated to myself. If only Sarah knew how few people he actually knew. The only friends he really talked to were Vic and Sarah, and that was usually because of my efforts to arrange a double date with them.

His mother had died when Mike was a child,

and his father a few years ago.

Besides Vic and Sarah, when he wasn't with me, he was around his brother Rick, much to my dismay. Despite Mike only being a year older, he was lightyears more mature than his little brother.

"Fine," Sarah said. "No 'old man Mike' jokes. 'Papa Mike' jokes, maybe?" I grinned. "Are you doing that smiling acting trick on me now?" she asked, raising her voice with a laugh.

Someone from another cubicle shushed us. I nodded towards the break room. "Coffee?" Sarah nodded back.

The call center room was a large, open space with rows upon rows of cubicles. Each cubicle was partitioned off with cheap, flimsy walls, creating a maze of identical workspaces. The lighting was fluorescent and dim, casting a harsh, unnatural glow over everything. The carpet was old and stained, and the air was stuffy and stale, as if it had never been circulated. It was a miserable place to spend long hours working, and it was no wonder that so many people hated their jobs there.

Along the way I heard others on the phones. I didn't hear my colleagues as much as I did the customers berating them. One woman had her head on her desk, covering herself with her arms. Her body was juddering, and you could hear the faint sound of whimpering.

"This place is getting to me," Sarah said, watching the woman as she walked by. "It gets to everyone, except you."

I rolled my eyes. "She's new right? What's her name?"

"I don't remember," Sarah said. "She won't last the week at this rate."

I didn't respond. Sometimes it felt like it was everyone for themselves at the call center. With little support from Ron the manager, it was easy to see why. I made a mental note to talk to the new woman later. Hopefully some gentle words of advice could help her stay, if that's what she wanted.

The break room was located just off the main call center floor. It was a cramped and poorly ventilated space, with a few vending machines lining one wall and a small table and chairs in the corner. The table was usually cluttered with half-empty coffee cups, crumpled napkins, and spilled sugar packets. The chairs were uncomfortable and mismatched, and the room had a constant stale smell of old coffee and microwave popcorn. Despite its name, it was not a pleasant place to take a break, and most people avoided it if they could, typically taking theirs at their cubicles.

We entered and made our coffee. I glanced back and saw Ron checking his watch and looking at us.

No wonder why this call center had such a high turnover.

"Vic wanted me to ask if he should bring some cash for poker like last time," Sarah asked.

"I'm sure Mike would love to play," I said. "I'm going to the family cabin early to set up." I smiled again, this time authentically.

"Maybe you can give us a sneak preview of your upcoming play too. What's the date again?" Sarah said. "We still need to purchase tickets."

"I already saved you two. And I'd love to practice my lines. Mike probably knows them better than me at this point. Although he doesn't really set the scene well with his monotone voice." I laughed.

"Lady McBeth," Sarah said in an old English accent. "It's going to be fun to watch you act Shakespeare."

I nodded in agreement, mouth taut. I had worked hard with the play group to get a lead role. Lady McBeth was my first. Still though, it wasn't what I really wanted.

"You don't seem so happy about it," Sarah said, raising an eyebrow.

"Lady McBeth is fun. It's a great part. It's just, I wish women had more interesting roles. I mean, I play a woman overcome with emotions who goes insane. At least I get to play a villain. Bad guys get all the fun lines."

"It would be fun to pretend to be a villain."

"Of course, since I'm a woman villain, everything centers around me being hysterical and acting like a victim." I shuddered. "I hate that. You know, the director of the play told me they're trying to get the rights to make a play from the movie *Misery*. You know, the book by Stephen King."

"Don't know it," Sarah said, which wasn't surprising.

"A woman kidnaps an author, and keeps him until he writes stories the way she wants, with force." I shook my head. "Now that's a villain I would love to play. Just an insanely evil person. That would be fun."

"It sounds more interesting than old man Shakespeare. I never understood why people like him so much. All of his plays end with everyone getting killed."

"A tragedy, it's called in my world. Not all of his plays were."

"The only thing that won't make it a tragedy for me is watching you on the stage."

"Thanks, Sarah."

"I also think Mike and Vic get along so well," Sarah said. "They never hang out much by themselves, though. We need to set up a husband playdate."

I laughed. "Agreed."

"Speaking of play dates, who's watching Mike Junior?"

"My mom and dad," I answered.

"A weekend of fun, games and drinking at a cabin... with no children. This must be heaven for you."

I nodded. "Mike misses Junior when he doesn't spend a lot of time with him during the weekends, though. He's been super busy at work right now."

"Well, people are starting to hand over their tax info to old man Mike. Accounting season begins." Sarah shrugged. "He's not here. I can't call him that when he's not present?"

"I'm sure Mike, the Zen master, can sense your comments," I said, chuckling.

"I'm sorry we'll be there late. Vic and I can't wait to spend the weekend with you guys, though. Celebrate with young man Mike."

"I can't wait to surprise him with everything," I said.

At that moment, I was so happy. Ready for a weekend of fun with good friends. Our time at the family cabin was going to be a surprise indeed for different reasons. It would be a weekend talked about by news channels and reporters for months to come.

CHAPTER 3

After work, I ran to my car in a frenzy, excited to get to the cabin. Mike said he would drop off Junior at my parents after his workday finished. He still didn't know what I had planned for him or that we were even going to the cabin. I had him promise to be ready for a fun date night.

"You're working too hard," I told him the evening before. "We need a fun night. Just us."

Mike reluctantly agreed. He was more stubborn during tax time. Being an accountant, this was the start of his busy season. It was February, though, and knowing his business I knew the busier nights would be coming. At this time of year, he was still able to enjoy most weekends with me and Junior. The next few months he would spend mostly working, day and night.

I sighed, thinking of it as I drove.

Knowing his work the way I did made me worried. Lately he'd been saying he needed to work some nights at the office. Other times he

343

made excuses to leave the house, usually when Junior was in bed. He said most nights that he was going out with his brother Rick. Sometimes I wondered if that was true, though.

Did he just want to be alone?

How much time would anybody want to spend with Rick, after all? The man was obnoxious. A drunk. I had to use my smile technique every time I saw him to stand the man. It was no wonder he was single at thirty-nine.

"I have no interest in having a woman," Rick had told me on several occasions. I believed it was the other way round. I didn't think many women wanted much to do with Rick.

How could Mike's mother create him and Rick from the same womb? Two totally different people. Mike was successful. He'd become a partner at his accounting firm in his twenties because of the hard work he put in.

Rick made near minimum wage when he was employed, which was seldom. He wasn't the employable type. He had a tendency to tell his bosses to F-word off on occasion. Although sometimes that was something I admired him for. It was a fantasy to tell Ronald what I truly thought of him and his management abilities.

As I drove to the cabin I continued to think about Mike. What was happening to my husband? He moped around the house most of the time. We were less intimate than usual. We weren't arguing more though, which was seldom.

It was almost as if he was waving the white flag. Giving up.

The worst part was I couldn't get him to talk about it. When I asked him what was wrong, he would give short answers. I'm just tired. Hard day at work. Or my favourite answer, "Nothing's wrong."

He would do anything but talk to me about what was happening.

For the first time in my marriage, I was worried about us. Did he still love me? Did he want to stay in this marriage? It was what I wondered daily around him.

The worst part was, I'd thought we were happy. I thought our marriage was... perfect.

Mike only seemed happy when playing with Junior now. No matter how he was really feeling, he was a good father. When he spent time with his son you got the sense they were the only two people in the world. Junior was a young boy and still saw his father as Superman. I was thankful that he didn't see the side of Mike that worried me.

Mid-life crisis, I reminded myself. I'm five years younger than Mike. Perhaps I'll feel the same as I get closer to forty and my thirties are in the rear-view mirror.

Mike was not the type of person who would be open to counseling. His father was a hard man, and counseling made you weak. Only women could have emotions apparently.

It was easy to understand why his brother Rick was the way he was when you met his father.

Truthfully, I never enjoyed the company of Albert Nelson. The nights that Mike did open up to me about his childhood, I could tell his father was a cold man. Mike's mother left his family when he was six years old and never returned. All he had was his father to support him. Mike basically raised Rick himself.

When Albert passed away from a heart attack three years ago, Mike surprisingly took it well. Now, he barely mentioned his father.

My cell phone rang, breaking me from my thoughts. It was the birthday man himself.

"Hey!" I said excitedly.

"Hey," Mike answered. "I'm glad you talked me into having a date night. I really can't wait for it to be just me and you tonight."

I took a deep breath. "Bad day?"

"Did I tell you I hate numbers?"

"That's a real problem if you're an accountant."

Mike laughed. "It certainly is."

I smiled, nearly not turning with the road. Despite saying he only wanted to spend time with me, he seemed playful today. Maybe I had caught him on a better day. Maybe with his actual birthday coming next week, he'd come to grips with whatever was troubling him.

"Hey, Mom!" Mike Junior yelled.

"Hey, Junior!" I yelled into my phone. "Are you excited to go to Grandma's today?"

"Yep! Grandpa said he's taking me to a hockey game tomorrow. The Flames are playing the Goddamn Oilers, he told me."

"Hey!" Mike said to him. "I agree with Grandpa but no bad words, mister."

"Sorry," Junior said in a low voice.

"He's excited," Mike said. "And I'm excited for tonight."

I honked at a car ahead of me when they turned into my lane and nearly struck me. "Sorry! I'll be ready soon too. I just need to set up and we'll be—"

"Set up?" Mike repeated. "Where are you going?"

I sighed audibly. "I can't keep a secret very well. We're going to the family cabin for the weekend!"

"What?" he said, slightly annoyed. "I thought we were going into the city for a date night."

"What's wrong?" I asked. "You love going to the cabin. We haven't been in a few weeks."

"We're supposed to get heavy snow this weekend. Didn't you check the weather?"

"No…" I admitted. "I just want you to have a fun weekend."

"Well, let's just go to the city instead of the cabin," he said. "I wanted to try this new Italian place."

I sighed again. "I'm almost there," I lied.

"At the cabin?" Mike asked.

"Are you really mad at me, or something?" I asked. "I thought you would be happier. I wanted to surprise you."

"You didn't have to surprise me by going to the cabin."

"It's just Sarah and Vic are coming. I wanted us to have a good time together."

"Tell them to come out for dinner," Mike said. "We can hang out at home after. I have to get back at Vic for beating me in poker last time anyway."

I felt my plans crumbling before my eyes. I wanted a fun weekend at our family cabin, and that's what we were going to get. A whole weekend with friends and good times was just what my marriage needed.

"Well Vic and Sarah are already on their way too," I lied. "So please?"

"Stop fighting!" Junior yelled in a playful tone.

"We're not, kiddo," Mike said. This time he made an audible sigh. "Fine. I'll see you soon." Before I could say anything, Mike ended the call.

Made in the USA
Columbia, SC
30 May 2025

58706894R00191